Finding Faith

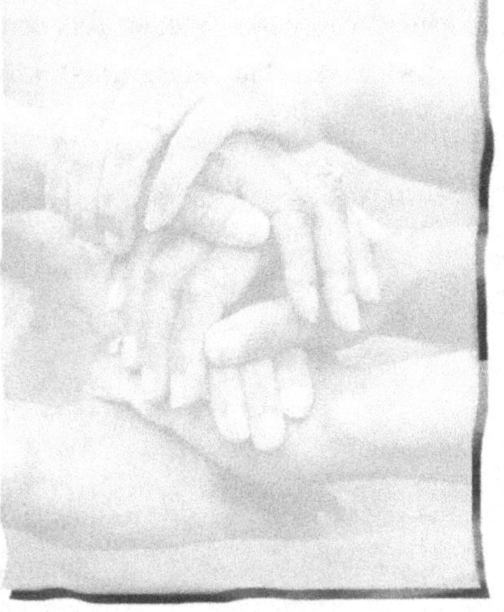

A Novel

ELLIE PULIKONDA

Published by
Applegate Valley Publishing
Grants Pass, Oregon 97527
info@applegatevalleypublishing.com

Editing by Constance Frankland

Book design by Deborah Perdue,
Illumination Graphics

Softcover ISBN: #978-0-9967565-7-0
Ebook ISBN: #978-0-9967565-8-7

DEDICATION

To my children

David LaMar, Lori Rogers, Lynda Snyder

Their faith in me has made all this possible

ACKNOWLEDGMENTS

Many folks have been instrumental in bringing *Finding Faith* to publication and I am grateful for all they added to the completion of this novel.

Just Friends Book Club members were my Beta readers and offered encouragement, helpful critiques and suggestions for improving the work. Members of Authors Innovative Marketing also offered encouragement and invaluable information about publishing.

Lori Rogers read and critiqued the first draft, providing corrections, feedback, and suggestions for improving the flow of the story. Lynda Snyder offered me vignettes of her days as a young nurse's assistant in a large nursing home, helping shape some of the stories related there.

Constance Frankland was a tough and educational editor; her corrections were unfailingly right on as were her suggestions for making it a better 'read'.

Deborah Perdue of Applegate Valley Publishing has been the personification of patience in guiding me through the publication process.

My gratitude goes out to all of these 'shepherds' who helped make *Finding Faith* a reality.

Chapter 1
Mae

Mae was a little pudding of a woman, barely five feet in height, with a figure well-rounded by a lifetime of her own good cooking. She had lost a pound or two since coming to this place, but it hardly showed. Her gray hair was confined to a casual knot at the back of her head, and her clothes were shapeless housedresses. Her most defining feature was the snapping black eyes that kept many people at bay.

Those eyes were certainly snapping now. She was talking to herself as much as her roommate, a woman who left her bed only to use the toilet and uttered little more than moans and grunts. The rocker recliner was swinging wide, and her feet stomped firmly with each jolt forward.

"I don't belong in here," Mae announced, and not for the first time. "No two ways about it. I shouldn't be here. Leastaways, not yet. I was doin' just fine on my own until Belle tricked me into signin' that paper. That's what done it for me. Now I'm in here for good and all, and looks like there ain't nothin' I can do about it. 'For your own good,' she said, but ain't nothin' good about it. I keep naggin' Belle to get me out of here. She don't like it none when I do, but even though I know it won't work, I hafta keep at her. It's pert near all I got left. They took everything else away when they put me here."

Mae looked about irritably. Her glance fell on a dime-store picture of cut flowers in a vase.

"I had just picked the last of my blue delphiniums…" she reminisced as she continued to rock. "I wanted the deep blue pitcher to show 'em off, and it was on the next to the top shelf. Climbed my little stool to get it, just like I always do, but the thing was farther over than I remembered. I put one hand against the cupboard to get my balance and got a finger around the handle of it. Well, it was kinda heavy, and the dang thing pulled me right down off that stool. Never knew nothin' till I woke up in that hospital.

"Belle told me she found me layin' on the kitchen floor. Guess I banged my head on somethin'. There was a mild concussion, the doctors said, kinda smirkin' when they said it. Said they'd keep me there a few days just to be certain. At least there was no broken bones or nothin'. They shook their heads at me as they walked away.

"I heard 'em when they said I should stay, but truth was I never felt comfortable but with my own things around me. So I fussed at Belle to take me outta there. Belle kept tryin' to make these silly arguments, sayin', 'Oh, now, Mama, you mustn't' … 'But you still need…'

And I just kept saying' 'Home.'" Mae pursed her lips; her chin stuck out firmly.

"So one day Belle comes in with these papers and showed me where to sign. I figured finally she was payin' attention to what I wanted and was gettin' me out of there. Any road, I still couldn't see too good, so I signed where she told me. Seemed odd… She had some fellow with her who asked me if I understood what it was I was signin', but I didn't spend too much time about that. Afterward she pats my arm and says, 'It's really going to be okay, you'll be just fine, Mama. This is best for you.'

"I just snorted. 'Of course, it's best. Isn't that what I been tellin' you? I just want to get home.' Belle picked up them papers and ran out of there. The next time I saw her was the day after I'd been set down in this place. 'Belle,' I told her, 'I want answers, and I mean now! What am I doing here? What in the devil is going on?'

"She looked kinda scared. 'Now, Mama, don't carry on so. You'll make your headache worse. The doctors didn't want to release you to go home, and you kept insistin' you wanted out of the hospital, so we brought you here for the time bein'.'

"Now I figured I was on to somethin'. 'We?' I said.

"She said, 'Yes, well, the doctors said it would be best for you to have someone with you now, and Arthur —'

"I said, 'Arthur, huh? I mighta known you'd listen to him instead of me. I didn't just want out of the hospital. I wanted to go home. Belle,' I told her, 'you take me home. Now!'

"She was lookin' fretful and sayin', 'Mama, please. Please, just for now? Until you can take care of yourself?' She was cryin' too, but she always did that, so I ignored it. I said, 'No, Belle, I want to go home now.'

"Belle started bawlin' for real then. 'You can't, Mama! Can't you see, you have to stay here now.' And she ran away like she always did when things didn't go her way. So I sat there for some time tryin' to figure out what was goin' on. I was scared, I'll tell you, but I didn't know why yet. I ain't used to bein' scared of anything. So I set that aside and thought about how to get outta here.

"I couldn't call a cab 'cause I had no money. Guess my purse was still at the house. I looked around but didn't see no telephone, either. Prob'ly have to go down to the lobby to call. But they'd be pay phones, and I'd need change for that. I needed to get ahold of my purse. Then I could start takin' care of myself. The next day when I asked Belle to bring my purse, she says, 'Mama, you don't need money here. Everything is paid for.'

"I said, 'Shoot, Belle, would you just for once do what I ask without arguin' with me? I want my purse. It's got my stuff in it. I never go anywhere without my purse, and I want it.'

"She stammered, 'All right, Mama. I'll bring it tomorrow, I promise. Have you made any friends here?'" As if on cue, Mae's roommate groaned in her sleep.

"Well, now, that was a good one. I hadn't seen anyone but you, and half the time you don't even talk sensible. Besides, I wasn't plannin' on being in here long enough to need friends.

"The next day Belle brought my purse, along with a armload of my clothes. 'Now, what'd you go and do that for?' I asked her. 'Just take those things right back where you got 'em.'

"She was shakin' some, but she just kept hangin' clothes in the closet. 'I thought,' she says, 'seein' as how you wanted your purse, you might want some more of your things. You know, so you'll have more changes?'

"I told her, 'Belle, so help me, sometimes I don't know what you do for brains. I'm goin' home. I don't need changes. Now, take those right back to your car while I finish gatherin' up the rest of my stuff. Then you can take me home.'

"She turns around to me. 'Mama?' she says.

"I told her, 'Get busy, Belle. I'm real anxious to see the last of this place.'

"But then she says, 'Mama, wait.' I tell you, I could almost see the gears turn in that brain of hers. 'You can't go home today,' she says. 'There's painters doin' up your house. They covered all the furniture so there's no place to sit or lay down.'

"I was real mad, I'll tell you, but I held myself in and asked, 'Belle, what have you done?'

"She started kinda pleadin'. 'Now, don't get mad, Mama. The place was so dingy and all so we're just sprucin' it up. It will do wonders for it. You can't imagine.'

"I said, 'No, I can't imagine. You had no right. You call right now and send 'em packin'. I want my house just the way it is. Right now, Belle.'

"But she says, 'It's too late. Everything is torn up, and they've painted some and, oh, it's just too late to stop now.'

"I was so shook up I couldn't think. Fear, pure and simple, spread all though me, and my hands was shakin'. I asked her, 'There's more, isn't there, Belle? You'd better tell me all of it.'

"But she shrugged and said, 'Oh, well, there's nothing much more to tell. They said it would take about a week, but you know how these things go. They're never done when they say they will be.'

Mae fumed silently as she relived the moment. When her room-mate stirred and muttered, she continued. "I could see her hands twistin' against each other like she always done when she was hidin' somethin' from me, so I knew there was more. But I didn't think I could take anymore right then, so I tried to believe her. Only a week, she said. I figured I could handle one more week as long as I knew for sure I'd be home at the end of it. So it wouldn't look the same … If needs be,

I'd hire someone to come in and paint it back the way it was. I just had to concentrate on gettin' home. Once I was home, things would be set back to rights.

I asked her, "A week, huh?"

"She said, 'Yes, or maybe a couple days more, but not much longer. It's all right, isn't it? I only want to do what's best for you, Mama.'

"Didn't seem to be anything I could do about it at that point. 'All right, Belle,' I said. 'I guess, like you say, it's too late to set things to rights now. But I want your word you won't ever do anything like this to me again.'

"She looked plenty guilty, but I figured it was because of what she had done. And she agreed. 'After this is all done, I promise I won't mess in your life anymore.'

"The next day there was a big to-do out in the hall, and then Belle comes in with two big busters carryin' Jim's recliner, this big ol' thing here." She pounded an arm for emphasis, and her roommate coughed, almost as if in response. "She had 'em put it in front of the window, and I never said a word to her. But she said, 'It was in the way at the house and I thought, seein' as how it means so much to you, you'd enjoy havin' it here. Since we had to move it somewhere anyways.'

"This here chair is a big, clumsy old thing. But I do love it 'cause I could just see Jim in it, kicked back watchin' a ball game or just waitin' for me to get supper on the table. It takes up too much space in this already crowded room, and I was pretty sure I'd run into it more often than not. Plus I figured I couldn't let up on Belle, so I said, 'Your promise yesterday didn't mean much, did it? Here you are makin' decisions for me without askin' what I want.'

"But she said, 'Oh, Mama, this isn't the same, is it? Aren't you glad to have the chair? I can have them carry it out again if you want, although I don't know where to put it.'

"I gave up. If I ran into it, I guessed I'd learn.

"That week went pretty good. I finally asked Belle about the paintin', and she'd tell me how things was going. I was beginnin' to look forward to seein' it when Belle told me it should be done by the end of that day.

"The next day Belle came in with another armload of clothes. I asked her, 'What the hell is goin' on here?'

"She said, 'Mama, please don't curse. What will people think?'

"And then I knew. The fear wouldn't be pushed aside anymore. It crawled up into my chest and lodged there, a cold hard thing. I looked her in her eyes and said, 'You'd better tell me.'

"Belle had to clear her throat twice, and even then the words came out strained. 'We sold the house, Mama. Yesterday. The people just loved it all spruced up and clean. They paid cash, more than we ever thought we'd get — enough to pay for your care for a long time.'

"I couldn't believe it. I said, 'You sold my house?' Belle nodded, swallowing hard. 'You can't just up and sell my house,' I told her. 'It's my house. I own it! My name is on the title — and only mine. What you did was illegal, and you'd —'

"She interrupted me right there and said, 'No, Mama, it wasn't illegal. You signed a durable power of attorney giving Arthur the right to take care of you. The doctor told Arthur you mustn't live alone anymore and that he should make arrangements for you. So he had a power of attorney drawn up, and you signed it that last day in the hospital.'

"I said, 'You tricked me? How could you?'

"She looked hurt. 'Mama,' Belle said, 'I only did it for you. I was worried about you. You don't know how scared I was when I found you layin' on the floor. I thought you were dead. I never, ever want to go through that again. Can't you see, I couldn't stand it? This way you'll be safe. It's for the best, Mama. I did it for you.'

"There was a roarin' in my ears, and I could see Belle was still talkin' but I couldn't make out the words. Didn't even want to. I couldn't take it all in. Belle meant for me to stay in this place the rest of my life. I never felt so tired in all my life. I couldn't imagine ever movin' again. Maybe I would just go ahead and die.

"I heard 'em whisperin' about it afterwards. The nurse said somethin' about mild shock. She said I reacted bad to havin' to stay here. And she said old people never take that news too well.

"Belle came back ever' day to see me, but I didn't want to look at her or talk to her. Truth was, I didn't want to do anything 'cause there didn't seem to be any point to it. Belle took it personal, just like she always did, sayin', 'You're punishin' me, aren't you, Mama? You're punishin' me, and all I ever did was to try to take care of you. Why are you doin' this? I only did what I thought was right. Arthur said you had to have somebody to look after you, and it looks like he was right. You surely can't take care of yourself anymore.'

"So that was it. No matter what I did now, Belle and Arthur would use it to show they were doin' the right thing."

Chapter 2
Carla

Carla paused on the sidewalk, letting her senses adjust to the quiet after the cacophony of the boom box blasting through the bus she had just left. Stepping out of the air-conditioned bus she was blasted again, this time with the steamy heat of the late June afternoon. She figured she was sweating like a hog and wondered if she smelled already. She casually pulled out the neckline of her tee shirt and sniffed. It wasn't too bad, so maybe if she got inside right away it would be okay.

She read the large wooden sign as she hurried past it. It looked like it might be more appropriate at a quaint country inn, with its white finials on the posts and a curlicue on top. "Sunnyside Haven. What a crock," she muttered to herself. "You'd think they'd at least give these places honest names."

She noticed movement at the corner of the building and saw an elderly woman wearing house slippers, pushing a walker. The old woman scurried around the corner, making a beeline toward the sidewalk. "Whoa. It looks like one of the inmates is making a run for it. You go, girl. They probably don't even know you're out here."

While Carla hesitated, wondering if she should try to stop her, the woman reached the street and pushed out onto the pavement, moving away from the building surprisingly fast. Carla shrugged and turned toward the front door with its promise of cooler air. There she paused, daring herself to enter, again having second thoughts.

This is the pits, she thought. *The last place on earth I'd pick to work is a nursing home for old farts who are half blind, nearly deaf, and stinky. But I got no choice, so I'd best pull up my socks and get on with it.* Squaring her thin shoulders, she pushed open the heavy door and walked up to the reception desk.

"I'm Carla Wills. I'm supposed to have a job interview." She knew her tone was somewhat abrupt, and she could feel the chill in the once-over the receptionist gave her. Carla was used to such appraisals — had been subjected to them for most of her life. Her unusual orange-red hair was tied up in a high pony tail, her mismatched clothing shouted thrift store, and she was small and skinny, all characteristics that normally resulted in poor first impressions. Once again she felt this was a waste of time. But the receptionist pointed toward an office behind Carla and said, "Over there," so she moved in that direction.

The slightly unpleasant smell reminded her of the escapee. She continued walking but tossed over her shoulder, "You might want to tell someone that one of your inmates has escaped, and she's hot-footing it down the road." Carla crossed the plush carpet, entered the office and, since no one was there, sprawled in a chair to wait. She glanced out into the lobby, an elegant space with delicately flowered wallpaper and soft deep rose carpet. *Not bad*, she thought begrudgingly.

Just then an old man slouched and shuffled his way aimlessly past, and Carla sighed heavily.

She heard the receptionist talking to someone and turned to look toward the front desk. The receptionist pointed toward her and then out the door. The other woman snatched up a phone and ordered someone to go out and bring back the escapee.

Carla stood up just as the harried-looking woman entered the office.

"You're here about the nurse's aide job, aren't you? Thanks for alerting us about the patient you passed. It's so hot out there — we need to get her back inside right away." She reached across the desk to snatch up a folder.

"Yeah, no problem. But hey, I'm thinking maybe this won't work for me."

"Oh, don't let first impressions put you off. It's really a great place to work, once you get used to it. I felt a little like that, too, when I started here, but now I'm really glad to be working with the elderly. And you've just shown us that you have the instincts to give quality care."

"Yeah? So what's the job like?"

"Well. As a nurse's aide, we would give you two weeks training at minimum wage. When you finish training, your salary would go up a dollar more an hour. That's not bad, is it?"

"It's okay, I guess" she shrugged. "But what's the work like?"

"All right! There's a nurse in charge around-the-clock on each wing to administer medications, take blood pressures, and oversee patient health. The aides provide the rest of the care our residents get. In a typical day you will probably give sponge baths, deliver meals, and perhaps feed patients who are unable to feed themselves. Some days you'll take them to craft class or rehab or to special programs that we have from time to time. Most importantly, you notify the nurse of anything unusual you notice about a patient." It was a recitation she had obviously given many times. "How does that sound?" Her cheer was almost contagious. Almost.

"Yeah, well, I guess I could do all that. So when would I start?"

"Well, we're somewhat shorthanded around here just now, so we'd like to put you on right away. Your training will be in the daytime, but your actual work hours will be the afternoon-evening shift. That's from 2:00 to10:00 p.m. and includes a half-hour meal break."

Carla's gut clenched at the hours, but she stifled the urge to grimace. "Yeah, okay, guess I could work with that."

"All right then! I do have a couple of questions for you. You're somewhat smaller than our usual applicants. Sometimes you'd have to help patients in or out of bed or into wheelchairs, that sort of thing. We'd train you to do that properly, but do you feel you're strong enough to handle that?"

"Oh, well … I used to help out with an old woman in our building before she died, and we had to lift her around some. I'm pretty strong, I think."

The woman beamed at Carla. "Then you've had experience at this kind of thing! You probably have a fairly good idea of what the job will be like."

"Yeah, I'm thinking maybe I do."

"Well, um," she glanced down at the application in the folder, "... Carla ... like I said, I'm sure you will learn to love it here. You'll probably get along just fine."

"Okay, so do I have the job or what?"

"Yes, I think we'll give you a chance. We have some other new hires starting next Monday. Can you start then?"

"Yeah, sure. What time should I be here?"

"The class starts at 8:00 a.m. We'd like you to come in a bit early the first day to fill out some paperwork. Okay?"

"Yeah, I'll be here."

As soon as Carla left the building, she took a big gulp of fresh air. Being here wouldn't be a picnic, but nothing else had worked yet. Turned out that fast food places didn't pay enough or give her enough hours.

She didn't have the right kind of clothes to get a job clerking in a store. This was it. The hours were lousy, but at least when school started she'd still be able to make it to her required classes and be done in time to get to work. She walked to the corner to wait for the bus thinking, *One good thing — the buses run all night.* Then she thought about what lay ahead.

The main thing was having a job, that's what she had to focus on. Ma had threatened to kick her and Faith out if Carla didn't start bringing in a paycheck. No way Ma would budge on that. She could maybe get welfare for her and Faith, like Ma had done with her, but Carla just didn't know for sure if that was possible. If she didn't get enough to help pay the rent, Ma would kick her out when her own ADC checks stopped.

She had to do this for Faith so her baby would have a better life than Carla. She had to figure out how to make that happen. For sure this job wasn't the real deal, but maybe it would get her through the next couple of years. After that, she'd be able to find something better. She'd lied about her age and had to hope they didn't check up on her, but it seemed as if they would have done that already if they were going to.

"Maybe Lotte can help me figure it out," she muttered aloud. Her one ally seemed to be the upstairs neighbor who had been an RN before an on-the-job injury ended her career. Her workers' comp was all Lotte had to live on, and she and Ma had bonded over bottles of cheap wine and more. But Lotte never got as drunk as Ma, and she had befriended Carla sometimes when things were really bad between Carla and her ma.

Carla braced her feet as the bus made a wide turn and then stood as her stop came into view. She was anxious to get back to Faith. Leaving her with Ma was scary. Between school and work, she'd be away too much of the time and never know if Ma was sober enough to do for Faith. So maybe she could talk to Lotte about that, too. Maybe Lotte would kind of keep an eye on Faith in the evenings and see that she got fed and all.

Getting to classes should work out okay, because she'd only be at school about four hours and could see to Faith between then and when she had to go to work. It was the evening, when Ma got stinking drunk, that was the scary part. Okay, okay, Faith was just a tiny baby; she'd be safe in her basket for now, even when Ma was drunk. So if Lotte would look out for Faith some, it might just work. Carla had survived in Ma's care when she was a baby, so maybe there was hope. But she didn't know if Ma was drinking so much back then.

Shoot. Every hopeful thought just got shot down by more what-ifs.

◈

Carla endured the two weeks of training, only paying attention with half her mind and, with the other half, worrying about whether Faith was okay. The instructor made a mental note of her seeming indifference but was impressed with Carla's high mark on each daily quiz and her ability to reconstruct a routine after one demonstration.

Miss Wilson interviewed her again at the end of the training. "Carla, you're bright, but I'm concerned that your attitude might get in your way. Give yourself – and us! — a chance. Drop the attitude, and apply yourself. This is honest work, and it can be rewarding. But we won't tolerate attitude where our patients are concerned."

"Yeah, okay. I'm thinking the work has got to be more interesting than the training, anyway."

"All right," Miss Wilson sighed. "You did very well in training, and we're putting you on a regular assignment. Just remember that these people depend on you and need your positive energy. So ... Your salary will go up now, and you have some benefits. You can buy health insurance, for example. Are you interested in that?

"Not on what I'm earning, I can't."

Miss Wilson sighed again, then smiled, Carla noted, already geared up for more cheer. "Well, we'll see you next Monday at 2:00, then."

On the long bus ride home she argued with herself about going back. Training wasn't bad, but then she hadn't had to deal with old people these two weeks. That would be harder.

She fingered the first paycheck in her pocket, knowing it was more money than she had ever seen before. But much of it went to Ma, and she had to cover Faith's and her own expenses from what was left. Plus she needed to figure in some decent clothes for work. She had worn jeans and tank tops to training but was expected to have white tops and pants on the floor. Maybe she could find something at the thrift stores. Oh, and white shoes. Well, she could polish her old sneakers and try to get by for now. She could almost hear a door slamming behind her, sentencing her to a life she had always planned to climb out of some day. She had only a slight hope that it would work out all right.

Squaring her shoulders, she decided to walk by Check-Rite on the way home. Having cash in her pocket made her feel better — for a little while, anyway.

Chapter 3
Mira

Mira could never remember feeling sure of herself. She had continually watched and studied her mother, who never doubted herself, and tried to understand how Mama always knew just what to do. Mama always pointed out when Mira was wrong but never told her how to know which way was the right way. She was pretty sure that was why she never fit in anywhere, and she was afraid she would never figure out how to get things just right. But she never stopped trying.

She looked at herself now in the mirror. She wasn't homely … maybe not beautiful, but she thought her face was okay. *Just okay, though, not pretty enough for people to notice or like me.* But she was always very careful with her makeup, just in case someone did notice her. Makeup helped her feel more like everybody else. Her hair was thick and wavy, definitely her best feature. She was not tall — taller than Mama, who was such a little bitty thing, but at five feet four inches, there was less of Mira than most everyone she knew.

After graduation she shortened her name to Mira, having suffered all the permutations her classmates had found for 'Mirabelle.' And she thought Mira was more sophisticated than the 'Belle' Mama and Daddy shortened it to. At least no one at work made jokes about her name, but then no one seemed to notice she was there.

When she felt her job was reasonably secure, she moved into her own tiny apartment and allowed herself to feel that she was finally getting her life right, being in control. Only every time she went home to Mama and Daddy, she felt like that gawky little kid again. So she tried not going home, but something just pushed her to go back every so often, and she didn't know how to shut out that something.

She liked her job, though, and she thought it was because so far this was something she could do right. She was in the typing pool of a large insurance firm, and that was pretty straightforward. She wouldn't say she was happy, exactly, but she thought she was content.

After several years on the job, she had been summoned to the office of Arthur Timkins, the head of the clerical department. All her old doubts welled up. Was she wrong about being able to do the job? Was she going to be reprimanded for something — or worse, fired? She first met him when she interviewed for the job, and it didn't seem to her as if she had made much of an impression on him. She remembered him, though, a trim man, not much taller than she was, with a formal bearing and a distant expression on his face.

She arrived for the meeting filled with the old anxieties, almost unable to concentrate on what he was saying. She finally understood that he was looking for a new secretary and was considering her for the position. She left the interview, her heart soaring — unable to remember much that had been said, but elated at the possibility that she might be promoted. But the job went to someone with more experience.

Instead, Arthur asked her to have dinner with him. Well, that was good, too. She hadn't had many dates. The few boys who asked her out were put off by Mama and Daddy, and they never asked for a second date. But Arthur was a man of the world; surely he wouldn't be fazed by them. Anyway, he didn't even need to meet them. At least, not right away.

Still, Mira remembered how she suffered through their first few dates, worried that she would do or say something wrong without even knowing it and that he, like everyone else in her life, would see that there was something wrong with her. She just knew he was far superior to her and that when he realized this the dates would end. Desperately, she spent hours choosing what to wear and other hours practicing what to say. But

Arthur never seemed to notice either one and spent all their time together talking about himself, telling her about his plans and his future. She was so grateful to have been chosen that she listened breathlessly.

But, oh, how she panicked when Arthur said it was time he met her parents. She was glad he'd said so, because that could only mean the relationship was moving to a new level. Mira hoped against all hope that this was true. By now she was sure they were meant to be together. Maybe it was because he so rarely criticized her. And when he did, he carefully explained where she had gone wrong. And it was such a relief to think that in time she could be like everyone else.

Mira could tell that Arthur wasn't happy at their first visit. Mama and Daddy were not impressed with him, either, and she was thankful that they didn't say much. As they left the home, Arthur was quick to say he had taken offense at their manner. And he told her that he was surprised that such a lovely, gracious person had sprung from such common parentage. She was thrilled by his words, hoping it meant he still wanted to see her, and she was relieved when it appeared that he did.

When he proposed, Mira was over the moon. He told her that after the wedding they would have little, if anything, to do with her parents, and she was so relieved that he wanted to marry her that she didn't think much about whether or not she herself wanted distance from them.

Arthur was adamant that no wife of his would ever work, so two weeks before the small, quiet ceremony she left her job. She didn't mind, because she had no friends there. Then, too, she would be so busy setting up their new home that a job would be impractical. Arthur gave her a very generous budget to furnish the home, and then gently told her what to send back and what to keep.

By the time Mira finished, their home looked as elegant as any interior decorating magazine illustration, so she felt truly proud of herself. She still worried that, as hard as she tried, she could never get it quite right all on her own. She was certain there must be something crucial missing in her, something that kept her from seeing things as clearly as Mama and Arthur. But Arthur continued to be patient with her, and she was so grateful that she stopped worrying quite so much.

She thought, or at least hoped, that they would soon have a baby and, oh, she wanted that with everything in her. Surely Mira's own child would be something she was good at. But month after month went by, and her periods were as punctual as ever. She worried that maybe she was too old to conceive. She began to fret that Arthur, in spite of his patience with her, would find her lacking and would ask for a divorce. She startled when he spoke to her and became so anxious and upset when he asked her what was wrong that he insisted she see a doctor. She truly believed that what he really wanted was to find out if she was barren but, true to her nature, she dutifully went to see the doctor he picked out.

The doctor found nothing physically wrong with her, but Arthur wouldn't let it go. He insisted that Mira talk about the problem. Finally, pathetically tearful, which Arthur hated, she confessed that she was worried because she couldn't give him a child. Arthur stared at her for so long she was sure he was too angry to speak. Finally, he told her that he never wanted children, so the fact that she was incapable of conceiving didn't come into the picture.

She was so relieved that she threw herself at him, crying gratefully into his shoulder. She quickly recovered and sat back, trying to stop crying. He handed her his handkerchief and made no comment on her outburst. They never talked about it again.

But it was so hard to fill up her days. There was little housekeeping to do, especially since Arthur was the tidiest person she'd ever known. Daddy had dropped his things wherever he happened to be, and Mama patiently picked up after him. But once Arthur was finished dressing for work, it was hard to tell that he had even been in the room. Then, too, he hired a cleaning lady to come in once a week and do the heavy cleaning, mopping floors, washing sheets and towels, and vacuuming the carpet. There was little for her to do except tidy her own dressing table and cook dinner each evening.

So, to fill part of the days, Mira began to go home again in the early afternoons, careful to be back early enough to have Arthur's dinner ready for him promptly at 6:00. She never told Arthur about these visits but figured he had said 'they' wouldn't have much to do with Mama and Daddy, and this didn't involve him at all.

For a time Mama seemed to tolerate her being there, and Mira was the happiest she had ever been. She tried to help with the housework, but Mama just told her that she did it all wrong and made more work for her. By then, Daddy had taken early retirement for some reason. He just seemed to shrink into himself after that, spending most of the day kicked back in his recliner watching ball games or quiz shows. So she sat with him, watching him watch the television, until it was time to go back home.

Then they found out that Daddy's withdrawal was due to early onset Alzheimer's disease. It progressed very rapidly after that, stealing first his memory and then his speech. The weight of his care fell squarely on Mama; she refused to even consider Mira's tentative advice to put him in a nursing home. She said he took care of her all her life, and she guessed the least she could do was take care of him now.

Oddly enough, Daddy's illness helped Mira have a place in their lives, and she was happier than she could ever remember. She made tea for Mama when Daddy was finally down for a nap in the afternoon. She was happy to tidy up after him when he knocked over his water glass or dropped food on the floor. Sometimes, though, she felt a little guilty that it took her father's illness to help her fit in.

When Arthur found out she was going there almost daily, he was very quiet for some time. But she told him they needed her, and it wouldn't look right if she didn't help them. He agreed it was all right to do her duty to her parents, but that when her father died, he expected her to live up to the agreement they made. She was so sure that Daddy would live many more years that she agreed. As it happened, he lived only seven brief months after that.

After the funeral, both Mama and Arthur pushed her to stay home.

Mama claimed she needed some quiet and space to get her thoughts around her and mourn her husband. Arthur reminded her of her promise. Mira stayed home.

But her days seemed endless, and she worried about Mama being alone. She went one afternoon for an hour, and it seemed to go well. She tried a couple more times, and it seemed to be all right. So she started to go more often. Oh, not every day, but once or twice a week she'd drop by to be sure Mama was managing on her own. She was very careful not to give Mama a reason to tell her not to come back, and it seemed as if Mama actually accepted her in a way she never had before. Arthur just didn't need to know. Mira was as content as she could ever remember being.

Then one day she found Mama unconscious on the kitchen floor and called for an ambulance.

She was so upset from the accident that she forgot Arthur didn't know she was visiting Mama. He scowled at her when she told him about finding Mama. She got things twisted up and out of order, partly because she was upset and partly because she had disobeyed Arthur. But then he calmed down. He told her to slow down and catch her breath. And then he asked her what the doctor said.

"Mother has a slight concussion, so she's going to be okay. But, don't you see, Arthur, this could happen again. And next time it could be more serious. I'm so worried about her, but I don't know what to do."

Arthur took her elbow and steered her to the sofa. "Sit down and we'll talk about it. I'm sure there's something we can do to prevent this happening again."

He was so calm and in control that she just felt relieved and glad she had him to turn to. Mira didn't know what to do, but she was sure he would. Mama was just so determined to go home, and Mira knew she would never have a moment's peace for worrying about her now.

Arthur talked about legal actions they could take to keep Mama safe. He told her they could have her declared incompetent to take care of herself, and then they'd be legally authorized to make arrangements for her. She was shocked. She couldn't do that to Mama, couldn't sit in court and say Mama was senile. She just couldn't. And she wasn't, not really ... She was just stubborn and set in her ways. So then Arthur said they could have her sign a power of attorney so he could handle her affairs. Mira knew that her mother would never do that. Mama was so used to telling everybody else what to do, she'd never agree to let someone else make her decisions. Arthur said he'd think about it and figure out something. She thought at that moment that she truly loved Arthur. She couldn't just let Mama go back and have another accident. She needed Mama. She had to keep her safe, no matter what it took. And Arthur was sure to come up with something.

So when Arthur showed her the durable power of attorney he had drawn up, she was willing to consider that. He explained that since

Mama's glasses were broken in the fall, she wouldn't be able to read, so she'd assume it was her discharge paper from the hospital and sign it. Then they could move her to a safe place.

She didn't like deceiving Mama in this way, but Arthur was quick to point out that otherwise she'd go right back home and put herself in danger again. He seemed as concerned about her care as Mira was and told her she was only doing what was necessary to protect her mother. He even volunteered to find an excellent nursing home to move her into. Mira was so grateful that Mama would be safe that, just maybe, she didn't think through it all as well as she should have.

Chapter 4
Mae

At first Mae was irritated with the constant muttering that came from her roommate, Ruby. She had grown used to the quiet since Jim died. But now Mae figured she'd talk over the stream of sound herself, so it wouldn't register much at all.

She slumped back against Jim's recliner and turned to look out the window toward the front of the nursing home.

"There's that skinny little kid again," she said to Ruby, who didn't seem to notice the kid or Mae. "Wonder who she comes to see? By the looks of the mad on her face, I'm glad it's not me.

"Well, ain't she somethin'? She does that ever' time — gives that sign the most disgusted look. Guess she thinks she's better'n us. Say, she's stronger than she looks, I reckon — can throw open those doors easier than I can. Not that I'm allowed to try. Wish I could walk fast enough to get to the front and see where she goes. Ain't much to do here 'cept see who's comin' and goin'." Mae drummed her fingers on the recliner arm. "S'pose I could go listen to the evangelical hymn singers of a Tuesday evening, but they're a tad too self-righteous, if you ask me. Wrinkle their noses all the time they're here. Way I figure it, they come mostly to remind their selves that they're better off than us. And I sure don't need them to remind me of that.

"Course, Belle says I'm takin' things too personal, that I should just close my eyes and ears to what I don't want to see. And my nose, too, I s'pose. She may be right, though. Some of the folks in here seem to be able to do that real well. Like you." She studied her roommate for a moment, then shook her head. "You done it up right well, didn't you?" She could almost see her daughter, her posture wilting, and replayed in her mind another painful recent visit.

"Made Belle cry again that time. It upsets me some to make her cry but, dang it all, she's gotta know I don't like it here. We been gettin' along a bit better, and that's good, but not if it means I gotta stay here forever. Not that I'm makin' much headway, you know. Leastaways, when she's cryin' she's not being so durned cheery. It just cuts against the grain for her to keep sayin' how good it is in here. If she likes it so much, why don't she move in?"

An elderly woman shuffled into the room, cuddling a baby doll to her withered breast. "Hey, Bert, you come to talk? You shoulda seen that little bitty thing that just come in a minute ago. Talk about someone with a chip on, she was somethin'. Glad she's not comin' to see me, I'll tell you — and glad you came by, Bert." Bert smiled uncertainly. "Not much to keep me goin' of an afternoon, what with lunch bein' so early in the day. That's another thing that galls me — lunch and supper when they want, not when I'm hungry. Wish I could get home.

"Tell me somethin', Bertha, how's come you happen to be in here? What crime did you commit to be jailed in here?"

Just then the day nurse came through the door. "Oh, heck, here you are with your pills again. Don't want 'em, don't need 'em, won't take 'em."

"Now, Mae, we go through this every time. You know the doctor has ordered these meds for you. They're for your own good. Why do you fight me every day?"

"The doctor orders what you tell him to, and you give me stuff to keep me quiet, just like all the others. 'Quiet and docile,' I hear 'em say."

The nurse erupted into a harsh laugh. "Quiet and docile, that's a good one! There isn't anyone in here less quiet and docile than you. Guess if I'm giving you meds for that, they aren't doing any good. C'mon, now, we go through this every day. This one is for high blood pressure…"

"Which I didn't have till I came here."

"...and this one is for arthritis. You need these to keep you healthy."

"Not much point in stayin' healthy when you got nothin' but this to look forward to. And I see you don't never tell me what this blue one is for. Why not?" But the nurse ignored her question, motioning for Mae to get on with it.

As soon as the nurse left, Mae headed for the bathroom, sat on the stool and carefully fished the blue tablet out from under her tongue with her thumb and forefinger, dropping it between her legs into the toilet. With a small sense of triumph, she peed on top of it and flushed. When she came back out, Bertha was gone.

"Well, guess I'll just sit here and talk to you a spell." She sighed heavily and tipped her head toward her roommate. "Same as talkin' to myself a spell. Maybe have a look at *Garden Flair* and see if I missed anything. You'd think Belle would figure out once she gave me that magazine that it's mine. But, oh, no! She goes and takes the old copy down to the lounge without so much as a by-your-leave. And you'd think maybe she'd get a couple more magazines for me, but she don't seem to think of that. Not that I'll tell her. The only thing I want from Belle is a ride back home."

She glanced out the window, wondering if she would see Miss Priss leaving, but Mae saw nothing but the drying grass and the cement sidewalk leading up to the building. It looked to be a typically hot July day. There wasn't even much traffic on the street in front of the building, and nothing interesting ever seemed to happen. Still, she kept an eye out, not wanting to miss anything that *might* happen. Behind her, Ruby droned on, and the noises from the hall and the nurse's station filtering into the room lulled her to sleep.

She awoke with a start when the supper cart stopped outside her door. Mae hated sleeping in the day, because then she slept poorly at night, and nights seemed endless when she couldn't sleep. But here she had slept nearly two hours, she reckoned. Sounded like Ruby was up and in the bathroom. Two hours! Mae would have to walk around the halls after supper and try to tire herself enough to offset the nap. She had tried to go outside once but was caught and firmly returned to her room with a stern warning: If she tried again, they would have to restrain her. Best to avoid that.

The nurse's aide brought in her roommate's supper tray and sat it on her tray table just as Ruby emerged from the bathroom. The aide ignored Ruby, cutting up the meat on the plate and taking the lids off the other foods. She was new, but old enough to know something, and Mae could tell by the set of her shoulders that she didn't want to be here. Ruby rolled herself over to the tray and began to pick up the food with her hands, stuffing it in her mouth.

"Hey, don't let her eat like that! She just went to the bathroom, and she has crap on her hands. Look at her. Clean her up." Mae's voice was sharp with anger.

The aide shrugged. "Already started. No point worryin' about it now."

Mae lunged for her buzzer and pushed it repeatedly, shouting at the aide all the while. The aide stalked back out into the hall and picked up Mae's tray as the nurse came hurrying into the room.

"What's your problem, Mae? You've got the whole wing in an uproar."

"That idiot didn't wash Ruby's hands before letting her eat. Just take a look at her hands. I can't believe —"

But by this time the nurse had taken a look at Ruby's hands and stopped Mae mid-tirade.

"Johnson, what is the meaning of this? You let her eat like this? Don't you know that she'll get diarrhea? Do you have any idea of how much cleaning you'd have to do then? Well, this is nothing compared to that. Get a warm wash cloth, and clean up her hands."

The nurse moved the tray beyond Ruby's reach, and Ruby was stretching for it and screeching in frustration while the nurse tried to restrain her without actually touching her hands. The aide looked at Ruby, shrugged again, and said, "This ain't what I bargained on," as she shoved Mae's supper tray back onto the cart and walked away.

The nurse grabbed the handles of Ruby's chair and wheeled her back into the bathroom. Mae heard running water and a running monologue, and when Ruby came out again, her hands were clean. The nurse carried her tray back to the cart and selected another one for her. Then she left the room without saying anything to Mae. A short time later another nurse's aide came up to the cart and pulled out Mae's tray, bringing it into the room.

"Oh, it's you, eh? So you're a nurse's aide. Too bad for us, I'd say."

The skinny little aide stopped in her tracks and eyed Mae. "I ain't too happy with you, neither, so best you just zip it up. Thanks to you, Ruth Ann just quit. Now I got to do her work and mine."

"You probably never had to work much in your life, that it? Lazy, huh?"

"Look, old lady, what I am ain't no business of yours. Just shut up and eat your supper." With that she wheeled and left the room, her carrot-colored ponytail bouncing along after her. Mae watched her go with something like grudging admiration. At least the kid had spunk. And she did bring Mae her meal.

Mae looked over the supper tray. There was nothing on it that she favored, nothing like what she used to fix for herself. But she knew she'd eat it anyway, more for something to do than because she was actually hungry.

"Don't know how a body can work up an appetite when you got nothin' to do, anyways." She ate the food slowly, making the activity last. Since she had decided earlier to take a walk around the halls, maybe she'd stop by Bertha's room and talk a spell. It occurred to her that she talked an awful lot since she'd come here. At home she had grown used to the quiet and used it to live in her memories. But here the noise and bustle left no room for memories, and she used words to cover the loneliness.

In spite of her walk, Mae had trouble sleeping that night. She knew it was because of the long nap she had taken, but she relished in blaming it on the skinny aide who looked in on Ruby about every half hour. Looked like the nurse had told her to check on Ruby to see if she developed any problem during the night. She just didn't like that girl, despite her spunk, and she hoped they would have someone else tomorrow. Maybe she wouldn't have been so quick to complain if she had known what would happen. Well, yeah, she would have: She didn't think she wanted to be in a room with Ruby *and* diarrhea.

Just then Ruby let out a huge fart. At least, that's what Mae thought it was, but as the room filled with the odor she knew it had to be more. She pushed her buzzer and waited. The skinny aide came just to the door and asked, "Yeah, what do you want now?"

She must have noticed the odor because she didn't wait for Mae's reply. "Did you shit in your bed?"

"Not me, but I'd guess Ruby did. Maybe you want to check it out."

Instead, the girl turned on her heel and fled the room. Mae looked at her clock. Ten-o'clock; must be shift change. That little brat was going to leave it for the next shift. Mae picked up her buzzer and pushed it again and again, but no one appeared for about ten minutes. When another nurse's aide stepped into the room, Mae turned her face away and pretended indifference. Let her figure out what was wrong.

Chapter 5
Carla

The swaying bus made Carla even angrier. The ride home seemed tortuously slow, and she held the metal bar across the seat in front of her tightly, wanting the bus to outrun the guilt that rode with her. She knew she had been wrong to leave the old lady in her mess, but she also knew that staying to clean it up would make her late getting home to Faith. As it was, she was always worried about Faith, helpless in Ma's care. She knew, though, that she would be in for it when she saw Mae the next day. That woman hated her for no reason. Not that Carla liked Mae any better, but then she had found she didn't like any of the old people she worked with, just as she had expected.

When she let herself into the apartment, her mother was watching late night TV, pulling on a beer. Faith was wailing in her makeshift bed.

"Prob'ly hungry. Outta formula. You get any?"

Carla rushed into her bedroom. The baby was wet, dirty, and hungry. Angrily, she took a diaper from the package and began to change her. Faith wailed still as she was carried, cradled in her mother's arms, through the living room to the kitchen.

"Ya got paid today, right? Where's my money?"

Carla fixed a bottle of fruit juice and soothed the baby as she sucked greedily. No telling when Ma had fed her last. "Yeah, I got paid. You'll get yours, don't worry. First, I got to go get some formula. She's starving."

"Do her good to be hungry once in a while — toughen her up. You're spoilin' her. You'll be sorry."

Carla slipped out the door, holding Faith. It would be harder to carry the baby and the formula back from the all-night drugstore, but she needed to keep Faith with her for now.

When she returned to the apartment, her mother was exactly where she'd been earlier.

"Gotta phone call from Welfare today. Caseworker's comin' in the mornin' to check us out. Be here about ten. You know the drill."

Yeah, Carla knew the drill. Her staying here was only good as long as the welfare checks continued to come in. Carla had to keep the caseworker from knowing about Faith or her job for that to happen. During her pregnancy, she'd worn baggy sweats to hide her condition. Fortunately, Faith was tiny even at birth, weighing in, Lotte told her, at probably only a little over four pounds. That's no doubt why it seemed no one could tell she had been pregnant. After she and Ma reached an agreement on her staying in the apartment, they'd devised a plan: Carla would take the baby up to Lotte's apartment any time the caseworker came, then Carla would swear she'd definitely be back in school come fall.

Later that night, while Faith slept in the laundry basket beside her bed, Carla figured. She cleared about $170 for the week. Sixty of that went to Ma for rent and babysitting, and about $40 for Faith's diapers, formula, and other stuff. She tried to get by on $30 for her own stuff. Oh, yeah, ten for bus fare. What did that leave? About $35 or $40 for anything else. Medicine and doctors if Faith got sick, clothes as Faith grew, and what else? Oh, lord, it wouldn't be enough. How had she gotten into this fix?

… She had been kneeling on the bathroom floor, emptying her stomach, wishing she had someone to turn to. It was always like this, her Ma either too drunk or too hung over to care that her daughter was sick. Now, when Carla had this horrible flu, Ma was sleeping off last night's binge. She rose up slightly and put her forehead against the cool porcelain tank. She hadn't even heard the door open.

"You're in for it now! If you got a lick of sense, you'll give it up the minute it's born. Won't even look at it. That's what I shoulda done, more fool me."

And so she came to know she was pregnant. Every morning she threw up whatever was in her stomach, and every day she endured the harangue.

"Think of it like a tumor. You go to the hospital, get it out, and let them get rid of it."

"Don't think for a single minute you can bring a kid here to live! I done my time, paid for my own mistake. I ain't payin' for yours."

"You can't even take care of yourself. If you could, you wouldn't be in this fix. Don't think you can handle a brat, 'cause you can't."

Carla thought back to the night this had all begun. The boy had pestered her every day at school to meet him for a date some evening. He had dirty blonde hair and was skinny and pimply, but he was popular with a certain crowd, and she was flattered by his attention.

Finally, she agreed to meet him late one evening in a small run-down neighborhood park, and before the evening was over she was no longer a virgin. He had promised her that since this was her first time she couldn't get pregnant, and she had believed him. Then he used her panties to wipe himself and threw them toward her as he left.

After that night, however, he no longer spoke to her. He walked by her in the hall smirking but otherwise ignored her. She finally understood that he got what he wanted from her, and she didn't matter to him at all. She worked at forgetting about that night and was succeeding until Ma had told her what her 'flu' really was.

Eventually, the morning sickness ended. The lectures continued, though, until she finally agreed. The baby would have to go. She'd put it up for adoption. Yes, yes, yes, she'd get rid of it. She would give up her baby as soon as it was born. All that time, she told herself it was best for the baby, best for the baby, best ...

In the end, she couldn't do it. She went into early labor in the middle of the night, and although still a bit short of sober, Ma's drinking buddy Lotte helped Carla deliver the baby girl. Lotte guessed the baby's weight at a little over four pounds. When the tiny girl cried for the first time, something twisted tight in Carla. She held out her arms, Lotte put the baby into them, and nothing else mattered.

She was just sixteen.

Ma came into the room late the next morning, hung over but dressed up as well as she ever managed to be, and reached to take the baby from Carla's arms. "I'll be taking her to the hospital. You can leave a baby there with no questions asked. They'll check her out and then find a home for her."

Carla wrapped her arms more tightly around the tiny girl. "No, I've changed my mind. This is my baby, and I won't let you take her away from me."

"I told you, you ain't bringin' that kid up here. You wanna keep it? Then you two just go off and have yourselves a grand ol' life. But you ain't doin' it on my dime."

Carla dragged herself out of bed and pulled on her grimy sweats. She was more scared than she'd ever been in her whole life, with no idea how she would take care of her baby but determined to try. She struggled upstairs to Lotte's apartment, hoping Lotte would let her stay a couple of days, just until she could figure out what to do. Although clearly not happy about the situation, Lotte didn't turn them away.

And then, after a couple of days, Ma had come up and laid out another plan.

"Okay, you won't listen to what's good for you. You always was a stubborn little brat. So, I been thinkin'. You get a job and pay me for the trouble this makes me, and you don't say nothin' to Welfare about havin' this brat, maybe we can work somethin' out."

So Carla lied about her age and unwillingly took the only job she could find, tending old people. She quit breastfeeding Faith and suffered through the pain of having her milk dry up. She went to work each day with fear for her baby's welfare going right along with her and came home each day with the same anxiety. So far, it had just about worked out all right, though, and nothing terrible had happened.

◈

Lori Martin grimaced as she scanned the case her supervisor had just laid on her desk. Her caseload was already way over the maximum, because the state had put a hiring freeze on the department.

When two of her co-workers left, their caseloads were divided among the rest of the staff and now, when new cases came along, they were dumped on top of the tottering pile. There had been no salary increases for three years, and she knew others in the office were looking for better paying jobs. She thought a lot about joining them but had yet to follow through.

Her mind, only half on what she was reading, wandered back over the past six years. She joined the Department full of optimism and energy, convinced she would make a difference. She no longer thought so. She barely had enough time these days to handle the legal requirements and paper work, let alone counsel and advise her clients. She felt lucky if she could squeeze in the requisite home visits. She plodded from one crisis to the next, sandwiching maintenance matters in wherever possible, taking files home to spend her evenings documenting but never catching up.

She realized that she was going from a naive, optimistic social worker to an angry, exhausted bureaucrat, and she didn't like it. But she could see no alternatives, the way things were. "Just do the job and move on," she was told. "Don't spend a lot of time trying to solve everyone's problems. It won't do any good. You can't win with these people, ever."

She was finally beginning to believe it.

She glanced at her watch. She had a home visit at 10:00, the Wills woman. It was a case that had given her real problems when she first came to the Department. She was sure the woman was drinking up much of the ADC check she got each month and probably selling some of her food stamps to get more liquor. She had one daughter, now a brash, skinny 16-year-old who seemed to take care of both herself and her mother. Carla had missed some school last spring, and although she was old enough to legally drop out, Lori was sure her mother pushed her into attending at least enough so the checks would keep coming. It galled Lori to think that the girl would probably end up just like her mother. There was intelligence in the wary eyes that glared back at Lori's questions, but not enough, she thought, to keep her from repeating her mother's life. Wearily, she reached for her briefcase and left the office.

Gertrude and Carla Wills lived in a second-floor walkup in a low-income inner-city neighborhood. As Lori picked her way up the cluttered, malodorous stairway, she thought briefly about how desperate people must be living here.

The apartment was no different than any other time Lori had been there. Although she had made an appointment, there was no indication that Gertrude Wills had made an effort to tidy up the place for the home visit. The room was cluttered and filthy, as always. The broken-down sofa emitted a cloud of dust as Carla sat down to join them. Magazines were piled haphazardly beside the greasy recliner where the Wills woman lounged. And the card table, which Lori assumed was meant to be their dining table, was covered with piles of odds and ends that seemed to have no earthly use.

Gertrude was no role model for her daughter. Her greasy gray hair was tied back in a low pony tail, and her ratty sweatpants and over-sized tee shirt were long overdue for the wash. She was no more and no less hung over than she had been on previous visits and no more or less taciturn. Lori had to work to get any information out of either of them.

"Carla missed quite a bit of school last spring. Why was that?"

"She had stomach troubles." The pale blue eyes regarded the case-worker slyly. "She's always had what you would call a delicate stomach."

"How are you feeling now, Carla?"

"Feelin' all right."

"So what year will you be this fall?"

"Junior."

"I see. Well, even though she's old enough to drop out legally, Ms. Wills, you know that your ADC checks only apply if she's enrolled in school."

"Oh, she's enrolled, all right. I see to that. An' I get her there as often as I can, but it's hard bein' the mother of a teenager, I can tell you."

"Yes, well, just so you understand. Do you have anything to report?"

"No, can't think of a thing." Her eyes slid back to the television set that had neither been turned off nor muted.

"Well, I guess that's it for now, then. Carla, I'm glad you're feeling better. Definitely get back in school as soon as it starts. It's really important for you to get your education."

"Yes, ma'am." Carla looked down at her feet as she nodded assent. Lori wished she would look up at her so she could see if the child was telling the truth. She felt sure that her mother was lying with every word she spoke and that the daughter could provide evidence of those lies if she would. Lori knew, however, that it would take more time than she had now to break through the wall of complicity. Just get the job done and move on, as she had been told to do.

Lori rose from the wooden chair, the only seat she trusted to be clean enough to sit on. "If anything at all changes in your circumstances, be sure to notify me. If Carla drops out of school, you must let me know right away. It's important for you — otherwise, you could be charged with fraud. Do you understand that?"

The mother nodded, her eyes still glued to the television talk show as she turned the volume up. Lori let herself out and mentally sighed over the life she imagined for Carla. But there was nothing she could do about it, and that was that.

She turned her thoughts to the next interview.

Chapter 6
Mae

The room was too quiet. Mae glanced around uneasily, seeing Ruby's empty bed made up with tight corners and no wrinkles. That skinny aide could make a bed pretty good, at least. Mae wondered why she missed Ruby, when she had done nothing but sleep and mumble, often at the same time. The old woman had been taken to the hospital when she didn't get better. Mae sighed. "Don't miss the smell, though, I'll tell you."

Without someone to distract her, Mae's mind kept turning over the fix she found herself in. Although she probed it like a sore tooth, nothing came to her on how to make things right. The more she thought about spending years in this place, the angrier she got. "It just ain't right. It ain't fair. I never did nothin' to Belle to deserve this. Why'd she go and treat me this way?"

But nobody was there to hear her, and nobody answered.

She and Jim had always been able to talk about things and figure out a way to make them come out all right. *Wasn't nothin' we couldn't fix, once we set our minds to it.* She missed her Jim, missed him more in this awful place than in the home they had shared.

"Jim built that home for me," she mused. "It was mine and his, and all we had together is gone. I got nothin' left of him."

She slumped into the recliner, trying to pull Jim's presence around her like a thick comfy shawl, but it wasn't working. She tried to picture him in her mind but couldn't get a whole picture. She could see his mouth, but the rest of his face was vague. She concentrated on remembering his eyes and lost the clear picture of his mouth. Her heart pounded and her mouth was dry. Where had Jim gone? Why had he left her? Maybe he couldn't find her here in this place. How *could* he?

◈

It was the late '20s, and everyone was struggling to make a living. Jim's family had to struggle harder, and his widowed mother was forced to take in laundry to support her three. Jim was the oldest, and he had been working any after-school job he could get for several years. He had certainly looked "bad" — he was darkly lean and walked with a slouching grace, with hair just a bit too long, his clothes just a little too unconventional, and that scowl he wore with everything. The other kids taunted him, his friends in a boasting way and the others with mockery laced with fearful respect. "Jim, Jim Jameson's a *bad* boy." He had generally ignored it, but occasionally his anger boiled over and let the speaker know he was on dangerous ground. But he was touchingly awkward and caring in the first days of the crush they had on each other, and Mae knew they would fit together.

Mae's parents had been late middle-aged when she was born. Having already raised one family, they seemed not to know how to deal with this late-comer. She grew up a little wild, her bewildered parents unable to control her. They disapproved of Jim, partly because he was older than Mae, but also because he had those rough edges and not much chance to improve that they could see. They tried to impress on Mae that she was making a mistake, but she simply ignored what they said.

They made love for the first time that summer of 1928, and afterwards she burrowed against him and chanted softly into his neck, "Jim, Jim Jameson's a *bad* boy." She felt him stiffen against her and she laid her cheek on his, breathing into his ear. "I love bein' bad with you."

Two years after Jim graduated and found a job as a carpenter's apprentice, Mae dropped out of school and they eloped. She adored the small Craftsman home Jim later built for them and wanted nothing more than to live out her life there with him. And as the years went by, it looked like she'd have her wish.

But at forty-five Mae gave birth to their only child. Jim had filled her up and left no room for others, especially the timid little girl who seemed to hover about at the edge of their love. Like her mother, Belle had been born late in the marriage, a true change-of-life baby, and Mae had a hard time accommodating this intruder. So she saw to her safety and well-being but couldn't find it in her heart to give her much more than that.

Mae was relieved when Belle finally moved out to her own apartment a couple years after graduating from high school. Their lives, hers and Jim's, closed around Belle's leaving with scarcely a ripple.

A few years later Belle brought a man home for them to meet. Mae thought him overbearing and a poor choice, but she said nothing to Belle about it. She felt certain that he could take care of their daughter materially, and that seemed to be all that mattered. She and Jim were content in their own company.

Then Jim's skills started slipping away, taking with them his ability to do the work he loved so much. He retired and spent his days in the oversized recliner, slowly slipping deeper into the dementia that finally took his life. Mae cared for him at home until the end, in spite of Belle's protests.

"Mama, you should put Daddy in a home. You'll wear yourself out taking care of him."

"Well, since he wore himself out takin' care of me all these years, seems the least I can do is return the favor."

He didn't know her in the end, not really. But he followed her with his eyes, eyes that gleamed briefly when she laid her cheek against his and crooned, "Jim, Jim Jameson's a *bad* boy."

In all the time they had together, Mae never dreamed that Jim would be gone from her, and her most frequent companion would be the daughter she'd never really gotten to know. She was always relieved when Belle, having satisfied some notion of doing the right thing, would take herself back to her husband and leave Mae alone with memories of hers.

In the first years after Jim died, she was still seeking and finding his quiet enfolding in the silences of her home. She assumed that would be the substance of her days, the days she had left, and she accepted Belle's interruptions with grudging tolerance because she knew Jim would be waiting for her when Belle left.

Now Jim was gone. There was no place for him here. She had tried to find him, to talk to him, but except for the occasional vivid dream, he refused to visit her in this place. She tried once to explain to Belle why she could not stay there. "I can't find your father in here," she confessed.

Belle looked embarrassed.

"Of course not, Mama. He's been gone for nearly two years."

Chapter 7
Mae

Mae awoke unwillingly from the dream. She and Jim had been on a picnic, just the two of them. They were both very young and very happy. Jim had grabbed her from behind as she bent over to lay out the food. He had rubbed against her and she would feel his need for her. Oh, she wanted him, wanted to feel him deep inside her again, feel that connection that always made her certain of his love. She was turning to him, turning slowly, anticipating, wanting.

Someone was crying. No, no, no! They were all alone here; there was no one else, no one to be crying! She tried to burrow back under the covers and into the dream, but the crying went on. Against her will, Mae could feel herself waking up. Somebody was crying. Whoever it was, she was sitting in Jim's recliner, her fist against her mouth, sobbing softly but helplessly. The light was too dim to see her clearly, but Mae knew by the slim silhouette that it was Carla.

So Miss Smart Mouth had something to cry about, did she? Served her right. She probably got bawled out by the night nurse and was in here feeling sorry for herself. About time someone took a stitch or two out of that little piece of work. As Mae watched without moving she saw Carla's free hand come up and scrub tears from her cheeks. *Real tears — huh. She musta got royally chewed out*. Mae worked at savoring the moment, but something about the pathetic little figure in the oversized chair ate at her. Oh, shoot! She didn't want to feel sorry for her. Their running battle had been one of the few things that kept Mae going these days.

Mae lay still a few more minutes as the crying subsided and an occasional soft hiccough erupted. Still the girl sat in the chair, head down now, and Mae thought it had been a long time since she had seen anything look quite so pitiful.

"So what brought on the waterworks, missy? You get chewed out for bein' mouthy?" Mae spoke softly into the darkened room, but Carla started at the sound of her voice.

"Hah, that's all you know. Getting chewed out don't bother me. I never even hear it."

"What, then?"

"Why should I tell you?"

"You're sittin' in my chair, in my room, wakin' me up out of a sound sleep, I figure you owe me."

Carla was silent for a long time while Mae listened to the night noises, the click of her old clock as it turned over the minutes, the soft hum of corridor lights, the occasional frail, petulant voice of someone needing attention. *All the same to me,* Mae thought. *She don't tell me, I don't hafta think about it.*

"I worry about my baby. I gotta leave her with Ma when I work, and I know that's not good. Ma doesn't care much about kids, never has time for them, and I'm scared they'll find out and take Faith away."

As she spoke, she wiped her nose on the sleeve of her shirt. Mae sat up, leaned over, and picked up the box of tissues on her nightstand and extended them to the girl.

"Of course they're goin' to take her away! You don't even know enough to blow your nose when it's runnin'. You're just a snot-nosed little kid yourself."

Carla accepted a tissue but ignored the comment. She wiped her nose again and then scrubbed the sleeve of her shirt.

"So why don't you find someone else to take care of your kid?"

"It's not that easy. It would cost too much and be hard to find someone for the hours I work. But that isn't your problem, right? I'm … I'm sorry I woke you up."

Just then the night nurse appeared in the doorway.

"Carla, you in here?"

"Uh, yes."

Hands on hips, the night nurse was clearly annoyed.

"She was just helping me go to the bathroom," Mae interjected. "I was a little shaky and didn't want to try it on my own."

Carla looked at Mae, and in the dim light Mae could see the girl's mouth gaped open. Grudgingly, the nurse nodded and walked away.

"Guess I'd better get back to work before they fire my sorry ass. Then I really would be up a creek."

"Splash some cold water on your face, and try to stay out of sight until your shift's over. It'll be a dead giveaway if they get a good look at you."

After Carla left, Mae thought about what had happened here. She'd lost the promise of her dream, and she knew an ache of regret. But something seemed to have started, and even though it was tentative, Mae felt the first twinge of satisfaction she'd had in this place. The girl wasn't much but at least she had some spunk, reminding Mae of her younger self.

The delicate truce that began that night grew by fits and starts over the days that followed. Mae wasn't ready to let go of her anger, and she still focused it on the closest target; often that meant Carla. But Carla gave Mae's testiness back with interest, and Mae came to admire her for that, for standing up for herself.

This, at least, was a way to divide up their fear and reposition the load of it.

Mae began to look forward to Carla's visits after most of the nursing home residents were asleep. Carla would recount the day's more interesting moments, and Mae knew a small triumph at not being the only one who had lost part of herself.

"Had to clean up a real mess today. You know Bess?" Mae didn't know Bess nor did she wish to know her. "Well, she's got Parkinson's real bad, mostly in bed all day, but around the middle of the day, noon, she perks up a bit and someone walks her down to the dayroom for a while. Anyway, she was down there when I came on shift; guess whoever took her down forgot to take her back. She kept saying, 'I gotta go. I gotta go now.' I was just coming on and didn't have my check-in work done, so I didn't get to her as soon as I shoulda. The nurse said I had to take a stool sample when she did go, so I figured I'd better get her down there. Well, she was starting back into her frozen state and couldn't move very fast, so we didn't make it."

In fact, she had been outside the door of Bess's room when she heard the soft plop of feces landing near her shoe. Looking down in disgust, it occurred to her that it would really be easier to take the sample from the hall floor than from the toilet. But still, she had to clean up the mess, and that really ticked her off.

"Ain't much different than cleaning up after a baby, is it? You get mad when your baby shits?"

" 'Course not, but she doesn't know what she's doing. Bess does."

"Don't mean she can help it. Makes it all the worse for her, knowing what she's doin' when she can't stop it. Be better if she didn't."

"So I'm s'posed to feel sorry for her? She gets to walk away from it, and I gotta clean it up, and I'm s'posed to feel sorry for her? I guess you *would* say that, seeing as how you're pretty much in the same boat."

Mae glared at her, and Carla stomped away. *Twitches that little butt as if it's made of glass, don't she?*

Another time, Carla told her about ol' man Moses on Wing Three. "Got gangrene from something and never was right. So what do they tell me? 'You got to wake him up to eat and take his meds.' They knew he was dying, and still they push food and meds down him like he was gonna live forever. Guess he showed them. He up and died last night. At least it wasn't on my shift. I don't think I could handle going in and finding one of them dead." They sat in silence for a while, thinking their own thoughts, and then Carla spoke into the silence.

"Sorry about bringing up dying and all. I s'pose you're pretty sensitive about that."

"Nope."

"Well, I'd think you'd be scared. I mean, you're getting on towards dying, aren't you? That's gotta be hard."

"Shucks, dyin' ain't hard. You just stop."

"Stop? Stop what?"

"Everything. You stop eatin' and drinkin' and then your heart stops and then your brain. They say when your brain stops, you're truly dead. Brain dead."

"That is so scary."

"Death's not scary. It's livin' that's scary. 'Specially when you got more troubles than you can shake a stick at. I think you got those kinds of troubles, don'tcha, missy?"

"I don't know what you're talking about. I'm sure better off than you, a half-dead old woman who has to pee every five minutes."

Mae nodded and bit her lip. She knew Carla told the nurse on duty she had to take Mae to the bathroom at nights to cover the time she spent in Mae's room talking. Carla snorted out a laugh, and then Mae started laughing.

Mae slept better that night than she had since coming to the home.

◈

One evening, Mae asked, "How's your kid? What's her name, Faith? Funny name to give a kid, isn't it? You don't seem to have faith in much — includin' yourself."

"Ha! Shows much you know about anything. I named her after a friend I had when I was just a kid. She was the best friend I ever had. We did everything together. Then her family moved away, and I never had a real friend after that."

"Okay, so you had a friend a long time ago. Why choose her name now?"

"I just like the idea of it. Guess I'm hopin' we'll be best friends when she's a little older."

"Faith, huh? Poor kid's gonna have a rough time of it, livin' down a name like that. Did you even think of that?"

"Hey, it's better'n Belle. How'd you come to name your kid that?"

"Well, I didn't. Her name's really Mirabelle, but it always got shortened to Belle." Mae stopped for a moment, remembering. "Funny, my Jim picked it out. Said she was his little princess and had to have a name to fit. I hadn't thought of that in a long time. Bein' his princess, I mean."

The night nurse appeared in the doorway. "Carla, you get on down to Leo's room. He needs you to take him to the john."

Mae spent the next few minutes remembering when Belle was little and Jim had been so taken with her. At the time, she hadn't wanted to see that, hadn't wanted Jim to spend so much time with his daughter instead of her. What would have happened if she'd left Jim alone, let him hold Belle and cuddle her as much as he wanted? Would Belle be different today? She punched up her pillow, trying to get comfortable, but the thought just wouldn't go away.

"Not much sense in worryin' about that now … can't change what was," she whispered. "Belle's a grown woman now. She oughta be able to figure out her own life and get on with it."

Still, it was a long time before Mae was able to get comfortable enough to fall asleep again.

Chapter 8
Mae

<hr>

The nurse held Mae's hand and dumped the tablets into her palm. Mae thought the woman looked tired, but she resolutely refused to feel sorry for her. If people like her stopped working in places like this, they would have to close them, and that would be just fine with Mae. She sat there holding the pills.

"Take the pills, Mae. I've got to get on about my rounds, and I can't leave until you take them. Go on."

Mae took a sip of water and swallowed; then she put a pill in her mouth, took another sip, and swallowed the first one.

"Where's Ruby? Is she all right?"

"Don't you go worrying about Ruby. She's fine."

"If she's so fine, how come she ain't back here?"

"They're keeping her in the hospital a little longer to get her strength back. They had a hard time controlling the intestinal problem."

"Intestinal problem! The woman got diarrhea from eatin' with dirty hands."

"Whatever. Take the rest of those pills so I can be on my way."

Mae took another sip of water and swallowed the second pill. She looked at the blue pill in her hand for a moment. Finally she put it into her mouth, raising her tongue slightly as she slipped it under. She covered her mouth with her hand so the nurse would not see her maneuver.

She needn't have worried: The nurse was checking her watch again.

As soon as the nurse left the room, Mae fished out the blue pill and held it in her hand, looking down at it, but not really seeing it. Instead, she saw Ruby. Poor helpless Ruby was even more helpless because of the aide's carelessness. Fear that she could end up like that stabbed through her. She felt something akin to panic at the thought that she had no way to stop it. She hadn't come up with a plan to get out of the nursing home and didn't even know where she could go if she did. Her home was gone, her things had been sold, and whatever money she had was now under Arthur's control.

She could end up exactly like Ruby.

Again she focused on the blue pill. If she could get her hands on enough of those, she could make sure that didn't happen. There was little left of life that interested her and no chance that things would change. She wondered how many it would take. Maybe 30 or 40. She would need to be sure she did it right, because she knew she would never get a second chance.

If she had saved the pills instead of flushing them down the toilet, she'd almost have enough by now. No, they would have found them and taken them away. Then they'd have checked more carefully to be sure she was swallowing them every day. Someone, either Belle or housekeeping or the daytime aide, was always rummaging through her purse and the drawers that held her underwear. It was one of the things that made her mad. She had nothing anymore that was truly private. And if it wasn't private, it wasn't truly hers.

She wondered if Carla would save the pills for her and bring them back when she had enough. No, best not to ask her. Even if she would do it, they'd be bound to find out and punish her.

She rose and walked over to the closet, pushing the clothes around. There was a winter coat she would never use because she wasn't allowed to go outside. Maybe she could put the pills in the pocket. No, Belle might decide to give the coat to Goodwill since Mae couldn't use it. Clear at the back of the closet there was an old terry cloth robe of Jim's. She could put the pills in the pocket of that. No, they might be found before there were enough of them to do her any good. Had to be someplace else.

She fingered the big cuff on one sleeve, noticing that the stitching was coming away from one side of it. The hole it left was just slightly larger than the pills. She could poke a pill through the hole each day and then string them out around the cuff so there wouldn't be any bulk to give them away. It just might work. Slowly, she pushed the tiny blue pill through the hole she had found. Beneath the terry cloth, she could scarcely feel it, and only then because she knew it was in there.

Feeling triumphant, Mae went back to the recliner and sat down. No one knew, so no one could stop her. It wasn't much, but it was more than she had ever had here in the home. She'd lost control over just about every part of her life, but this was something she could decide when the time came. Now she just had to be sure to convince Belle to leave the robe in her closet no matter what.

◆

"Why are you here, anyway?"

The question caught Mae just as she was dozing off. She raised her head to see Carla entering the room. She recognized her silhouette easily now from all the nights they sat in the darkened room and talked. Funny how they could talk freely at night in the dark but still sparred during the day. Not that they didn't bicker some nights, too, but mostly in the nights they talked easily about everything.

"Last time I looked this was my room. Where would you want me to be?"

"No, I mean why are you in the home at all? Nothin' much wrong with you I can see, and you lived alone all that time before. So why are you here?"

"Mostly, I guess, because I was in the way."

"How could you be in anybody's way? You lived alone, didn't you?"

"Yeah. I haven't quite figured it out myself, but somehow I was in Belle's way. I guess because I was in Arthur's way. Between them they figured out to get me here, and then I wouldn't be in anybody's way."

"That doesn't make sense. Now me, I know I'm in Ma's way, but she keeps me because she wants the little bit of money I bring in. I don't like it, but I understand it. Least I think I do. But you? That doesn't make sense at all."

"Not much in this life does make sense anymore. Least of all to me. But that's the only thing I been able to come up with."

"How did you figure that?"

"Why, there I was, mindin' my own business, puttin' up with Belle when she took a notion to come check up on me, and lettin' her fuss over me some. It seemed to do her good to be able to fuss over me. But she took to comin' more often and stayin' longer, and I was gettin' a little put out about it. Once or twice she let it drop that Arthur wouldn't like her comin' so much, but she kept comin'. So I was about to tell her to stay away if it bothered Arthur, and that way we'd all be better off. Put it off too long, I reckon."

"What does that mean?"

"Well, about the time I was fixin' to speak to her, I fell and had to stay in the hospital a few days. That's when they got me. Had me sign some papers that said they could direct my life from now on, and there I was. Right where they wanted me, I figure."

"Why would you ever sign such kind of papers?"

"Shoot, I didn't know that's what they was. Belle brought 'em in and made like they was discharge papers for me to leave the hospital. I was right anxious to get out of there, so I signed. Couldn't read 'cause my glasses was broken. Never occurred to me she would put one over on me that way."

"Wow, you mean she tricked you? What kind of paper gives someone else the right to say for you?"

"Power of attorney, she called it. They up and sold my house so I don't have anywhere else to go now anyway, so they got me right good."

"That's not right!"

"You'll get no argument out of me about that. But it's what is."

They were both quiet for a while.

"So you're just gonna take it, not do anything about it?"

Mae considered her answer. She thought of the blue pills she had carefully worked into the cuff of Jim's old robe. Not enough yet, but they were her promise to herself and represented the only hope she had at present. She still nagged Belle to take her out of the home, but there was no reason to believe Belle was listening. No, there wasn't much she could do right now.

"Don't see what I can do. They got those papers, and they're sure not lettin' me get my hands on them. As long as they got them and all my money, I got about a snowball's chance in hell of changin' things."

"Still, seems as if there should be something you could do."

"Don't know what it could be. I wish there was, but wishin' don't make it so. Only makes you more foolish."

They were both quiet again, and then Carla slipped out of the room without saying anything more. Mae watched her go and turned her back to the door, trying to find a comfortable spot so she could sleep. There wasn't any.

A few nights later, Carla slipped back into the room and touched Mae on the shoulder to wake her. Disgruntled, Mae turned over and glared at her.

"Seems like I just get to sleep, and you come in here wakin' me up. Do you know how hard it is to get any sleep in this place?"

Ignoring her complaint, Carla sat on the edge of the bed. "You know what we talked about the other night, about you being here and all? Well, I talked to Leo about it, and he says you can fight that paper they got and make your own decisions. That's something, isn't it?"

"Who in the Sam Hill is Leo, and why would you talk about me to someone anyway? What, you just go around blabbin' to anyone and everyone about the people in here? You got no better way to spend your time?"

"Listen, you old bat, Leo says he can help you get out of here. Don't you want to know how? He says he can tell you how to go about it, if you want. I bring you good news, and you jump on me."

Carla rose from the bed and started to leave the room. Mae called after her, "Aw, come on back. I'm half asleep, and you just bounce in here and hit me with all that, and then expect me to be glad to see you. C'mon, Carla, tell me again. Who's Leo, and how does he know so much?"

"Leo's one of the patients over on the next wing. He's blind, but he's been everywhere and done everything. He's a neat old guy, and I talk to him when I can. Sometimes he even calls me at home and we talk. Anyway, he says he knows you can get the power of attorney set aside. 'Set aside,' that's what he called it. That means it isn't any good anymore. And then you can live how you want."

"Don't seem like it can be as easy as that. And where would I live? They sold my house, and I don't even know if I have any money left or not. You think you have all the answers for me, and I'm tellin' you, you don't know nothin'. And neither does this Leo."

"No, Mae, he's really smart. He *knows*. He's done just about everything you can imagine, and he learned so much. And he just knows."

"Hah! If he knows so much, why's he in here? Looks like he only thinks he knows. And he sure took you in, too."

"Well, if you don't even want to know about it, I'm sure not going to push you. Guess you like it here, letting someone else tell you what to do and when to do it. Pretty soon, they'll tell you when to go to the bathroom and why. Guess you'll like that just fine."

With that she stomped out of the room, and Mae watched her go. Hah, a lot she knew. How could Mae do anything, helpless as she was here — no money, no phone, no nothing? Angrily, she punched her pillow and let her anger settle on Carla. That girl had some nerve, talking to the other patients about her. Of course, she knew Carla talked about the others to her, but that was different. All of them were senile, didn't know up from down, and sure didn't know they were being talked about. But it rankled that she was talking about her and letting someone else in on her secrets. *Shouldn't of ever started talkin' to that girl. Shoulda minded my own business and left Carla clear out of it.*

Seems like there was a lot of *shoulda's* in her life these days. Too many *shoulda's* and not enough of the blue pills.

Chapter 9
Carla

Carla squirmed angrily on the seat of the bus. Just try to do that old fart a favor, and what does she get? All right, if that's the way she wants it, that's how it'll be. Didn't need her anyway. Just another old fart to make work for her. Why did she ever think different?

Suddenly Carla looked around and realized she had missed her stop. Shoot, she'd let that old lady mess her up again. Going the whole circle back to her stop would take nearly an hour, but it would probably take her ten minutes to walk back to where she should have gotten off. Quickly, she stood up as the bus pulled into the curb. She didn't give herself time to be worried about the longer walk back in the night.

The apartment was too quiet. Fear jolted through Carla as she let herself in. There was no television, no crying baby, no slurred voice scolding her for being late. She rushed to her room and found Faith asleep in her basket. She flopped back on her bed, feeling the exhaustion of her evening. Eventually her fear diminished a little and she slipped into an uneasy sleep.

When she awoke the next morning, it was to the whimpering cries that told her Faith was waking up, needing attention. Astonished, she glanced at the clock, noting that it was six thirty. Faith had never slept this long before! Now that she was awake, Faith's crying was more fretful than the full-blown squalls Carla was accustomed to hearing.

She touched her forehead, worrying about illness, but Faith felt all right to her. She just seemed listless and logy.

After changing her, Carla quietly slipped into the kitchen to warm some formula. Faith continued to whimper against her breast, rooting around as though she were hungry. "Shhh, sweetie. Mommy's getting your breakfast. It's okay, it's okay. Almost ready. Here you go."

Faith pulled at the nipple but, after one swallow, turned her head away. Carla nuzzled the bottle nipple against Faith's lips, trying to interest the infant in the milk. Again, Faith took a swallow and then turned away. Worried, Carla repeated the effort several times with almost identical results.

By the time Faith had emptied less than a fourth of the bottle, Carla gave up. She knew better than to wake up Ma and ask her what she thought. Maybe Lotte was awake. She might have an idea about what was wrong with Faith.

Lotte wasn't awake, but she woke up at Carla's knock. "What's wrong, honey?"

"I think Faith's sick, but I don't know what's wrong."

"Here, let me have the little darlin'. C'mon, precious, what's the problem?"

"She just whimpers, and she won't eat. I'm scared, Lotte."

"Hmm, she doesn't have a fever." Lotte put the infant over her shoulder and patted the baby's back, nuzzling her neck. "Did she take any food at all?"

"Yeah, she takes a swallow or two and then quits. Sorta like she thinks it's gonna be something else, and when it's not, she doesn't want it."

Lotte's head came up sharply, her eyes narrowing on Carla. Then she held the baby out and checked her over again. "Oh, honey, I think I know what the problem is. She'll be all right in a little while."

"What? What's wrong with her?"

Uneasily, Lotte looked down at the fretful baby. "Uh, I think maybe she's just a little hung over. She cried a lot last night, and I think Gert gave her a bit of booze in her milk to settle her down."

Carla's head whipped up. "You watched Ma give my baby booze, and you didn't stop her?"

"Look, kid, I'm not responsible for you *or* your kid. Remember that." Her voice softened a bit. "I do what I can, but you know your Ma. She has her own way of doing things. Chances are she gave you booze when you were a baby to hush you up, too, and it didn't do you any harm, did it?"

"Oh, God, I can't believe this." Carla snatched Faith back and sat down in a chair, rocking back and forth with her, rubbing her back. It was like a kick in the stomach, knowing that Ma had given Faith whiskey. Carla carried the baby back down to their apartment, her mind careening from thought to thought. She had to find a way to stop Ma from giving Faith alcohol, but if she wasn't here, how could she know it wouldn't happen? She couldn't care for Faith on her own and work, too.

Maybe she'd just go ahead and talk to the social worker and see if she could get welfare.

Maybe if she found someone else to live with, it would be enough until Faith was older.

But she didn't know anyone except Lotte, and she knew that Lotte wouldn't be apt to go against Ma that way. Maybe, though, Lotte would know of someone. She had to plan. Somehow she had to make things different for her and Faith. But right now she had to make Faith better.

Carla warmed up the formula again and spent the better part of an hour trying to tempt her baby to take more of it. Gradually, Faith seemed to get better and finally fell asleep in Carla's arms, but her sleep was fretful with little mewling cries that tore at Carla.

She slumped back against the old chair, not even smelling the dusty, used smell that came from it. She laid Faith across her chest, and the baby settled down even more. Carla returned to the fix she was in, trying to see a way out. She guessed she'd have to talk to Lotte first.

She heard sounds from Ma's room and glanced over at the clock. It was nearly noon. Soon she'd have to get ready for work. No, she couldn't go to work today, not until she was sure Ma wouldn't pull this stunt again. She'd call them and tell them she was sick. She wondered if they'd dock her pay but knew that it didn't matter if they did. She needed to be sure Faith was all right.

Ma shuffled out wearing a ratty old robe and slippers that once had been pink and were now a murky gray. She was scratching her left hip, her bleary eyes scarcely open. She headed straight for the kitchen and turned the gas on under the battered old teakettle. Carla knew she would make instant coffee and slurp it down, then have a shot of whiskey. It was her cure for the hangover that was rarely completely gone. She figured Ma didn't want it completely gone, that the drinking and the hangover were what got her through each day. As soon as she had the whiskey, though, Carla would be able to talk to her and lay down some rules.

The thought of telling her Ma anything surprised her. Carla wondered where it had come from. She had never been much good at standing up to Ma, the two or three times she had tried. But now things had shifted, and she knew she had to try again. And she knew that somehow, she had some leverage this time. She pushed that around in her mind while she waited for Ma to finish her coffee and whiskey.

"Ma, did you give Faith whiskey last night?"

Ma eyed her with something like annoyance in the look. "Can't remember. Used to give it to you when you was peevish. Always worked. Yeah, I think the kid was fussy, and you know that don't set well with me. Yeah, prob'ly gave her a little in her bottle to put her to sleep. Won't hurt nothin'."

"Don't you ever do that again! You hear me? Don't you *ever* give her booze! You can put her in her bed and shut the door, or go to Lotte's to drink so you don't have to hear her, but don't you ever give her booze again."

"Who you think you are? You don't tell me what to do. This is my place, and it's my rules. You don't like it, you can walk out. I don't got to put up with your crap."

"I'm gonna walk just as soon as I can find something. But till I do, you remember what I said."

"Oh, yeah? How you gonna make me?"

"The way I figure it, Welfare could get you for fraud if anyone told them what's really going down here. I don't figure they'll find out as long as Faith doesn't get any more whiskey. You wanna make a deal on that?"

"You don't know nothin'. You rat on me to Welfare, your ass is in the crack, same as mine. You never told what you know, so you're in this as deep as I am. They'd take your baby away in a minute. How'd you like them apples?"

Carla was shaken, but she kept her voice level and her eyes on her mother.

"Maybe, maybe not. But at least she'd be better off than she is here with you feeding her booze. I ain't having it. So make up your mind."

There was a long silence while they eyed each other, each waiting for the other to back down.

"Awright. Waste of good booze, anyway. Don't think this changes anything. You don't run things around here, so don't get too big for them britches. Hear?"

"Don't want to run things. I just want Faith to be safe. Long as we understand each other, I'm all right with it." Carla felt triumphant. She had Ma's promise, and she had bested her for the first time.

It felt good.

She decided to go to work after all, now that she was fairly certain Faith would be safe. Funny, she should have taken the excuse to stay home, but somehow she knew she wasn't going to. She wasn't sure why. True, Faith was sleeping peacefully, and she would have time to give her one more bottle before she had to leave so she would feel okay about leaving her. And she wasn't sure if they'd cut her pay for not coming in, and she couldn't afford that, especially now if she was going to try to find another place to live. All of that was reason enough to go on in to work. But it was somehow more than that, and that puzzled her.

Chapter 10
Mira

Mira stood before the mirror, carefully applying blusher to her cheekbones. She used little: Arthur liked for her to keep her makeup tasteful, so she concentrated on getting it just right. She reached for the mascara wand and began to stroke it over her lashes. As she did so, she looked briefly into her own eyes and quickly looked away from the reflection. With a start, she looked back up. Why did she shy away from looking at herself?

Suddenly, it seemed important to answer that question. She looked straight into her own eyes and tried to read what was there. The longer she stared, the more uneasy she became. Something was there, but she wasn't sure she wanted to see it. Maybe she was feeling guilty about tricking her mother. But it was for mother's own good, she reminded herself. True, the way she'd had to go about it didn't set well, but hadn't Arthur assured her that, in this case, the ends justified the means?

The last few times she had visited her mother, it seemed that she looked older, as if she was going downhill. It looked like they moved her into the home just in time. Mama wasn't her usual take-charge self. She was surely slipping. And then that business about not being able to find Daddy in the home. Too, it seemed as if Mae was accepting the situation now. Mira truly only wanted her mother to be content and safe.

She would like to reassure herself by talking to her mother about it, but whenever she gently brought up the subject, Mae either ignored her or made some biting comment. That hurt Mira's feelings. Why couldn't Mae understand that it was for her own good? Why was she being so stubborn?

For that matter, why had Mae been so stubborn her whole life? Mira remembered the many times in her childhood when she tried to tell her mother something important, only to be rebuffed. Not that Mae had ever been unkind, exactly, but she hadn't listened — or when she did listen, she had been dismissive, as though Mira didn't know what she was talking about. Why, she even did this now that Mira was grown.

"What's wrong with me?" she wondered aloud. "I don't seem to matter ... even to my own mother."

That was the core of it. All her life Mira had tried to win Mae's attention, but no matter what she did, Mae seemed to keep her at arm's length. Daddy had been more affectionate, especially when Mira was small. She had a very old memory of her father carrying her and giving her little hugs and pats on the head. But not her mother. Mae seemed to almost forget she had a daughter sometimes.

And Mira had tried so hard. Was she still trying hard to ... to what? *Oh, Mama, why don't you love me?*

Tears washed the carefully applied mascara down her cheeks. Mothers were supposed to love their children. Mira knew if she ever had a child, she would love him with all her heart. She could never tell Arthur, but she would love a baby more, much more, than she loved her husband. She felt affection for him and respected him, and she guessed that was enough. But a parent should love her child more than anyone else. And some days she just wanted someone to love who would love her back in that same way.

Arthur loved her. At least, he had said that he did, and she had no reason to doubt it. Except ... Arthur seemed to want her to be something else, too. No, that wasn't true. He just wanted her to be better than she was, and he ... he what? Something nagged at her, but she couldn't quite get it clear in her mind.

Now, how had she gotten into this maudlin mood? A look in the mirror told her she would have to clean her face completely and reapply the cosmetics. A glance at the clock told her she would have to hurry, or she would be late at the nursing home. She always tried to go in at the same time so that Mae would know when she was coming. Mira figured it helped her mother to have regularity in her days. She was still doing her best to make her mother happy.

It was a good thing Arthur wasn't here to witness her lapse. He didn't like crying, to begin with, and seemed to have limited patience for her sense of responsibility toward her mother. Maybe it was because his parents were dead and Arthur had been on his own for so long before they married.

But *her* mother was still alive, and Mira knew it was her duty to look out for her. She rarely did anything she knew would perturb Arthur, but in this one thing she was determined. Still, she was grateful to Arthur for solving Mae's problems. He was truly intelligent and good at working things out. Even though he didn't understand what Mira felt for her mother, he had helped take care of her. She thought maybe that he respected Mira's feeling of responsibility, but she knew he didn't really understand why Mira took it so seriously.

Heaven knew he had no reason to feel neglected. Their house was always spotless, and she willingly took on the jobs he gave her. Even though she was timid about entertaining his colleagues, she managed to play the hostess role whenever he asked it of her. She was always careful to be home before he came from work in the evenings, always listened carefully to whatever he wished to tell her about his day, always sympathized when things weren't going as smoothly as he preferred, and praised him over his small victories.

But she sensed that he thought she should be doing more. So she was careful not to mention her mother unless she had a problem that she couldn't solve on her own. Whenever that happened, Arthur quickly appraised the situation and invariably came up with the perfect solution. Mira thought she was getting rather good at judging when to ask for Arthur's help and when to allow the situation to correct itself.

With that thought she perked up a little, quickly repairing her makeup and checking her appearance in the mirror. She still had time to get to the nursing home, spend an hour with her mother, and be home before Arthur. Maybe today Mama would be in a better mood and they could have a nice visit. Mira wanted more than anything to have a nice visit.

◈

Mae sat on the old recliner while Carla perched on the edge of the bed.

"I don't know why you won't just go talk to Leo. What harm can that do? Just listen to what he has to say, and then you can ignore it if you want to. Although why you would want to is beyond me. He can help you get out of here. That's what you want — or at least that's what you *say* you want. I guess you're just battin' your gums, huh?"

Mae was madder than she'd ever been so far with Carla. Who did she think she was, poking her long nose in other people's business? Pushing and poking her to do something just because *she* thought it was a good idea. Mae certainly wasn't going to tell *her* what she was doing to get out of here. First thing she knew it would be all over the place. Mae glared out the window and obstinately refused to answer.

"All right, if that's the way you want it, guess I'll just leave you alone from now on. Don't know why I tried to help you. You're just like all the other old farts in this place. Haven't got sense enough to look out for yourself, anyway."

Mira paused just outside the door. What was the girl talking about? Why should Mama have to worry about taking care of herself? That's why she was in this home, so she could be taken care of. Mira pushed into the room.

"What are you two talking about?"

Both of them jumped and turned to look at her. Carla seemed incapable of explaining the conversation. Mae enjoyed her discomfiture for a few seconds and then spoke to her daughter.

"Carla's tryin' to talk me into going to the craft class. I ain't goin'."

Mira spoke to Carla sternly. "I'd think you would show more respect for your patients than that, calling them names. And I'll thank you to be more respectful of my mother. If I ever again hear that kind of language from you, I'll report it to administration."

"Why, Belle, don't tell me you're getting some gumption after all this time! You might want to save it for your own self, though, instead of wasting it on Carla, here. She don't mean nothin' by what she says."

Carla slipped out of the room.

"Mama, whatever are you talking about? I took the girl to task for being disrespectful to you. You'll have to admit that what she said showed disrespect."

"No, I don't think it did. I think it showed that she *does* respect me, a whole lot more than you do."

The righteous indignation left Belle's face, leaving her crestfallen and sad. Tears leaked from the corners of her eyes. She rummaged in her purse for a Kleenex and dabbed at her eyes, careful not to spoil her makeup.

"Ah, hell, there you go cryin' again. How about pickin' up some of that gumption you had a few minutes ago and usin' it here?"

"Mama, I swear I do not understand you. That little smart aleck was sassing you — and you stood up for her. I try to come to your rescue — and you turn on me. I simply do not understand you."

"That's for sure. But I guess, truth be told, I don't understand you either, so maybe we're even."

"Well, let's just put all this behind us and talk about something else for a while."

"That's pretty much what you always do, isn't it, Belle? Put things behind you instead of figurin' them out. Don't think about it, and it will be all right."

"Mama, you are determined to ruin my visit. Please don't do that! I don't have much time … Arthur will be home soon, and I have to be home when he gets there. Please, can't we just have a nice talk and forget this unpleasantness?"

"All right, Belle, you win. You think the weather is going to change?"

"Well, this is Indiana. The weather changes frequently, as you very well know. I don't want to talk about the weather. You know, Mama, I may not approve of her tactics, but that nurse's aide did have a point. Why don't you get involved in the activities here? It would be so nice for you to make friends and enjoy your time."

"Is that what you call having a *nice talk*, Belle? I ain't much interested in that kinda talk. Nor probably much else that you would bring up. Let's talk about gettin' me outta here and into my own place. Now, *that* I'll talk about with you."

"Oh, Mama, please don't be difficult. You know you can't live alone anymore."

"I don't know nothin' of the sort. You're the one who's convinced I can't live alone. You're the one who tricked me into this place. You're the one who's not lettin' me run my own life."

"Oh, Mama, it's for the best. Why can't you see that?"

"Because it ain't the truth. Never was, never will be. You keep tellin' yourself it's for the best, but that's a lie. A lie you tell yourself. Think about that, Belle. Think about that real hard, and maybe next time you come here, we can have a real conversation."

And this visit ended as most of them did, with Belle running from the room in tears. Mae rocked in the recliner and thought about Belle. She had never liked the man her daughter married; if Belle felt too little of herself, Arthur was too full of his own importance. Mae knew the first time Belle brought him to the house that he was someone she wouldn't ever care to know. And since then it seemed that Belle lived in his reflection, carefully gathering the scraps of attention he doled out so ungenerously. Mae knew she had been right in keeping Belle at arm's length, and there was no reason to try to make a relationship now.

But there was something about that girl Carla that drew her. Perversely, it seemed that the more Carla argued with her, the more Mae respected her.

Chapter 11
Leo

"Mae, you asleep?"

"No." She spoke clearly but from the depths of the covers, with her head turned toward the wall.

"I came to apologize. I guess I just let my hopes, and wanting to help, run away with me. I won't bug you any more about going to see Leo." Mae pulled herself into a sitting position in the dark.

"Been thinkin' on that," she said. "Maybe it wouldn't hurt none for me to just talk to him once, see what he knows. I can't see how it's goin' to help any, but guess it won't hurt, neither."

Carla sat down on the edge of Jim's recliner. "Do you mean that, Mae? I'll take you over tomorrow if you mean to talk to him. He's such a neat old guy. You and him are about all that makes it so I can stand working here. Well, maybe one or two others, but mostly you guys."

"It's been a long time since someone told me somethin' good about myself. I guess that's worth somethin' right there. Sure, I'll go with you tomorrow. Now, get out of here and pretend to do some work for a change."

Carla giggled. "I work. Who'd take you to the bathroom every night if not for me?"

Mae lay back down, turned over, and pulled the blanket back over her shoulder. Yeah, she'd go talk to Leo. But she wouldn't flush her blue pills just yet.

◈

Their first meeting did not go well. Leo was sitting in a chair near the window of the room, relaxed but alert, as though he, like Mae, enjoyed watching whatever was going on outside the home. Then he turned toward them, and Mae had to bite back her reaction. It was not just that he was blind, but that his eyes were covered with a milky film that made her think of childhood monsters.

Carla introduced them to each other as though he were a normal person. "Hey, Leo, this is Mae — the lady I told you about. She decided to come and talk to you about getting out of here."

"Oh, I don't want to bother Mister ..."

"Leo, ma'am, just Leo. Glad to meet you." He extended his hand and, reluctantly, Mae placed her hand in his. Instead of shaking hands, as she thought he would, he simply held her hand for a few moments. "You're nervous."

Mae laughed nervously. "I, ah, reckon I am a little."

"Now why would that be? Haven't you ever seen a blind man before?"

"Now that I think on it, I guess I never did. Not really."

"You probably saw one at a distance and never thought about him being a real person, did you?"

Mae was silent. She didn't know how to answer that question. Leo sat silently waiting for her response. He didn't appear to be concerned about her hesitation, nor did it seem that he was angry about her reaction. After what seemed like a very long time, Mae turned to tell Carla that she would go back to her room. Carla wasn't there. But Leo had obviously sensed her movement, and he broke the silence.

"If you're afraid you'll say something wrong and I'll be upset, don't be. I've been blind since I was a teenager. I've heard it all, and I had to learn very early not to let any of it get to me. You'll probably say some things that you'll wish you hadn't, like, 'Why can't you see what I mean?' or something like that. Doesn't matter. Just talk to me like you would someone who can see."

Mae studied him, noting now that his face was lined and that the lines were gentle somehow, as though he had an endless reserve of patience and understanding. Odd, when she looked at the rest of his face, the eerie eyes didn't seem to be so off-putting. And maybe she could talk to him without actually looking at his eyes. She could try.

"Carla says you've traveled all over the country. How'd you do that?"

"When I graduated from the Indiana School for the Blind, they wanted to put me in a sheltered workplace of some kind where I could be looked after. Wasn't having any of that, so I just packed my stuff and took off."

"But you couldn't see. How did you take care of yourself? How did you even know where you were going?"

"Didn't matter where I went, all places pretty much looked alike to me. Heh, heh! A little 'blind humor' there. Well, that's not entirely true. I did want to go to some of the places I read about in my classes, so I got someone to make me a cardboard sign that said 'Chicago' and I held it up and hitch-hiked to Chicago. That's where my real education began. Chicago. Always wanted to go back, but I never did. Too many other places to explore."

"But what did you do? I mean, how did you support yourself? You had to have money to eat. And clothes and a place to stay."

"Well, as to that, I took odd jobs wherever I could. Some places had some industry for the blind, and I could work there. They'd find me a place to stay while I was there, and I made out all right. Then when I wanted to move on, they'd tell me about other places in the direction I was going … Someone would print me up a sign to hold up, and I'd be off."

"What kind of work could you do?"

"Oh, make brooms, for one. Made and sold them on street corners and got to keep part of whatever I made. There was other kind of work I could be trained to do by touch. Never did beg, but I was lucky not to have to. Got enough from working to buy food when I was on the road. Sometimes I'd find a place to stay, but I slept out many a night when I was between places. A few times I got rolled for whatever I had, but not so many times that I stopped traveling. I just learned to be more careful where I picked to bed down."

"I can't imagine it."

"No, I don't suppose many people can. But it was a good way to live my life, something I could do since there were so many things I couldn't do."

"What made you quit?"

"The times are changing, for one. Not as safe out there as it used to be. But mostly it was a matter of health. Got diabetes and couldn't keep it under control when I traveled. My sister was worried about me, so I promised her I would come home. And I did."

"But livin' in a nursin' home, after that kind of life?"

"It's a change, I'll tell you. Guess I ended up in a place where people could take care of me after all. But now I have my memories of what I've seen and where I've been. Wouldn't change that for anything."

"I wish I could live in my memories and block out this place, but the memories are gettin' dimmer all the time."

"That's because you're sight dependent. I have the advantage over you in that. Since I've never seen many of the things I remember, I made up my own pictures of what they look like, and they never fade."

Mae didn't like his statement. It made him seem better than her somehow. She rose from her chair and started toward the door.

"Thought you wanted to talk about getting out of here."

"Yes, well, I think someone who's stuck in here himself wouldn't know much about gettin' out, so I'll just let it go."

"I could leave, if I wanted to. My sister wants me to come live with her, and I could do that, but I have just what I want here. I'm here by choice."

"Well, I'm not, but I think I'm stuck here just the same. No way out for me."

"You could be wrong. Carla told me your daughter tricked you into signing a power of attorney. That's illegal. You could have it set aside and make up your own mind where you want to be."

"Oh, sure, and how do I have it set aside?"

"You get a lawyer, and they take care of it for you. In fact, even if you signed it willingly, you can still revoke it. It's your choice."

"Got no money. How could I pay a big fat fee to some lawyer to get this done?"

"Well, I assume you have some money from the sale of your house, and social security, and maybe a pension, don't you?"

"I did, but my son-in-law took over all that when I signed the paper, so now I don't have any way to get ahold of it. See, there's nothin' I can do."

"Sure you can. A good lawyer would take the case and let you pay after you get back control of your money."

"Ha! And how am I gonna find a good lawyer, sittin' in this place without even enough change to use the phone?"

"I have a phone. You can use that."

"And who am I gonna call?" she argued. "I don't know no lawyers, certainly wouldn't know a good one from a bad one."

"Mae, are you sure you want to get out of here? All you do is throw up objections. I think maybe you've decided to stay here where you're safe."

"You don't know nothin' about me. You just keep throwin' out these ideas, and none of 'em work. Then you blame me because they don't work."

"It's no shame to be afraid. I've been afraid plenty in my life, believe me. But you can't let the fear keep you from doing what you want to do."

"I ain't afraid. I'm tellin' you, I'm in a fix here, and there ain't no way out."

She should just walk out and quit arguing with the old goat. He might know something about the law, but he didn't know anything about her setup.

"Mae, I can help you get back the control over your life, if you want it. I know someone who would be glad to take on the legal battle for you. Once you had control of your money, you could figure out where you want to go. There are even people who will help you with that. But you have to make up your mind."

"There's more than one way to get out of here. You ever think about that? Maybe I'm workin' on my own plan. I got nothin' more to say to you."

Back in her own room, Mae fussed and steamed. What did he know anyway? Making out like he could put her life back the way it was, when he didn't know a thing about her. She threw herself into the old recliner and heard the dinner cart coming down the hallway. *Another tasteless meal. Maybe I just won't eat any of it. Maybe I just won't eat anything again, just starve and be done with it.* She knew that wouldn't work, that they would just force-feed her by sticking tubes in her and make her live whether she wanted to or not.

The only out she had was the little blue pills. She got up and went to the closet, pushing clothes aside until she found the robe. Carefully, she felt around the cuff to make sure they were still there. They were.

She waited a few moments for relief to claim her, but it didn't come. *Damn that old man, he's messin' it all up.* She pushed the robe to the back of the closet and went back to the recliner.

Jim, where are you? I need you, honey. Never needed you so bad in my life. It's no use anymore. I don't want to go on livin' like this, just want to be done with it. Help me. Please help me."

But instead of Jim's voice, she heard Leo's: "I can help you get back control of your life, if that's what you want."

Chapter 12
Mae

"Carla, I'm tellin' you, that old fart doesn't know nothin' about gettin' me out of here. He's just rattlin' his gums."

"How can you tell that when you don't try anything he said? Why don't you try? What're you afraid of that you won't even try?"

"You don't know nothin' either. I got to work this out for myself without some interferin' old fool messin' around in my life. Got too many people messin' around in my life as it is. Don't need any more."

"Carla!" The voice was sharp and loud, and Carla jumped up from the side of the bed and whirled to face the door. The nurse stood there glaring at her, hands on her hips. "You have other residents to see to, if you want to stay employed here. Mrs. Roberts has been pushing her call button for nearly five minutes, and you sitting here passing time with Mae. Get a move on, girl!"

"Yeah, yeah, I'm on it. Five minutes isn't long to wait. She probably just wants to tell me she has to pee. She can go by herself, but she has to tell somebody first."

"Well, if she pees her chair, you're the one who's going to have to clean it up, so think about that, huh?"

"I said, I'm on it." As she walked to the door Carla glared back over her shoulder at Mae, whether to blame her for getting chewed out or to show her anger at Mae's stubbornness was hard to tell.

Mae chewed on the idea that she was afraid to leave the nursing home. Maybe she was. She had no idea how to go about putting her life back in order. She did real well before, but everything was pretty well set. She had her house and her garden and her own way of doing things. She didn't have to think about what she wanted; she had everything she wanted right there.

She knew she wanted out of the nursing home, but everything else was so vague it made her uneasy. She thought about the blue pills. With them, it was pretty much settled. Nothing to worry her ever. There was something comfortable about that. If there was an afterlife, she would be with Jim again. *'Course, there isn't no way to know for sure.*

But if she did what Carla and Leo wanted her to do, she'd have to start setting up her life again. Make decisions about how she wanted to live. She'd never had to do that before; everything had just sort of fallen in place with Jim. They didn't think about how they would live; they just did. Ah, hell, she was just too old to start coping with things like this. Best to just take the blue tablets and let it go.

She looked up as Belle came into the room. Right on time, she thought. As long as I stay here, I'll have Belle here at 2:30 every weekday, telling me what she wants me to think.

"Hello, Mama. How are you today? I hope you're not as fretful as you were the last time I was here. It surely makes it more difficult for you and everyone else."

"Hello, Belle. Come to try and brainwash me again?"

"Whatever are you talking about? Mama, your conversations keep getting stranger and stranger. Are you sure you're all right? Maybe the doctor should take a look at you. Maybe you need some kind of medication."

"Sure, somethin' that will make me dopey and easier to get along with, huh? Why don't we just skip that and go for brain surgery, like that guy in the movie? Easier all the way around, and then I would just sit here and smile at you ever time you came. Guess you'd like that a lot."

"Mama, I made up my mind I wasn't going to let you get to me today or ever again. I think you are just getting a little cranky in your old age, and I should overlook it and forgive you."

"Belle, when I want your forgiveness, I'll ask you for it. In the meantime, I'd really like to get you riled up enough to think. Is that possible?"

"Mama, I just told you I'm not going to let you twist me up any more. I'm sure I'll feel better if I just ignore the mean things you say to me."

"Then we're gonna do a whole bunch of ignorin' each other, 'cause I ain't plannin' on listenin' to you much either, when you spout all that crap about how lucky I am to be here."

"Oh, Mama, please stop picking at me. I'm trying so hard to bring you some pleasant moments each day, and you go and spoil them."

"So, you admit that my day doesn't have very many pleasant moments in it, huh? I guess at least that's a start. Maybe we can work with that."

"Speaking of pleasant moments, I almost forgot. Your new copy of *Garden Flair* came this morning in the mail. Now where is the old one, and I'll take it out of your way."

"Damn it, Belle, why do you give it to me and then take away?"

"But, Mama, you've already read it! I know how much you dislike clutter, so I'm just getting it out of your way. Look, here's the new issue. Doesn't it look great? All those wonderful flowers on the front. Puts me a little in mind of your old garden."

"Yeah, I used to have a garden. Now all I have is a picture of one, and even that's on loan for a month."

"Now, Mama, I don't believe you could keep up with a garden now. You're just not as perky as you used to be before the fall. I wonder if there's some kind of residual damage that you haven't gotten over yet."

"Oh, look, Belle, it's getting late. Better scurry home before Arthur gets there. Wouldn't do for you to neglect him."

After Belle left, Mae let her thoughts dwell on her daughter and son-in-law. She had never liked the man Belle married, and since that day Mae had avoided Arthur as much as he'd avoided her. That seemed to work for everybody, but why was it that Belle had no self-respect?

More than ever now, Mae knew she would make no attempt to develop a better relationship with her daughter. But even as she rejected Belle, she felt drawn toward Carla. There was something about the girl that Mae admired even as she continued to spar with her. Carla had gumption, and Mae approved of gumption. To be honest, Mae wished her daughter was more like Carla.

Chapter 13
Mae and Leo

Carla wasn't going to let it go. She would walk into the room, take up the argument and, when Mae proved intractable, she would stomp out of the room muttering that she would never bring it up again. But she always did.

Mae found it harder and harder to work up her defenses against Carla's arguments. Dang it, she was getting on in years, and that girl should have a little respect and not this constant nagging. It was wearing her down.

She wondered if she had enough of the blue pills to do the job yet. She wasn't sure. She guessed that was why she put up with Carla's nagging.

"You are so stubborn. What is it going to hurt to see if Leo is right? What are you so afraid of?"

"I ain't afraid of nothin'. You don't know everything. I'm workin' on my own plan to get me out of here. What do you think of that, Missy?"

"What plan? You never talked about a plan before. I think you're bluffing just so you won't have to actually do something about it."

"I ain't talkin' about it anymore. I got my plan, and you don't need to know about it."

"What? You're just going to walk out of here some day? Where you goin'? How're you gonna live? You think I'm gonna help you escape?

My job would be on the line if I did that, so don't count on it."

"I ain't countin' on you for nothin', so don't get your knickers in a twist. I'm handlin' this on my own."

"Oh, sure. You are so *full* of it. You just don't want to take help when it's offered, so you make up stories about having your own plan. You ain't got nothin', so why don't you talk to Leo again? C'mon, Mae, give his idea a chance."

Carla glared at Mae and then lifted her brow as an inspiration hit her. "Listen, go talk to Leo. If what he says doesn't work, you can always fall back on your plan. If you have one. Which I don't believe, anyway. What do you say?"

"All right, all *right*, I'll go back and talk to Leo. Anything to get you to quit yammerin' at me."

"All right! I'll be back as soon as I get a few minutes and take you over to his room."

"Hadn't you better ask him first?"

"Nah, he asks me every day when you're coming back. He's waiting for you to get up the nerve to do something. He'll be glad to see you."

◆

Leo *was* glad to see her again. "Hey, Mae, I had about given up on you. Listen, if you don't want to keep on with this idea, that's fine. I don't mean to force you to do something you'd rather not. But I enjoyed talking to you and was hoping you'd come back and spend some time with me."

"Yeah, well, Carla finally said somethin' that made a bit of sense. She is so full of it most of the time, but once in a while she actually comes up with a good idea. So if this doesn't work out the way you both think it will, I can always back off and work on my own plan."

"That's the spirit. You're right, that does make sense. Okay, open up that cupboard and pull out the telephone book. I'm going to give you the name of my attorney. She gives you good advice and better assistance. You got the phone book? Look up Lynda Falkner, that's Lynda with a *y*. You're going to really like her, I guarantee it."

Leo and Carla left the room as Mae placed the call. She was surprised when the person answering identified herself as Lynda Falkner.

No secretary, no receptionist; the call had gone through to the attorney. For some reason, that reassured Mae as little else would have done.

Mae told the attorney who she was and that Leo had suggested she call. She told her about the power of attorney and how she had ended up in a nursing home even though she was quite capable of taking care of herself. The attorney listened quietly, interjecting a few questions of her own, neither promising anything nor negating what Mae was telling her.

Talking on the telephone to someone she didn't know, who seemed to be listening carefully to her, lessened Mae's reticence to talk about her situation. She found herself telling the attorney that she was desperate to get out of the nursing home but worried about how she could find a place to live and take care of the hundreds of details of moving into her own house again.

"You know, Ms. Jameson, there are folks who are skilled at helping you do just that, and I know it's doable, so let's don't worry about it right now. Why don't we concentrate first on having the power of attorney set aside? And finding out what your assets are so you can determine where to go from here? Does that sound about right to you?"

Mae nodded and then realized the attorney couldn't see her gesture. "I guess that seems about right. To be honest, I don't know much about legal stuff."

"I think that's why you find yourself in your present difficulties. But, don't worry, I *do* know quite a bit about legal stuff, and I'm fairly certain we can work this out to your advantage. Let me start by filing a change in the power of attorney and getting your finances back in your own hands. I'll stop by to see you tomorrow morning so you can sign the papers that will take care of that. Then we'll go from there."

"Can you do that without lettin' on to my daughter?"

"Neither she nor her husband will know about it until it's signed and served. I'll make sure that when he is served with papers he'll be required to relinquish all of your funds. Once you get control of your money, we'll put you in touch with people who can help you set up to live on your own again, if that's what you want. Now, I'll just need you to give me some information so I can draw up the paper."

Chapter 14
Carla

ori reached for the phone to call Carla's high school counselor. The teenager had enrolled as promised and signed up for the heavy classes in the morning with gym and study hall in the early afternoon. It wasn't standard procedure to check up, but Lori just needed to know if Carla was moving forward. Just then her supervisor stopped at her desk with another load of intake files.

"The file on top is urgent. Set aside whatever else you were planning to do today and get it started, will you?" She made a mental note to follow up on the Wills case the next day and pulled the urgent file towards the middle of her desk. She couldn't quite stop a heavy sigh of resignation, noting that her supervisor hesitated in mid-stride but then continued on her way without comment.

Turning to the new file, Lori read the first few items and found that, with her mind still on Carla Wills, nothing penetrated. Perhaps she should go ahead and make that call; it would be a quick one and might relieve her mind. She dialed the school counselor's number and waited for her to pick up.

"Hello, Gloria, Lori Martin here. I'm calling to check up on Carla Wills now that school is in session."

"Hi, Lori. I've been doing some checking up myself and can tell you that Carla is in school almost every morning. She sometimes makes it to gym after lunch, but mostly skips it. She never makes it to study hall, but her teachers tell me she's doing okay in her four classes, so maybe that's the best we can hope for from her."

"Sounds pretty good to me. If she's going to skip, I'm glad it's not academic stuff. I sure do want to see her graduate and move on to something better. I wish I could check up on her more regularly, but my caseload seems to be growing exponentially these days."

The counselor chuckled. "Tell me about it. Listen, why don't we set it up so that I call you if I notice anything starts going south on us? That way you can get this one worry off your shoulders and focus on your other cases."

"Gloria, I'll name my firstborn after you, boy or girl! That would be a big help to me right now. Thanks for offering."

Lori finished the call and turned to the urgent file once again. Of course, everything here was urgent, but when her supervisor made note of it, she knew it was top priority. She soon lost herself in the new case and allowed the worry about Carla to fade away.

At that very moment, Carla was confessing to Mae that she was making a real effort to stay in school, hold down her job, and take care of her baby. It was all wearing her out.

"How long before you graduate?"

"I have this year and one more, but I lost some time last year early in the pregnancy because of morning sickness. So my first period class was incomplete, and I don't know if I can just make up the work I missed or if I'll have to take it over. If I have to take it over, I'm thinking of trying to do it in summer school so I can still graduate next year."

Mae, who had not graduated herself, didn't see much point in Carla's pushing herself so hard just to get a diploma and she said so.

"Maybe it worked out for you," Carla huffed, "but you had a husband and no child when you started out. I don't have anyone to depend on but me, and I want better for my Faith than what I've had."

Mae admired her grit but still thought she was just setting herself up for failure. "Why don't you just get on welfare like all the others do? That way you could stay home and keep your baby?"

"That just shows you don't know diddly about welfare. My mother's been on it all my life, and it barely covers the necessities, let alone any extra to help you get a little bit ahead in the game. Of course, it would go farther if she wasn't drinking up some of it, but it's no easy life, I can tell you."

Mae fell silent as Carla swept out of her room. It touched her that the youngster was so determined to make a better life for her child, but Mae thought it would never happen. She was sure Carla hadn't looked ahead to the next year and a half, working full time, caring for a child, and trying to get an education. Carla would almost certainly give up sooner or later, and the thought of her failure made Mae a little sad.

She shook herself out of the contemplative mood. "Ain't none of my concern. I got enough to worry about without pickin' up the load of her problems." Still, the concern just wouldn't completely go away.

Carla also thought about their conversation as she rode home that night. It had felt good to know more about something than the old woman did. But now, remembering her words, she once again felt that gnawing fear she got whenever she thought about her own situation.

It was getting harder to take care of Faith, make it to school for five hours, and hold down a job. She crammed homework in on her breaks and dinner hour, getting just enough done to make decent grades. She wondered fleetingly if her mother was right about giving up Faith; she'd had no idea how hard it would be. One good break she had was that the home's administration allowed her to eat leftovers from the kitchen on her dinner break. Even cold, it was better food than she ever got at home, and she had even put on a little weight. She felt better, except that she was just so tired all the time. Maybe now that Faith was sleeping through the night it would be a little better.

But that brought up another worry. The baby would probably start crawling in a month or so, and Ma was more interested in drinking than in caring for a small child. The idea of all the things Faith might get into scared Carla. Maybe she didn't really have a choice about going on welfare.

The bus pulled in to her stop as she gathered up her things and left by the back door. Suddenly, she heard someone running up behind her. She turned and braced for an attack, but the man ran right on by. She could see by then that he was dressed in running garb. She let go of the breath she was holding and started running, too, wanting to get home quickly.

As she walked in the door she heard Faith crying, and tears formed in her own eyes. She picked the baby up and cuddled her, knowing that she needed to feed her. She had planned to give her a bath tonight and had hoped to get in at least another hour of study for an exam tomorrow. She was so tired.

"Told ya to give up the brat when she was born. Ain't too late. You could go down your next day off and set it up. You don't have what it takes to raise a kid, so just get rid of it. Then you could work more hours and bring in more money. It's past time you pulled more of the weight around here."

"So if I give Faith up, I'd just have to work more. Don't see how that helps me any." Carla swiped the tears off her cheeks.

"Yeah, but you wouldn't have no kid to have to tend to. 'Course, you'd still have to make it to school sometimes to keep the welfare check comin' in."

"Faith is the only good thing I got. There's no way I'm gonna give her up, just so you can have more drinking money! You want to keep your welfare check coming in, you'd best be leaving me and Faith be!"

"You'll be singin' a different tune soon enough. I can wait a while t'say I told you so."

As she prepared for bed later, Carla was still thinking about how tough it was to do what she was doing. There had to be a way to make this better, but darned if she could see what it was. She searched her mind yet again trying to figure out something, anything that would make this better or easier. Maybe she would talk to Leo tomorrow about it. She hadn't yet told him about Faith, but maybe he could help her figure out something. It looked as if he had finally got Mae started in on a solution to her problems. Just maybe he could help her. With that thought, she allowed herself to drop off to sleep.

Chapter 15
Mae

For the first time since she entered the home, Mae woke up with a sense of expectation. For a moment her foggy mind groped to remember what she had to be hopeful about. Then she remembered that Lynda Falkner was coming by today to start getting her life back the way she wanted.

She would like to have talked with Carla or Leo; she felt like she could actually trust them enough to talk about what might happen. Mae was so nervous over what the attorney would tell her, afraid she might learn that there was some glitch that would make this impossible. For instance, what if Arthur and Belle had used up all her money, and she couldn't escape the home even if they did change the power of attorney. Or any one of many other what-ifs that would condemn her to live out her life in this place.

As soon as she had gone to the bathroom and washed her hands and face, she heard the breakfast cart coming down the hall. Even if she had her regular appetite, eating right after she got up was almost more than she could face. There had always been some small chores to do at home besides cooking breakfast that helped her work up an appetite, but now even just the time to get hungry was denied her. Well, at least it would give her something to do besides get nervous about the day. She just hoped that the attorney would come early so she could quit fretting about what was going to happen.

And Lynda did come early, in fact just after Mae finished her breakfast. After checking in at the reception desk she made her way to Mae's room. Mae was sitting in the recliner looking out the window and was a little startled when Lynda announced herself as she walked into the room, her hand extended.

"Hey, Mae, it's really good to meet you. I'm Lynda Falkner. I'm as glad to be getting this process started for you as I'm sure you are."

Mae had hoped to see Lynda walking up to the building so she could size her up, so now she stalled for a little time. "Can't say I don't have some worries over how this is goin' to work. Before I sign them papers, I got to have more to go on. When they're all done and stuff, where will I stay? Don't I need to start with findin' a place to live first? And I'm real nervous about doin' it at all, because how do I know this will all work out how it's s'posed to? I ain't never had to do nothin' with legal stuff before, and I'm right nervous about how it's gonna come out."

"Mae, I can certainly understand why you're apprehensive, considering the way you were tricked into your present situation. We won't know your financial situation until we get this present power of attorney set aside and we're able to get a look at your assets. As far as where you will stay, you could continue to stay here until you find a place that's suitable for your needs. That way you'll have some time to look for a place that suits you, one that you can afford.

"So there's no way to get that goin' now?"

"Well, actually, this is the first step of working on that. I understand your concern, and I think that's natural, given all that's happened to you recently. I want you to remember that I will explain everything to you very clearly as we go along so you can decide at any given time if you want to proceed or not. But the only place we can start is with this paper."

Still Mae hesitated. Somehow she had thought the attorney would just take care of everything and she wouldn't have to do anything but pack up her things and move into a new home. If Arthur got these papers and could figure some way out of them, he would really blow a gasket, and it seemed to her that he could make her life even more miserable. What would she do if that happened? But then she remembered the little blue pills; there were almost enough now. If all this didn't work out, she still had her back-up plan. Lynda sat quietly and waited for Mae to digest what she had said.

"Are you sure Arthur won't have no chance to get even with me on this? He don't like me very much as it is, and I'm sure this will make him madder'n hops. I don't want him to do worse to me than he's already done."

"Your son-in-law will be unable to do anything once we serve him with these papers," the attorney answered firmly. "They take away every right he has to determine how and where you will live and to manage your finances. And I will go with the process server and make sure he turns all your financial papers over as soon as possible. As of the minute he's served, he will have no more legal authority to do anything of a financial nature with your assets."

"So then does that make you my power of attorney?"

"No, Mae. That makes *you* your power of attorney. From that moment on, you and you alone will be making the decisions about your life. That's not to say that at some point you may want to have someone else made power of attorney for your affairs, when things get to be too much for you. But all that can be put aside until we work through what you're going to do now."

"Okay, where do I sign?"

"Not so fast, Mae! First I want to go over every part of this document with you to be sure you understand it. From now on, don't sign anything unless you read it first, no matter how big a hurry you're in to change things. If you don't feel confident in your own ability to understand, please call me before you make a commitment to anything. Will you do that?"

Somewhat ashamed and not sure why, Mae nodded her agreement. "Never been one to want too much to do with this kind of thing, but guess I don't have much say about that now, huh?"

Lynda regarded her new client with compassion. This was all so new and probably confusing; she could understand Mae's feelings, but she hoped Mae would trust her to look out for her best interests. Carefully, she explained the document she'd brought for Mae to sign. Then she called down to the office on her cell phone to ask someone to come and witness her signature. She almost hated to leave the older woman, knowing that she likely still didn't understand exactly what was going on, but she gave Mae enough coins to place a phone call as well as a business card with her number on it.

As soon as she left, Mae began to have second thoughts. That young lady didn't know Arthur; he was pretty slippery. What if he outsmarted her? What if she didn't have much money left? Maybe Arthur had taken most of it to begin with. Now that she'd signed, she'd let hope well up in her; finding that she had been fooled again would just about finish her. She thought again of the blue pills, but even that failed to comfort her just then. Then she thought of Leo. Maybe he could explain this to her so she could understand and quit worrying about it.

She walked over to Leo's room, but he wasn't there. She turned to leave and there he was, standing in the door with his white cane. "Hello, Mae. Haven't seen you for a couple of days. Everything going okay?"

"How'd you know it was me? I never said a thing. You're kinda spooky, y'know that?"

He chuckled. "Mae, everyone has their own distinct aroma. You smell like talcum powder, and even though there are several ladies in here who use talcum, you're the only one who uses that particular scent, to my knowledge. So that's how I knew."

Mae wasn't sure whether to be satisfied with that or not, but she passed on to the point of her visit. "Saw that attorney friend of yours this mornin' and signed the paper that would take me out from under Arthur's thumb and let me do my own life like I want."

"Good for you, Mae. I know that took courage, but I was sure you had it. But I suspect it was still a bit frightening, eh?"

"You got that right. I was hopin' you could help me sort out what this all really means. I ain't never had much occasion to get into legal stuff, so I'm kinda scared about what I done. Will it be all right, you think?"

"So, you signed a paper revoking your son-in-law's durable power of attorney over your affairs, right?" Mae nodded, turned red, and said, "Oh! Yes." Leo went on, "And why are you worried about that?"

"Why, he's got all my money and all my papers, and I don't know what all he's done with any of it. Don't know if I have enough to live on when or if I can find a home of my own. I guess I'm just really scared of what will happen, how all this will turn out."

"Mae, how old are you? Hope you don't mind my asking, but it will help me help you sort this all out."

"I was sixty-nine my last birthday."

"So, you are drawing social security, I'd guess."

"Yeah, I got a check ever' month since Jim died. It's not much, but I never needed much. My home was all paid off, and lights and water are about all I needed. Ain't never been sick much or needed lookin' after before that fall that started all this. I reckon Arthur gets that social security check now, though, 'cause I don't see it anymore."

"And when they sold your home, how much did you get from that?"

"Don't know, they never said."

"Do you have any other income?"

"Well, Jim had a pretty good pension from the union, and when he died, it came to me."

"So, before this, you were easily able to live on your income."

" 'Course. Even managed to save up some ever' month in case somethin' happened that I needed help. Nothin' ever did though, 'til now."

Leo was quiet for a moment, and then nodded his head. "Mae, you will start receiving the income from those sources again yourself, and that should cover your living expenses as it did before. It's hard to believe that your son-in-law could have gone through all the proceeds from your home this quickly, so try not to worry about that. Besides, Lynda is the most capable person I know to handle this kind of thing, and I guarantee you that she is one-hundred percent on your side. She will do her best to get everything that's yours back from your son-in-law, and she'll help you set up your affairs so that you decide when and if to have someone else take care of things for you later on. I'm thinking you could know by tomorrow how things stand and how much your assets are, and then you can start planning."

"So meantime I just gotta wait it out, huh? Reckon I'll head back to my room and think this out as best I can."

"All right, Mae. But if you need to talk to someone about it, feel free to come back any time. I listen real well."

Chapter 16
Carla

<hr>

" Mae, you awake?"

Just as she was nearly able to fall asleep, Mae heard Carla's voice. Irritated at first, she started to grumble, but then thought maybe talking to Carla would help her work things out in her own mind. "Ain't asleep now, that's fer sure. Why do they call this a *rest* home? Don't seem like a body can get any rest around here."

Carla ignored Mae's grousing. "Did the attorney come today? Did you get your things back? When will you be able to get out of here?"

"Whoa, missy, it don't work out like that." Mae felt kinda good about knowing more than the teenager about something. "Yeah, the attorney came by and I signed the papers she brung, and now I just wait, I guess, till she comes back to tell me what comes next."

"Oh. Well, when will you find out? Did she say?"

"She said she'd be goin' to Arthur's office tomorrow to serve the papers. I guess once he turns over all my stuff to her, she'll let me know. Maybe I'll know somethin' tomorrow, but I ain't sure of that."

"I was hopin' for some good news for a change. Sure need somethin' to make me feel better about things."

"Why? Has something happened to you?"

"Nothin' new, but Ma's putting more pressure on me to give up

Faith. She sees how tough it is, and she just makes it tougher. Now she's sayin' even if I did give Faith up, I'd still have to keep workin' and goin' to school so she can have my pay and the welfare check, too. The only thing I wouldn't have is to take care of Faith. Taking care of her is hard for me, and I'm so tired all the time, sometimes I think I should just give up. But Faith feels like part of me, and I can't imagine not having her now. She's the reason why I keep going, so then I think none of the rest of this matters unless I can keep her."

Mae was silent for a moment. "Don't seem to me like you really got much choice. How long you reckon you can keep up with ever'thing?"

"That's the hard part. I keep thinking if I can make it 'til summer that it'd be easier for a while, and then I'd only have one more year of school to get through. But there's more. Soon Faith will be crawling, and maybe she'll get into something that's dangerous. Ma doesn't do real good looking after her now when she's always in her bed, so it will just be worse when she can get around. Am I being selfish to keep her? I just can't figure it all out! It all just goes round and round in my head. I only know I don't want to let go of her, but I don't know if I should keep her."

Mae waited for her to say more, but Carla seemed lost in her thoughts.

"I reckon you're gonna have to make a decision at some point. You can't just keep goin' on like you been doin'. It's just askin' for trouble."

"Maybe I could talk to Leo about it. He sure knows a lot, and he helped you out when things looked hopeless for you. At least now it looks like you might get things worked out so's you can get out of here. He's smart, and maybe he can think of something I never thought of."

"Wouldn't hurt nothin' to ask him, I reckon. But I wouldn't count on him bein' able to figure it out. He ain't never had a baby or a family to take care of. Seems to me he don't have experience with this kind of problem."

"Yeah, you're right, but I got nothin' else, so guess I'll give it a try."

◆

The next day Carla hurried into Mae's room a few minutes before her shift was due to start. "You're not going to believe this! Leo's in the hospital."

"What happened to him?"

"He's just so danged independent! He hates to have an aide with him in the shower room when he showers, so he usually talks her into waiting just outside the door. So, this morning he was alone in the shower and he fell. The nurse said it didn't look like he broke anything, but there was somethin' not right about his shoulder, so they took him in to check it out."

"Well, shoot! How is he?"

"Don't know. They told me they haven't heard yet. But the aide got chewed out royally for not doing her job. Sure glad it wasn't me, but it coulda been me 'cause he's awful good at convincing you he can take care of himself."

"So, whatcha gonna do now?"

"About what?"

"About figurin' out what to do with your baby and all. I thought you were gonna talk to Leo about that."

"Guess I'll just have to keep hanging on for now. When Leo comes back, I'll still ask him what he thinks about it … but 'til then I'll just have to hang in there."

"Wish there was something I could think of to help you, but I'm plumb outta suggestions."

"Yeah, I guess it's my problem, and I'm gonna have to figure it out."

After Carla left the room, another aide came in. "I'm s'posed to take you down to the pay phone. I guess maybe you got a phone call or something."

Mae stood up too quickly and overbalanced somewhat, but the aide caught her arm and steadied her. "Hold on to me, and I'll walk you down."

Mae hated to be dependent, but she was anxious and more than a little fearful. She was certain it was Lynda calling to tell her about what happened with Arthur, and she still had that nagging worry that Arthur was trickier than the attorney. As they walked down the hall they passed Carla, who gave Mae a thumbs up, but the worry didn't get any less. By the time they reached the pay phone, Mae was tense with fear. Lynda's first words quickly took care of that.

"Mae, this is Lynda. I have excellent news! Your son-in-law has been served and has already turned over to me all your financial papers."

"How in the world did you get him to do that?"

"I didn't give him any choice. He's smart enough to know that the whole affair was not handled as it should have been, so there's no way he could fight it."

"So, what now?"

"Mae, you certainly have reason to be angry with him for his manipulation, but I will have to say that he appears to have been very above-board in the way he handled your finances. I haven't studied them in depth, but the records appear to be complete, and the bottom line is that you now have a great deal more wealth than you did when he began to handle your finances."

"How come he gave them papers over so quick?"

"He actually kept them in his office, so when the server and I went to see him, he only had to go to his files."

"Was he mad?"

"I'm guessing he wasn't the happiest person at the moment, but he was very controlled and seemed to handle the whole thing as just another business transaction."

"So you're tellin' me I have enough to live on in a house of my own."

"I'm pretty sure that you do, but we won't know exactly how much until we have someone look over the financials."

"Can't you do that?"

"That's not what I do, Mae. I can recommend a financial advisor who could help you understand how much you have and also handle your investments to the best advantage to you. But I want you to think about your next move before we start the process. My question to you is this: Do you see yourself moving from the nursing home immediately, or are you all right staying there until you find just the place you want?"

"If you'd of asked me that even a week or so back, I would have said I wanted out of here right now! But now that I know I don't have to stay here the rest of my life, I'm thinkin' I can handle it a bit longer, y'know? I'd like to stay long enough to know for sure how Leo is, for one thing."

"Leo? What's happened with him?"

"I heard he fell in the shower this morning and maybe hurt his shoulder. They took him to the hospital to check it."

"Oh, my, I'm sorry to hear that. I'll check with the administrator about how he's doing. So, meantime, you're okay staying on there a few more days?"

"Yeah, but what happens next?"

"I want to set you up with a social worker who can help you decide exactly that."

"You mean a welfare worker?"

"No, you're not really income eligible for a welfare worker, but there are other agencies that are set up to help folks figure out where to go from here. They're staffed by volunteers, so there's usually no fee involved. I'll line you up with one of them, and they can get you all set."

"My goodness, I don't know what to say! I don't even know how to thank you."

"Having you get your life back on your own terms is thanks enough for me."

"But don't I have to pay you somethin'?"

"No, my services are free through the Legal Aid offices. Now, if you'd ever like to make a donation to Legal Aid, I'm sure they would be happy to accept it. But that's not something you need to think about just now. Seems like you have enough on your plate at the moment. Good luck to you, Mae. I'd love to hear from you in the future, once you're settled and on your own again."

"I'll be sure to call you. Thank you again for helpin' me!" After hanging up Mae just sat there thinking about what had just happened. She wanted to talk to Leo to thank him for what he did. She wanted to tell someone, almost anyone, that she now had her life back again. She stood up and started walking back to her room. Hardly anything around her registered with her. Just then, she saw Carla hurrying down the hall toward her.

"What happened, Mae? Did the lawyer fix things up for you?

Are you moving out right away? I'm gonna miss havin' you to talk to, y'know?"

To her surprise, Carla threw her arms around Mae and gave her a little hug. Mae found herself hugging Carla back even though she had never been a hugger.

"It's all fixed, Carla. Lynda got my papers back from Arthur, and he can't keep me in here anymore. I ain't movin' out right away, though. Got to figure out where I can go first."

"So, how do you figure out where to go?"

"Lynda's fixin' me up with a social worker who can help me. 'Course, I just wish all this had never happened and I had my own little house back, but what's done is done, I reckon. So I'll be here a while longer. And I need to thank Leo for all his help. Never would have done this without him pushin' me on."

"Oh, I almost forgot, Leo's back. He had a dislocated shoulder and they were able to put it back where it belongs. He has to have physical therapy for a while, but they can do that here, so they brought him back this afternoon. I think he's asleep right now, but you can go visit him in the morning, I bet."

Chapter 17
Mira

Mira sat in front of her mirror, her mind filled with dread and indecision. She didn't understand exactly what had happened, but she knew that her marriage was at risk. Arthur was livid when he came home last night, and he made it clear that he blamed her for the problem. She thought back on it, wondering how she could have been at fault.

Arthur had let himself in promptly at 6:00 as usual, but he was obviously extremely angry. His eyes burned into Mira's for several endless seconds before he strode over to their small bar and poured a generous glass of whiskey. Mira trembled in her chair, unable to even ask what was wrong. Arthur never drank large glasses of whiskey — in fact, he seldom drank at all. The bar was more for accommodating business acquaintances who were invited to dine with them from time to time. He seemed to contemplate having another, but instead placed the glass firmly on the bar and turned to face her.

"Is something wrong, Arthur?"

"Is something wrong, Arthur?" He mimicked her voice. "Oh, no, not unless you consider it was *wrong* to be accosted in my own office by an attorney your mother hired! Or if you feel that being all but accused of trying to take advantage of a helpless old woman is *something wrong*! Or if you consider that everything I've done to help your mother is being scrapped so she can kill herself is *wrong*! But except for that,

I wouldn't say anything was *wrong*!" With that he folded himself angrily into a chair across from her and glared at her contemptuously.

Although he had not raised his voice, Mira trembled at the venom in his words. She could tell that he blamed her. Her mind raced. How had this happened? Her mother knew nothing about attorneys and things like that.

"But, Arthur, how could she do this?"

"Exactly what I asked myself. After all the trouble I went through to take care of her, your dear mother made a fool of me. And I'll be damned if she'll ever have a chance of doing that again."

"Oh, dear! But, I mean, how could she have arranged this? She knows nothing of lawyers and that kind of thing."

"Well, somehow *your mother*," he spat the words out, "found an attorney to draw up papers setting aside my power of attorney over her affairs. The lawyer and a weasel of a process server came to my office — to my *office!* — and served me with the writ. She immediately asked me to hand over all the records, financial and medical. She knew that taking this matter to my office would put me in an untenable position with the company so that I could not argue my case with her. I'm almost certain that her move will jeopardize my standing with management. It was a thoroughly repugnant situation."

The more he related, the move livid he became.

"Oh, Arthur, I'm so sorry this happened. I can't understand why Mother would do such a thing! After you went to so much trouble to be sure that she had a safe place to live out her life … I'll go tomorrow and try to talk some sense into her."

"No!" The single word exploded into the room. She cringed back in the couch and waited for him to explain.

"Now, listen to me, Mira, and listen well. After all I've done for you and your mother, today's experience was a disgusting repayment. I will have nothing, absolutely nothing more to do with that woman!"

"Oh, Arthur, I'm so sorry! How can I make up for this?"

Arthur seemed to consider her question for a moment. "There is only one thing you could possibly do. Swear to me that you will cut that woman out of your life and never again have anything to do with her as long as she lives."

"But ... but, Arthur, she's my mother. How can I possibly cut her out of my life? Why, she needs me more than ever, now that you're not looking out for her financial wellbeing. What kind of daughter would I be if I didn't take care of her anymore? Oh, dear, I know this has been awful for you. And I'm so sorry, but if you're never going to allow it to happen again, it shouldn't matter if I continue to see her."

"Mira, would you just listen to yourself? What has she ever done for you? Compare the way she's treated you to all that I have given you. How you can even want to see her again is beyond me! I've seen from the first how she and your father ignored you, treating you like you were a piece of the furniture whenever we were with them. And now, when she has taken my generous effort to keep her safe and comfortable in her old age and thrown it in my face, why you would even want to see her any more is beyond me. I will not tolerate her in my life in any way — and that includes your having any relationship with her whatsoever. I *forbid* you to ever see her or talk to her again."

Mira cringed back against the couch. Arthur was right. Her mother had never lavished love and affection on her, so why did she even want to keep seeing Mae? She had no good answer to that question, but she knew that she still did want it with all her heart.

"Oh, Arthur, she's my mother. A daughter has to love her mother, no matter what."

Arthur glared at Mira. Clearly, he hadn't anticipated her resistance. "Have you not heard a word I said? Her stupidity could have cost me my position. It could still cost me my position, our very income. I don't know about you, but I refuse to let that happen. It almost certainly will put my promotion in jeopardy, and that's my next step up in the company. I've worked long and hard to get where I am, and she has come close to demolishing everything I've worked for."

Seeing that she still hadn't grasped the seriousness of his ultimatum, he threw up his hands and strode over to where she sat, looming over her. His voice was cold and calm as he delivered his ultimatum.

"All right, Mira, here's the bottom line. Either you promise me that you will never see her again, ever, or our marriage is over! Understand that, Mira. It's either her or me. I will not have any connection, even indirectly, to that ungrateful old bitch. Either you 'divorce' her, or I'll divorce you. Is that clear enough for you?"

With that declaration he turned and left the room. Mira sat where he'd left her, riveted to the couch in shock. How had this happened? She couldn't have both her mother and her husband. How could she choose? She needed her mother; Arthur had to see that. Someday her mother would realize how much Mira loved her. And some day she would need Mira, and Mira had to be there for her. But giving up their marriage was unthinkable; it had given her something, if only the feeling that she was, after all, just like other women. How could she go back to what she had been? Arthur wasn't the most demonstrative man, but she needed to be a wife. She needed to be … somebody.

She collapsed back in the chair in fear, a sudden fatigue enveloping her. She felt nauseous and needed to lie down, but she was afraid to go into the bedroom for fear of disturbing Arthur. She finally pulled herself out of her chair and went into the kitchen, turning off the oven and leaving the food there to spoil. She walked slowly into the guest room, laid herself rigidly down atop the bedspread and allowed the evening's events to overwhelm her. The shock and fatigue won, and she fell into a fitful sleep.

When she woke in the morning, stiff and chilled, Arthur was already gone. Or maybe he had left the night before without her knowing it. She couldn't seem to work up the energy to think about it one way or the other. She showered, dressed carefully, fixed her hair, and applied her makeup just as she did every morning. Then she sat on the vanity chair and wondered what to do next.

She wished somebody would tell her what to do next.

Chapter 18
Mae

<hr>

Mae could scarcely bother with her breakfast. She took a few bites and pushed the tray away, certain she would hear about it from the nurse later. She was anxious to get down to Leo's room to find out how he was and to tell him what had happened. She also wanted to ask him some questions about getting her life back in order. When she got there, Leo was still in bed but was awake and seemed happy to have her company.

"How ya doin', Leo?"

"Well, now, I've been better, but I'm been told it could have been a lot worse so guess I'll make do. I just hope the aide didn't get into too much trouble for bending the rules for me."

"Ask Carla about that. The aides seem to take care of each other some, so she'd know. I bet they all keep a closer eye on you from now on, though. I hear your gal got royally chewed out for not stayin' with you, but Carla didn't say anything about her gettin' sacked."

"Good, I hope not. Now, what's happening with your plans?"

"That Lynda is just amazin'! They served them papers on Arthur yesterday, and she called me right away to tell me it went good. Guess he didn't take it too kindly, but he gave 'em ever'thing she asked for. And the best part is, she's pretty sure I'll have enough to get back to a place of my own. So now I got to figure out what it is I want to do."

"What's there to figure? You said you wanted to go back to living on your own. Have you changed your mind?"

"No, not exactly. Just don't seem to know how I want that to be yet. I don't reckon I've ever had to do all that decidin' on my own before, and I'm a little scared of doin' it now."

"C'mon, now, Mae. You're a stronger woman than that. Did Lynda have any advice for you?"

"Well, she said there was some kinda social worker who could help me figure what I maybe could do, and once I made up my mind, they'd help me get set up. Don't know, though. I'm not sure I want a social worker messin' around with my life. I just wish Belle hadn't done this to me and I was back in my own house and all."

"Now, Mae, wishing won't do you any good. You're a strong woman — you just have to believe in yourself a little bit. Do you think a social worker is going to take advantage of you somehow? I can tell you from experience, I've never yet asked for help and then felt like I was taken advantage of. Your fretting about it will just make it take longer. I know you can do this. Just tug up your drawers and get it done."

"Huh, I reckon I don't have much choice. Reckon I'll just go and call Lynda and have her set me up. But, for sure, Leo, you doin' okay? I kinda worried about you."

"Oh, now don't you go worrying about a tough old geezer like me. I just got some healing to do, and I'll be right soon enough."

"Well, I'll come back after I talk to Lynda and let you know how things are, okay?" Mae paused for a moment, a little uncertain. "Say, I wanted to ask you about Carla. How much do you know about her situation?"

"I know she is living with her mother. But she hasn't shared much more of her story with me. Why? Has something happened to her?"

"Well, she has a baby. Named her Faith. Maybe I shouldn't be tellin' you, but she needs some sound advice. See, her ma's been puttin' pressure on her to give the kid up. I reckon it's because she's havin' trouble keepin' up with school, workin', and the baby. And Carla's all worked up just thinkin' about losin' her kid. Then her ma lays it on her good, says she'd still hafta keep her job to pay for herself even if the kid is gone. Don't seem right to me that her ma's gettin' welfare to pay

Carla's way and still wants Carla to earn money and give it to her. How can she get away with that, anyway?"

"Hmm, I don't really have any experience with how welfare works. Maybe I can talk with Lynda about it, not naming any names, just to see what her take would be."

"Hadn't thought about that. She knows a lot about social services, so maybe she could help. And for sure, don't tell her any names or nothin'. Carla has enough troubles without the state takin' over on her."

"Let me think on it some. I know Lynda can be discreet, but I'm thinking there might be some welfare fraud going on here, and she'd be wanting to get that straightened out. But I'll be careful."

"Yeah, go on and do that. And don't tell Carla lessen you do get some good news. She don't need any more bad news in her life, I'm thinkin."

Mae thought about their conversation as she walked slowly toward the office to make her call. Just talking with Leo made things seem more reasonable. She was anxious now to set up the appointment with a social worker and get things rolling.

Chapter 19
Mira

Mira stopped at the door, hesitating to go in. If Arthur found out she had gone against his demand, would he do just what he had promised? She was more fearful of that than of anything else just now. Even so, she couldn't just never see her mother again. She had to let her know that she was doing what she had to do to save her marriage. She wasn't even sure her mother would care, but Mira cared. In spite of everything, she cared.

Mae was sitting in the recliner looking out the window. Mira wondered if she had seen her coming up the walk and was deliberately ignoring her. Hesitantly, she stepped into the room and cleared her throat.

"Mama, I'm here."

"So I see. Why are you here after all you done to me? Why aren't you off somewhere with that connivin' husband of yours? Come to stick it to me one more time?"

"Oh, Mama. Please don't do this! We were only trying to make your life easier and more comfortable. We did it for your own good. Why can't you see that?"

"Mostly because it *wasn't* good. I think you did it for your own reasons, and I know for certain that Arthur wasn't thinkin' of me at all. So now that I can put things back the way they belong, why don't you just get on with your life and leave me to mine?"

"Mama, please, I need you. I don't know how I can say it any differently. I've always needed you, but you never seemed to believe that. So when I thought you needed me and I could do something to help you, I felt good about it. Now you've gone and made it a terrible mess."

"Belle, did you ever once consider what *I need*? What *I want*? Oh, no, just what you want. You're the one who made this mess you're complainin' about. I never did understand you, and I purely don't understand you now."

Mira began to sob, her carefully made up face becoming ugly and pitiable at the same time. She could not imagine how she could go on, losing her mama and probably her husband in the same day. Mae watched her closely, a little shaken to see her daughter so torn up. She tried to steel herself against pity, but she was truly unsettled by the heartrending sobs. At that moment Carla came to the door, studied the scene for a moment, and then slowly backed away.

Mae softened her tone. "Belle, go home to your husband. I 'spect he won't want you to have anything to do with me now, so go on home and tend to your marriage. I'm gonna get on with my life. You should get on with yours."

Still sobbing, Mira gathered up her purse and walked slowly out of the room. She knew she would tell Arthur about disobeying his orders, but she would explain to him that it was definitely the last time she would see her mother. Perhaps he would forgive her for trying one last time. But the Arthur who confronted her yesterday was not someone she even knew, and she was very much afraid she couldn't count on it.

◈

Mira had been right about Arthur. When she told him that she went to see her mother one last time, his face became a mask. "I had my doubts about you from the first, but I thought you could be trained, that I could make you into something. It seems I was wrong about that. I should have known that coming from such a low class family you couldn't measure up to my standards. You are a simple-minded fool, and I am finished trying to teach you some grace and class. You're a huge disappointment to me, Mira. I was willing to give you one more chance, but you couldn't wait to throw that in my face, could you? I'm not surprised; you never got anything right. All that blather early on about wanting children. If you had any sense at all, you'd know off-spring are of no interest to me. Children are vulgar little animals who suck the life out of you and then turn on you. But you couldn't even fig-ure that out. So, to make sure that never happened, I had a vasectomy before I married you."

Mira gasped. There was a roaring in her head, and although Arthur's mouth was still moving, she couldn't hear him. All she heard was her own thought: *My life is over!*

Arthur watched her crumble. His disgust was written large across his features. "I'm going to a hotel for the night. By the time I come home from work tomorrow, I want you and your pitiful possessions out of my house."

"But, Arthur, where will I go? I have no job and no place to live."

"You should have considered that before going against my explicit instructions. Oh, and one more thing you need to know: The papers you signed before we were married are an iron-clad prenuptial agree-ment. You'll get nothing from me — which is appropriate, because you brought nothing *to* me. You may take your clothes and personal items, as I have no use for them, but don't even touch anything else, or I'll have you in court for theft. I own the car you drive — you'll have to take a cab wherever you're going. My attorney will contact you about the divorce."

With that he turned and left the house. Mira sat there in a stupor for some time, wondering how things had become so twisted and wrong, and where she could go from here. She had nothing and no one to turn to.

Chapter 20
Carla

Leo was sitting in his chair, enjoying the feel of sunshine on his face and listening to his favorite music when Carla walked into his room.

"Hey, Leo. Glad to have you back. I guess you're pretty sore from what happened, huh? I'm just glad it wasn't anything worse."

Leo smiled in the direction of her voice. "Hey, Carla, it's good to see you again. What's happening in your corner of the world?"

"Not much of it good, I'll tell you. I was wondering if I could come back this evening and ask you some questions. Would that be all right?"

"Fine with me. I'm sure not going anywhere. Don't you go getting into trouble for doing that though, you hear?"

"Oh, I know how to handle that. I just tell the nurse you needed some help with something, and she doesn't ride me too much."

"Well, you gotta be careful with stuff like that. Even though you're a good worker, folks don't like being fooled, and it could get you into hot water."

"Sure, I'll be careful. But I really need your advice. I'll see you around eight, then."

Leo was in bed when Carla returned that evening, but he was awake, waiting for her. She had cut her dinner break short so she wouldn't be taking quite so big a chance.

"So, little Carla, what's the problem?"

"Whew! Okay, I never told you I have a kid. She's beautiful, name's Faith, and she's just about all the good I got in life."

Leo grunted assent. "Go on."

"The problem is, we live with Ma. She gets welfare for me, so she said I could stay there if I pay her for taking care of my baby and pay all of Faith's expenses. And, I have to stay in school so she can still get welfare for me. You see where this is going?"

"Yeah, and it's not good. Aside from the legalities, you're probably sinking under the weight of all of this, aren't you? How long do you think you can keep going like this?"

"Well, that's the problem. Or one of them. The biggest one is I worry about Faith when I'm not there. Ma likes her booze, and she doesn't much care about anything else. So Faith will be crawling before too long, and I'm worried she won't be safe when she can get into things."

"Yep, and when she crawls, walking won't be far behind. Can you make things as hazard-free as possible for when you're not home?"

"Yeah, I can set things up, but no telling if Ma would leave them that way. I could maybe get a baby-gate and confine Faith to my bedroom during my working hours, but Ma might take it down and forget to put it back."

"Okay, so it's not a perfect set-up, but what other choice do you have?"

"I don't know. Maybe I could go on welfare on my own and move out, but I'm under-age and don't know if they'd just take Faith away from me if I applied. How can I find out about that without taking a chance on it happening? Do you know how welfare works?"

"Nope, not really. Never had to use it myself. I could talk to my attorney friend about it if you want me to, not telling her any names or things, and see what she knows. Or she may know someone else who could give us some answers. I'm certain we can trust her to keep it in confidence. But I don't know any other way to start finding out."

Carla let out the breath she was holding. "I'm scared of even doing that. But I'm more scared for Faith. I guess I'll just have to take a chance for the baby's sake. Yeah, go ahead. Call your friend and find out what you can. The most important thing to me is Faith's safety."

"Sure, little Carla. Listen, I'm not making any promises, but I'll bet we can get some help for you one way or another. So let's just sound her out and see what we can come up with. You okay with that?"

"I'm real scared, but I'm more scared of what could happen to my baby if I don't. So, yeah, I'm okay with that."

Chapter 21
Mae

Mae slept poorly that night. Something nagged at her about Belle, and she was having a hard time figuring out what it was. Belle hadn't changed — she was still the helpless, whiny, clingy person she had been since infancy. But even something about that seemed to eat at her, and she puzzled over it. She tried to just shut it out and go to sleep as she usually could, but sleep wouldn't come. She was almost starting to think maybe she should have done different by Belle somehow.

"Don't see how I coulda done anything different, though. Belle just always wanted too much, right from the start." Her mind went back to those days. Mae had been angry to learn she was pregnant, had not wanted to share Jim even with a baby. She and Jim were perfect together, had been for more than thirty years, and a baby would surely take that away from them. And she felt too old to care for an infant. Then Belle had turned out to be a colicky baby, crying almost non-stop some days, taking away any chance of quiet time between Mae and Jim. Mae resented how Belle changed their lives. Her time with Jim had become their time struggling to care for Belle.

Jim helped her out as much as he could, sometimes walking the floor with Belle during the night so Mae could get some sleep. But Mae couldn't sleep when he wasn't in their bed. She resented more and more that their life together had been pushed aside to make room for the baby she never wanted. Now, instead of lovers, they were parents. She wanted to tell Jim what she was feeling but couldn't figure out how to say it right. By the time the colic finally ended, Mae's resentment had lodged deep inside her, and she pushed Belle to the fringes of her attention.

She figured out things like how she could prop Belle's bottle up with a pillow during the day so she could get done the things she wanted to do. That way her evenings were free to spend completely with Jim. It seemed like a good plan, but Jim was purely taken with Belle. As soon as he came home, he picked up his daughter and held her, rocking her gently and cooing to her. Mae simmered resentfully.

So she started keeping the baby awake during the day as much as possible so she would be asleep when Jim got home. Jim just moved the cradle over next to his chair and gently rocked it as he watched her sleep. Mae didn't know how to explain to Jim that she needed him so much more than a tiny baby ever could. Her resentment deepened, all of it focused on Belle. She fed her, changed her, bathed her, but resolutely ignored her otherwise.

"You get enough attention from my Jim," she thought. "I ain't givin' you no more than I hafta."

Gradually, though, as Belle grew older, Jim's relationship with her changed. Mae never questioned why this was. She just began to make sure Belle was safely asleep by the time Jim came home. As Belle grew older she grew quieter, spending more time just watching her parents as she sat with her toys around her. For Mae, things seemed to get back to where they had been before Belle was born, just like she wanted.

Mae recalled all this now with a slightly different perspective, and it rankled her some, thinking of Belle sitting quietly all alone. "Still don't see how I coulda done different," she reasoned aloud. "She was always just too much. And she still is." Angrily, Mae punched her pillow and tried to drift into sleep. But just as she was about to drift off, a realization startled her. She sat up fully awake. She had treated Belle pretty much as her parents had treated her, as an intrusion into their lives — and she remembered how lonely and unwanted she had felt.

She sat quietly for a few minutes with the thought, but then dismissed it. "So what? I didn't get all mopey with my folks — I just made my own life and lived it. She's a grownup now! She should just pull up her socks and get on with her life, just like I did. Any road, I can't go back and give her a different childhood, so none of this don't matter none now." She nodded with satisfaction at her conclusion and whispered, "She's gotta learn to figure out her own life."

Maybe, if Belle ever came around again, she would tell her just that. With that she lay back down and settled herself to sleep. But she slept in fits and starts that night, and by morning she was so irritated she snapped at the aide who came in with her breakfast tray and mulishly refused to eat. She spent most of that day in Jim's old recliner arguing aloud with herself.

Chapter 22
Mira

Mira had her own long night. Unable to sleep, she had spent the night packing up her things. She was somewhat surprised at how little was "hers" and not even sure what really *was* hers. Arthur had picked out most of her clothes, so she knew they would always be an unpleasant reminder of all that had happened, and she considered leaving them. Practicality forced her to pack them, but she promised herself to discard them as soon as she found work and could buy things she liked.

When she finished, she had two large suitcases of clothes and personal items. She had enough money in her purse for a taxi, and maybe enough for a night at an inexpensive motel. Then she remembered that Arthur had regularly deposited money in a checking account in her name for household expenses. There might be enough money to rent a room at least for tonight. She would have the taxi driver stop by the bank so she could find out.

To her surprise there was a fair amount in the account, enough to see her through the next two weeks or so. She withdrew most of the money, worried a little that Arthur might find a way to give her grief over that. She just had to take that chance.

She briefly considered going to the nursing home to let her mother know of the change but decided that Mae probably wouldn't care. She checked a phone book in the lobby of the bank, found an inexpensive motel nearby and went there, grateful that things seemed to be working out.

Then she started job hunting. However, finding a job turned out to be harder than she anticipated. When potential employers checked her reference with the insurance company, they were told no one by that name had ever worked there. In desperation she turned to an employment agency, but they were dubious of finding a job matching her qualifications without a prior work record. Finally, they both agreed that she would take any kind of job just to be employed. At last she was offered a position as a night auditor in a large motel close to the city center. The salary was barely adequate to pay for an apartment and other living expenses, but the requirements were within her capability so she accepted it.

The apartment she found was in a seedier part of the city than she would have liked, but she didn't have much choice. It was fairly close to her new job, it fit within her new budget, and she could ride the bus to and from work. She was frightened but determined to meet the challenge of her new life. She had a small office, which turned out to be a converted storeroom with space enough only for her desk and a chair. Small though it was, the idea of having her own office made her feel as if she had already taken a step up in the world.

Mira found the auditing job easy enough, and her co-workers were a friendly group, totally different from the pool at her old job, so she began to breathe more deeply. Coffee breaks were spent together with the other employees, filled with laughing and teasing, and Mira found that for the first time in her life she was accepted in the group. She had told them very little about herself or her life up to now, and they seemed to be okay with that. Some nights when the auditing load was light and she was bored, she volunteered to help out elsewhere in the hotel just to make the time pass more quickly. Her co-workers appreciated the help, and she found that it gave her more camaraderie with the group.

One morning as she rode the bus home, she realized that she didn't even think about Arthur these days. She liked being able to buy clothing that appealed to her, and she found that she also liked not being so unsure of her taste. She felt like a different person from the woman who was married to Arthur — and she liked who she was now most of all. As she thought about it, she realized that doing things on her own schedule was very satisfying, and not having to worry about whether Arthur would approve was exhilarating.

She thought about how Arthur would disapprove of her socializing with her co-workers and laughed out loud. This independence was heady stuff! No one was telling her she couldn't, or shouldn't, or frowning at her as though she were a teenager with no sense. She was enjoying the new Mira very much, gaining confidence with each new task. Socializing with coworkers after hours included good natured bantering and even a little flirting. Arthur would surely have frowned on that. Her life had never felt so good.

She thought vaguely about telling her mother how good her life was now, but then she remembered almost every word of their last conversation and decided that Mae wouldn't care. Even that couldn't completely ruin the exhilaration she felt. She had new friends who clearly accepted her as she was, not expecting her to meet some hidden criteria that she couldn't figure out, and giving her the confidence to just relax and be herself. It seemed that from now on she could create her life to suit herself. And that thought made her very happy.

Chapter 23
Leo

"Hey, Lynda, good morning! Leo here. I have some questions for you, if you've got a minute to talk with me?"

"Of course, I always have time to talk with you, Leo. How are you doing, by the way? Are you fully recovered from your fall?"

"Seem to be. But they're watching me much closer now than before, and I'm not very happy with that."

"That's what happens when you break the rules, my friend. I do understand that you're more concerned with your independence than your safety, but nursing homes have liability issues, and you can't blame them for being careful."

"Okay, okay, now you sound like an attorney. But I didn't call you to get the lecture. There's another troubling situation that I'm hoping you can help out with. You game to take on another wounded soul?"

"Tell me about this 'wounded soul'!"

"One of the aides who works here has some serious problems in her home life, and I'm hoping you can help figure out how to help her or tell me who can. Here's the thing … her mother gets welfare because the girl is underage. But the mother is pushing her into an impossible situation, and she's scared out of her wits about it. How do we find out what options she might have?"

"Well, Leo, this sounds complicated. Why is she working as a nurse's aide if her mother gets welfare for her? And why isn't she in school? That's surely one of the requirements for eligibility for welfare. Is there more to the story than what you've given me?"

"Of course there is. It's just that she's so scared of what could happen that I promised her I wouldn't tell you more than you need to know. But you certainly need more than that. Okay, here goes! I don't even know all the details, but I'm fairly certain the mother is an alcoholic. The girl seems to have pretty much raised herself and taken care of her mother in the process. Now, however, she's a mother too, and she's worried about the welfare of her baby."

"Wait a minute. She's a mother, and her mother is still getting welfare for her? Why hasn't the mother just applied for welfare for the girl's baby? And why is she working if she has a baby? I'm guessing the welfare worker doesn't know about the baby."

"I suspect you're right, and I think therein lies the problem. I'm filling in details I'm not sure about, so bear with me a bit. It seems the mother has threatened her with being kicked out on the street if she doesn't work and turn over her paycheck. The thing that scares her the most, though, is that the mother babysits while the girl's in school and does her shift here at the home. She worries about her baby's safety because the mother gets drunk every evening, but she thinks she has no other options."

"Okay, I'm with you so far. There are certainly some welfare issues here, but we'll set that aside for the moment. How old is the girl?"

"Never asked her, but I'd say I'd guess about sixteen."

"That's important. If she's sixteen and a mother, she possibly could be emancipated from her own mother and be eligible for welfare on her own, I believe. Or she may have to have a guardian of some kind until she's eighteen. I'd have to check on that with Child Protection services to be sure of the laws. Since you're concerned for her, I'm guessing that you believe she deserves better than she's getting."

"Yeah, for sure. I think she's a fairly bright young lady and, with the right breaks, could make a success of her own life and raise the baby capably. The baby will begin crawling soon, so Ca — uh, the girl's even more worried about the baby's safety. She really needs to know if there's any way out of this mess."

"I'd have to have more to go on to give you any valid advice. What more can you tell me?"

"Well, not much. But I could talk to her when she comes on duty and find out whatever else you need to know. The thing is that she's scared they'll take her baby away, and it's apparent she really does love that kid. So it's a little like tiptoeing across broken glass, trying to get information out of her. What else would you need to know?"

Lynda outlined some of the information she needed to move forward and suggested that Leo talk the girl into making a call to Lynda herself.

"I'm not sure she would do that. She's even afraid that my talking to you will result in her somehow losing her kid."

"Leo, tell her she doesn't even have to tell me her name. But I can't find out pertinent information without knowing more about her. Her age, for example. Things like that. Please try to convince her to call me."

"Will do, Lynda. And thanks for taking on yet another of us walking wounded. You're the best!"

"Ah, shucks. Your pretty talk will turn my head, kind sir." They both laughed as she ended the call.

◆

"Are you saying that I have to talk to that lawyer myself? I don't *think* so! How do I know she won't somehow figure out who I am and let Welfare know? She's probably sworn an oath or something to do that! And if the Home found out I'm not eighteen yet, I'd lose my job. There's got to be a better way than this."

"Carla, I've trusted Lynda with my secrets for a very long time, and she's never let me down. You saw how she helped Mae — Mae was worried about her son-in-law finding out what she was doing, too, but Lynda handled that with total discretion. There's no reason to believe she would fail you."

"Leo, you're a great guy, and I really, really trust you. But I just don't know about this. Man, I've got so many things to worry about now … What if she rats on me to Welfare? Then my mom would throw me out for ratting her out, they'll take my baby, and I won't have nothin'. Nope, I just can't take the chance."

"Well, I can't guarantee that none of that would happen. But, Carla, stop and think about where you are now. Your baby may soon be in serious danger if you don't do something, and if the worst happens, Welfare will be notified anyway. Then, you'll likely end up in foster care, and your baby will be in separate foster care. And even if that never happens, you must see that you are carrying a load that is about to overwhelm you. This may be a chance you just have to take."

Leo heard Carla crying softly, and he ached for the child's dilemma. She was obviously scared to go any further with the attorney and scared of what would happen if she didn't. There just didn't seem to be any good alternatives. He listened as she pulled a tissue from the box, blew her nose, and scrubbed her face.

He heard her stand up and walk toward the door, tossing a tentative "I'll think about it" over her shoulder. He closed his eyes and thought how tough her young life was. He hoped she would make the right decision but, at this point, he had no idea what the right decision was.

Chapter 24
Mae

"Hello, Mrs. Jameson. I'm Brenda Marshall. Lynda Faulkner asked me to stop by and speak with you. I understand you're about to make a big change in your life and you'd like some help. I'm from Senior Services, a non-profit organization that helps older folks meet some of the challenges they face. Would you like to talk about that?"

"Yeah, I s'pose so. But how much is this gonna cost? I got to be careful about that sorta thing now, y'know."

"Of course you do. I brought a brochure about Senior Services and what we do, so you can refer to that as we go through this process. But let me point out that Senior Services doesn't charge clients for the service it provides. We are a fully-funded nonprofit organization, so all our assistance is free. That includes what we would do to help you find a place to live and help you get settled in."

"Reckon that sounds good enough. How do you go about it?"

"Well, first we talk. What kind of place do you have in mind? Do you want an apartment or a house or what?"

"I had a sweet little house, and I want one as much like it as I can find. My Jim was a carpenter, and he built that house for us. After he died, I could still feel him there. Now I can't feel him at all in this place."

"And you're hoping that when you're on your own again, you may feel him with you."

"That's what I want more than anything."

"Tell me about your little house. How big was it? How many bedrooms? What other rooms? Did you have a garden? What was your favorite part of the house?"

Mae and the Senior Services lady talked for a long time, Mae growing increasingly excited about the prospect of finally having her own place again. Finally, Brenda shook her hand and promised to start the search the next day and to keep Mae abreast of how it was going.

Again, Mae had trouble sleeping that night. She might be out of this place soon, and it couldn't be soon enough for her. She scarcely registered when Carla slipped into the room, although she was still wide awake. As Carla sank into Jim's chair, Mae noticed that she was unusually quiet.

"Cat got your tongue? Somethin's eatin' at you, ain't it?"

Carla sighed and slumped back against the chair. "It doesn't look like it's gonna work, after all."

"What ain't gonna work?

Carla wiped her eyes. "Leo didn't have anything that would for sure work for me. Said I'd just have to take a chance on gettin' everything straightened out. Said I didn't have much of a chance going on the way it has been, and I might lose Faith anyway if I don't try something else. But I can't even think about losin' her. Maybe it will all work out alright the way it is."

Mae lay in silence for some time. Finally, she asked, "So what did Leo tell you to do that won't work?"

"He wants me to talk to that lawyer you talked to. Says I have to lay it all out for her to even know if she can help me. But what if I tell her and she can't help me, or what if she's got to tell on me or she'll break the law, too? I'm sorta sorry that I even told him now. He already called her and told her too much, how I'm an aide here and all. I wish you'd have stopped me when I told you my idea."

"Humph. No way I could know how that would turn out either. But I guess I see your point. I never broke the law, so I don't have that to worry about. I guess old Arthur is the one who broke the law, but I don't care much about that now I got myself outta his trap."

"Well, things are sure all messed up for me, so I don't know what will happen now. But I do know I'd take Faith and run away before I let someone take her away. That's maybe what I should have done in the first place." And with that, Carla rose and left.

Mae found it ever harder to get comfortable enough to sleep after that. Just seemed like the bed was too hard and lumpy, the noises from the Home were louder than usual, and she couldn't find a good position to lie in to sleep. She finally turned over onto her back and lay there thinking about all that was happening and how it would turn out.

" 'Course, I ain't got any way of knowin', not for me and sure not for Carla," she said to herself. "So, guess I'll go over and talk to Leo about it tomorrow." She thought again about whether or not she should get ahold of Belle and let her know what was happening. It rankled some that she even had to consider that, since Belle put her in this situation and therefore was responsible for her sleeplessness.

Well, she didn't have to decide that right now. Belle was getting on with her own life, and that suited Mae to a tee. Maybe after she got moved, though, she would need to let Belle know where she was. Or maybe not. She'd think on it some.

Chapter 25
Mira

Mira leaned back in her chair and looked around at the group of people with her at the table. They had left work at 6:00 a.m. and gathered at a nearby restaurant to have breakfast together before heading to their homes to sleep. Having breakfast together was something they now did frequently.

She couldn't remember ever being this light-hearted, laughing at the corny jokes her co-workers told, reacting with mock anger when Ernie reached over and swiped a piece of bacon from her plate, and simply soaking up the camaraderie that enveloped the whole group. She couldn't remember ever having this many friends or feeling like she was part of a group like this.

She thought sleepily that she wouldn't mind staying in this job for the rest of her life, just to have so many friendly people around her. Mama would …

She sat up straighter, realizing that she hadn't thought much about her mama lately. Hadn't worried about why Mama wasn't appreciative of her help and company, hadn't fretted about pleasing her mama so she would love her. When had this happened? How had it happened?

Ernie noticed her withdrawal. "Earth to Mira. Are you falling asleep already? Do we need to help get you on the bus home?"

"Goodness, no! I just thought of something strange, and it surprised me a little bit. I'm not at all sleepy now."

"Wanna talk about it?"

"No, I need to think about it for a while. It's maybe important to me to figure it out. I'm not even sure what it means yet."

"Well, if you ever do, I'd be willing to listen."

As if this signaled the end of the gathering, her co-workers began to fumble for cash to pay their checks and go out to catch a ride home. Slowly Mira did the same, her mind still on the realization that something had changed in her feelings toward her mother. Actually, it was more as though something had shifted in Mira, and her mother's opinion just didn't seem so important anymore. The thought made her feel good, and that amazed her, too.

She awoke with a start early that afternoon. She had been dreaming of Mama, and in her dream Mama just wasn't as overbearing as she had always been. Instead, Mira had a sense of some kind of respect coming from her mother that had not been there before. She probed this idea for some time, wondering why she would have this dream now. What had changed?

Well, she really didn't know for sure, because she hadn't seen Mama for … how long had it been? She tried to remember the date when she left Arthur and realized that it had been nearly three months since she had last seen her mother. And, amazingly, much of that time she hadn't missed the daily visits at all. Not since she started working and meeting new people and been accepted as one of the group.

Maybe she should go see Mama today. If something had changed, it might mean that she and Mama could be … what could they be? Friends? Somehow that struck her as funny, and she laughed out loud. But the word stuck in her mind, and she toyed with it. She liked the idea of being friends with her Mama, just as she liked the idea of being friends with her co-workers. But was that even possible? The more she thought about it, the more she felt compelled to find out.

As Mira got off the bus that afternoon at the stop nearest the nursing home, it occurred to her that her mother might not even still be here. She had been so insistent on getting out that she might have found a place and moved. But she was here now, so this would have to be the place to start. Besides, if her mother had left, they probably had her new address.

In fact, she was told that Mae had left the home some time ago, but the director refused to give her the new address without Mae's written permission.

"Well, if I knew where to find her to get her permission, I wouldn't need it, would I?"

"You know, I believe one of our other residents stays in touch with her by phone. He might be willing to give you a phone number. Would you like to talk with him?"

For a second, Mira hesitated. Her mother hadn't even bothered to let her know where she was living but was still keeping in close touch with some elderly man here. It didn't look as if much had changed after all. It was on the tip of her tongue to say, "No, thank you," but instead she heard herself saying, "Yes, please." The director went into her office and dialed up one of the rooms, spoke for a few minutes and then returned, saying, "Leo would love to meet you and tell you what he knows about Mae. He's in Room 117, just down this hall."

Mira thanked the woman and started down the hall. Strangely, she was aware now as she hadn't been in her earlier visits of the faint but definite odor associated with the building. Had Mae experienced this unpleasant smell? She wondered. Had that been part of her anger at being here? Before she could think further on this she came to Room 117 and knocked lightly on the open door.

"Come in, Belle! It's really good to meet you at last. Your mother and I have become good friends, and it's nice to finally meet her daughter."

Mira was surprised to see that he was wearing dark glasses even though he was indoors. "I'm sorry — the director didn't tell me your last name, Leo. But I'm glad to meet you, as well."

He didn't move from his chair, so Mira walked toward him, her hand extended. When he didn't reach out to shake hands with her, she wasn't sure what to do. Then he did reach out, groping for something on his bedside table and it struck her that he might be blind. Not knowing what to do with that information, she waited to see what he would say next.

"Mae's new address is on this paper." He held out the scrap of paper for Mira, and she started to open her purse to get out a pen and paper to copy it down. "No need to copy it, you can have this one. I have the number memorized." So, she had been wrong about his not seeing. He clearly knew when she reached into her purse. She accepted the paper, leaning in toward him to reach it. At close range she could see through the dark lenses to the eerie whiteness of his eyes.

He *was* blind! Dumbfounded, she was unsure of what to say next. He chuckled briefly and then apologized. "I'm sorry. I should have told you right away that I'm blind. It's unnerving, not knowing what to do or say, isn't it? I should have better manners at my age."

Mira just sat there, not knowing how to respond. She started to rise, thank him for the information, and leave the room. He sensed her movement and put out a hand. "Please don't go yet. I promise to be on better behavior. I'd like to meet you properly and chat for a while, if you have time."

Mira looked at her watch. She didn't have to be at work until 9:00, and she probably didn't have time now to try to find her mother's house this afternoon, so she might as well talk with Leo for a while. She settled back down into her chair and asked, "How did you and Ma — uh, my mother come to be friends?" Leo chuckled.

"Pretty unlikely, isn't it? Wouldn't have happened at all if not for a snippy little nurse's aide named Carla. She pretty much orchestrated our meeting. Your mama didn't really want to meet anyone in here, but Carla just kept at her until she agreed."

"I've met Carla and found her very pushy. But why would she do that?"

"Well, Carla knew your mama was unhappy just being here, and she thought that if she had someone she could talk with from time to time, she might feel more at home."

"But I came every day to visit with Mama, and she would hardly talk with me. Why would she talk with you and not with me?" Leo hesitated.

"Well, Belle, I think your mother was very unhappy with you for putting her here in the first place. I think she was afraid to be here and only wanted to find her way back home. That's the funny thing about older people — they want to be in a place they're familiar with, even though their ability to live alone may be compromised. They'd rather take the chance on dying in familiar surroundings than living by adjusting to new ones. Does that make sense to you?"

"No, not at all. I couldn't bear the thought of Mama falling again and maybe dying from the fall. I did what I had to do to keep her alive and healthy."

"So you did. But do you realize that you did what was right for *you*, and not necessarily what was best for your *mother*? You just told me that you couldn't bear the thought of her falling and dying, yet your mother was apparently very willing to take that risk to live out her life where her memories were. You didn't even have a conversation with her about what her preference would have been."

"Because I knew what she would choose, so there was no point in talking to her about it. But, don't you see, I love my mama. I needed to still have her in my life. I couldn't take the chance that she would be gone from me."

"Belle, have you ever had the feeling that you didn't have control over your own life? Have you ever felt that someone else was controlling parts of your life that were by rights your own decision to make? Well, now, that's how your mama felt."

Belle felt a roaring in her ears and a lightheadedness that seemed very much like she was going to faint. That was exactly what she felt her life had been until a short time ago. Is that what her Mama felt? Is that what she had done to her Mama? She gasped for breath and felt Leo's hand gently pushing her head down close to her lap. How could he have known she felt faint?

Tears rolled down her cheeks and a small sob escaped her. Leo held a box of tissues out to her, and she grabbed a handful. Somehow, she knew this would go on for a while.

Finally, she glanced at her watch and knew that she would have to leave before too long. It was just as well, because she didn't know what to say to this man. This was all too much to take in at one time.

"Leo, you've given me a lot to think about. I have to leave, but may I come back and talk with you some time? I won't be going to see Mama right away, not until I think through all this. And then I'm not sure if I could ever face her again. I'm afraid she'll never forgive me for what I did, and I'm not sure I could take that. But I'd like to come back and talk with you again, if it's all right with you."

Leo nodded, and then said, "Belle, don't be too hard on yourself. You must realize that your mother had a part in all this, too. She could have explained herself to you at any point, and you might have understood what she was feeling. That woman can be mule-stubborn, I know. But she has a good heart, and I believe you can both work it out. Don't give up before you try."

Mira nodded. "Could I ask you one more thing? Would you call me 'Mira'? It's what all my friends use now, and I'd like to think of you as a new friend."

Leo chuckled. "Mira, huh? I like the sound of that. Much more elegant than Belle, in my opinion. Okay, Mira, please come back soon. I'm looking forward to seeing you again."

As she left the room, Mira thought about how very much she was looking forward to seeing Leo again.

Chapter 26
Mae

Mae was settled into her new home. It didn't hold the memories her former home had, but it did give her back her sense of independence. The similarities to her old home helped to ease the sense of abandonment she had been feeling, and she was hopeful that, sooner or later, Jim would find her here. She had his old recliner, which again ate up far too much floor space for its usefulness, but she thought that whatever she had left of Jim was now to be found only in that old chair. She patted it gently whenever she walked by it, willing it to give him back to her.

During the six weeks since she moved in, she savored the time spent unpacking and placing things just where she wanted them, making it truly her home. The Senior Services people offered to help her with that, too, but she wanted to do it herself, feeling that each object put in place moved her closer to finding Jim here. So they brought in Jim's old chair, put up her bed, made it up with new sheets and blankets, and unpacked her teakettle and enough food to see her through a few days. Then they left her to her quiet, promising to check in with her about once a month.

The house was remarkably like her old house, but slightly larger. There was a picture window in the living room looking out over a garden space that reached around the house, and there was a low picket fence beyond that. Because it was late fall, not many of the plants in the garden were still alive, but she recognized some from the browning foliage and knew that she had some of her old favorites back again. There were even delphiniums. She breathed deeply, thinking it just might come out all right.

Each day she unpacked two or three boxes and spent the day deciding where to put the things. It turned out that, for some reason, Arthur had put her belongings in storage rather than selling them. More likely, Mae thought, he just didn't want to be bothered with them. So, what she was unpacking gave her more and more the sense that this was truly her home.

At first, cooking was a problem. She had forgotten many of the recipes that she always cooked from memory but remembered enough to get by for now. She was hopeful that some of the others would come back as she spent more time in the small kitchen and even more when she unpacked her old cookbooks. She reveled in making her own meals, eating when she wanted to, and even cleaning up. As soon as her phone was installed, she called Leo to tell him how glad she was to be back in her own place again. He congratulated her and asked her to describe the home. They chatted for a while, and then Leo asked her to call the office and give them her phone number so he would have access to it. When the conversation ended, she felt a brief pang that she wouldn't be going to Leo's room to visit with him anymore. She supposed she could call a taxi and go to the home — she thought that she might do that from time to time. But not now. Now she just wanted to let her little home wrap itself around her and comfort her. And give her back her Jim.

For as long as it took for her to get unpacked and settled in, the house did seem to comfort her. It surprised her that she missed some of the folks at the home, Leo in particular, and Carla, and even Bertha and her baby doll. But those were vague feelings, not the same as how much she missed her Jim. And now she was in a place where she could maybe find him again.

To her dismay, it didn't happen. She would sit in his old chair, close her eyes, and try to remember how he looked, how he walked, how he ate, even. But like the spirit that he now was, he avoided her. Maybe just a similar house wouldn't tempt him to come back. Maybe by losing the home he built, she had lost him entirely. As despair wove itself through her, she began to sob quietly. Jim was all she had ever had; now she didn't have him. She had been wrong. It wasn't just the nursing home that had kept him from her, it was something more than that. How would she ever find him again?

Tiredness like she had never known settled in on Mae. She slept fitfully that night, lying in Jim's old recliner and often awakening from a dream in which she was searching endlessly for him. When the volunteer came to check up on her, she was appalled by how listless and helpless Mae seemed to be. She talked with Mae for some time, urged her to see a doctor, perhaps get Meals on Wheels to stop by with food, or go to the gatherings at the Senior Services building.

Mae said she'd think about it. But she really didn't mean it.

Then, miraculously, Jim did appear. She had fallen asleep in his old recliner, and Jim came to her in a dream, something like the ones she used to have just after he died. He was holding her and gently rocking her as though she was his child, and she was reveling in the feeling of being in his arms. When she tried to raise her head to look at his face, however, he gently pushed her head back against his chest.

He didn't say anything to her, but she seemed to feel his thoughts as though he were speaking them.

"Mae, darlin', you can't go on this way. Pull up your socks and get on with your life. You've got to stop sittin' around feelin' sorry for yourself. You weren't even this bad right after I passed on. You think your life is useless, but there's work to do, and you'd best get on with it."

She didn't know what he was talking about. She had nothing that needed doing, no one but herself to look out for, no reason to keep going on. Jim gently shook her as these thoughts swirled through her mind. The shaking woke her up, and she was indeed shaking, but it was from being cold. The house was chilly, and she had not covered up before she fell asleep.

She found a blanket and pulled it over her, hoping sleep would come and the dream would continue. But she could not fall asleep again, so she started to rehearse the dream to plant it more fully in her mind. It was the clearest she had seen Jim in a long time. No, she hadn't really seen him … but she had felt him hold her and heard his words. Yet she hadn't really heard him, more like she was reading his mind, as if he were too far away now to come back fully as he had in the first days after his death.

She stayed that way the rest of the night, wrestling with what she had "heard" and what it might mean. What did Jim want of her? She had no work to do, no one besides herself to take care of, and taking care was really all she knew how to do. What else could he have been talking about?

She probed the matter like a sore tooth, pushing it this way and that, trying to figure out what he wanted from her. Well, who could she possibly tend to? Immediately, Carla, Leo, and even Belle popped into her mind.

"Jim, are you doin' this to me? How can I help any of them? I'm old, not much use to myself, let alone anybody else. Wouldn't even know where to start." But the thought just wouldn't leave her alone, so finally she stopped sidestepping and looked at it head on.

"Carla needs help about her mother. Can't see how anybody can do anythin' about that. Not about her baby, either. Belle ain't even been to see me in months, and I don't remember her phone number. Not sure I'd call her if I did. Nope, can't do nothin' for Belle, but I guess she's doin' all right or she would have called me.

"Leo? He's where he wants to be. But reckon I could go call on him from time to time, give him a bit a company. Not sure it would be really helpin' him, but guess it's easy enough to do. So I could try it and see what happens. I do like the old codger, and maybe he could help me figure out what it was Jim was tryin' to tell me."

With the comfort of that last thought, she finally drifted off to sleep, warm under the blanket and calmed in her spirit.

Chapter 27
Leo

True to her word, Mira did go back to see Leo, and they became closer. She confided in him, and he listened to her story of the ups and downs of her life without comment. Finally, one day she asked him why that was.

"Just seemed to me that what you really needed was someone to listen to you. No, not just listen but really hear you. It just seemed as if no one ever heard you. Does that seem right?"

Mira sat very still for a few minutes thinking about what he had said. When she tried to remember a time that she had been heard, she couldn't. Arthur maybe had listened to her some, especially about her fears for Mama, but not much else. Mama had never really listened, had always brushed her off. And Daddy was distracted and withdrawn for most of the time she could remember him. Now here was this kind man, no relation at all, and he listened to the things she told him. Not just listened, but heard what she said. And what she hadn't said.

"Thank you for hearing me. I think you're right. No one has ever really listened to me, so I never felt as if I mattered to anyone else. That sounds weird, doesn't it? But do you know what I'm saying?"

'Oh, yes. In a way, I have had the same problem. Because I can't see, it often seemed as if some folks weren't really seeing me, either. Not the real me, just 'the blind man'."

"Oh, my. That is so sad! Does it still happen?"

"Oh, sometimes, when people meet me for the first time. But now I'm better at making conversation, so most folks begin to treat me like a regular person after a while."

"I understand what you're saying. I've just recently realized that now I have folks who not only listen, but hear me. Being with them is like being with family, or at least what I thought family should be. Between talking with you and being with them, I feel like a different person. But I'm thinking I didn't really hear you at first, either, did I?"

"I understood. You had a lot chewing at you when we met."

"So, tell me some of *your* story now, will you?" And he did.

A few days later, Mae dialed Leo's number and waited for him to answer. When he did, she said, "Leo, I've a mind to come over to the Home and visit with you a while. Would that be okay with you?"

"Mae, you know there's nothing I would like better. How soon are you coming over?"

"I was thinkin' later this morning. I'll need to call a cab to get there. Don't do well at climbin' on and off buses anymore."

Swiftly, Leo calculated the time Mira might arrive if she came today. She usually came about mid-afternoon, so there was not much chance of Mae being here when Mira came. "Sounds good. You think about ten o'clock or so?"

"What, you got a date or something? Oh, maybe you got an appointment with Lynda?"

"No, nothing like that. Just don't want to leave the room and miss you."

"Okay, I'll try to get there around ten."

As Mae walked into his room, Leo held out both hands to greet her. She grasped his hands in hers and gave a slight squeeze. "Gosh, Leo, but it's been a long time!"

"Sure has, Mae. If I had known how much I was gonna miss you when you moved out, I maybe wouldn't have been so eager to help you."

"Oh, go on with you. Your room is as busy as a bus station. No way you coulda had time to miss me."

"Ah, but you know, not all the people at a bus station are good friends. Anyway, tell me about how things are going with you."

"Well, I done told you most of it, just gettin' moved in and stuff put away and all that. Kept me pert near as busy as I ever been. Now I'm about settled in."

"And how are you liking it?

"That's the strange part. I'm not nearly as happy as I thought I'd be. Just doesn't seem as good somehow as it did before I got put in here."

"Is it because it's not your old home?"

"I thought about that. Jim only came to me once in my new place, and that was really a dream. Better than nothin' but not exactly what I was hopin' for, neither. I'm thinkin' I lost Jim completely when they put me in here, and I'm afraid I might never find him again."

"Well, Mae, I'm sure you know that the presence of someone we loved tends to grow weaker as the days pass, no matter where we are. Jim has been gone for quite a long time now. Odds are you would have experienced the same loss of his presence by now even in your old home."

"I reckon you might be right. But my old home comforted me even when I couldn't feel Jim there. And this new house just seems empty somehow. At least when I was in here I had folks to visit with, so it helped me not to fret so much about Jim bein' gone. Jim and me was ever'thing to each other, and I don't know how to fill the empty feelin' I have now."

"You miss Jim."

"Yes, and now I got nothin' left of him to hang onto, to help bring him back to me."

"Mae, don't you know that part of Jim is still with you? Belle is his daughter. He's a part of who she is. Have you thought that you might be able to find Jim by building a relationship with Belle?"

"Leo, you got no feel for what's happened to me. See, my parents never wanted me, and I could tell. They never wanted me to marry Jim, either. They said he was a loser, and I was throwin' my life away. But Jim gave me the only happiness I ever knew in this life. When it was just the two of us, our life was perfect. When Belle was born, ever'thing changed!

She took too much of Jim away from me, and I always wanted things to go back the way they was before she came, but they never did."

"And you've never forgiven her for doing that, have you?"

"I reckon not, and I don't plan to real soon. She done me wrong when she was born and then again when she cooked up that scheme to get me into this home. That's too much to forgive."

"Mae, Belle didn't have a say in being born. How can you hold that against her? You're the mother, you're the reason she exists, so you're to blame for her being here. But, can't you imagine how she feels, knowing that no matter what she does, she can never win your love?"

"How do you know what Belle thinks? You never even met her. Don't go tryin' to make me feel guilty. You don't know nothin' about her and me and how hard it was."

"What I know is just what I've been told. Your parents pushed you away, but you found Jim. You pushed Belle away, but she is Jim's child. When you find him in her, you'll have him back again in a way. Think about it, Mae. You and Jim loved each other and out of that love, Belle was born. She is Jim's gift to you, proof of his love. In loving her, you could bring Jim back into your life again. Mae, you haven't lost Jim. You've just been looking for him in the wrong places."

"But what about what she done to me, sellin' my house and puttin' me in here? I can't never forgive her for that. She took away ever'thing I ever had."

"Well, let's see. You have a new, somewhat bigger house now. You have more control over your finances and your life than ever before. And because of what happened, you've learned how to handle your own affairs much better. And if you had never come, you and I would never have met. Maybe Jim is still trying to take care of you … through his daughter."

Mae sat silently, stubbornly pushing away Leo's words.

"Mae, Belle was wrong to do what she did, especially in the way she did it. But she believed she was doing the right thing for you. She was trying to take care of you, just as Jim did. She was also trying to tell you, in the only way she knew how, that she loves you. Don't you see Jim in all this? How he showed you his love by taking care of you?"

"She's nothin' like Jim!"

"Dammit, Mae, as long as you keep pushing her away, you'll never give yourself the chance to learn how like Jim she is."

Angrily, Mae rose from her chair and left the room. The visit had given her no comfort.

Chapter 28
Mira

Mira was in her small office just after midnight, going over the day's receipts, when she sensed someone leaning against the door frame. Looking up, she saw a man dressed in filthy jeans, a ragged tee shirt, and a crusty old coat she could smell from there. He was leering at her in a frightening way.

"I'll take that cash, sweetheart. Just push it across the desk toward me."

Shocked, Mira couldn't move, and her hesitation enraged the man. He produced a large knife from behind his back and stepped toward her menacingly. She was so alarmed that she was unable to think, pushing back from her desk to keep out of his reach. He laughed at her fear and lunged toward her, the knife just missing her arm. Still holding the knife out in front of himself, he gathered up the paper money from the desk and stuffed it into his coat pocket.

Mira gasped and half stood, moving forward to stop him. He lunged toward her again, this time stabbing her in her left shoulder. The shock and pain caused Mira to lose consciousness, and she slumped to the floor as the man fled with his take.

A few minutes later Ernie poked his head into Mira's office to remind her it was break time, but she wasn't at her desk. Thinking she must have already gone on break, he started to leave. Mira moaned softly, consciousness slowly coming back to her. Alarmed, Ernie moved toward the sound and found her lying on the floor behind the desk, blood flowing from her shoulder.

Stunned, he shouted for help, and almost immediately the small office was full of shocked people. One of them had the presence of mind to call for an ambulance, and then another said, "Better call the cops, too."

After the ambulance took Mira away, the officers started checking the office as the staff stood around in the hall talking about how this could have happened.

"No one could get in at this time of night without a key card. Maybe it was a hotel guest."

"Nope, don't think so. Anyone staying here would have to be stupid to do this and think to get away with it."

"Well, who else could have got in?"

"Guess we'll just have to wait until Mira can tell us."

Each employee was questioned by the police about what they had seen or heard, but there was little to tell.

It was far too early in the morning for Mae to be up, but she'd had a restless night. Try as she might, she couldn't get Leo's words off her mind. She recognized that they were similar to what had been troubling her thinking of late. And while she had been able to argue herself out of taking those thoughts to heart, she wasn't quite as capable of forgetting when it was reinforced by Leo.

She thought back to her own childhood and remembered the loneliness she had felt during that long period. *But I always just pulled up my socks and got on with life. Belle should do that, too.* Damn Leo, anyway. Why did he have to go raking up things best left forgotten? She still wanted to be mad at Belle for forcing her into that Home.

Of course, she hadn't had to face the problem of her own parents' aging. Her much older siblings had taken care of all that, adeptly putting her mother and father in a nursing home when the time came. Mae had never given a thought to whether or not this was what her parents wanted. She hadn't even gone to visit them, because she just really didn't care. Had they been as unhappy being in a Home as she was? And why did she even think about that now?

Well, shoot, it looked as if Belle had finally grown up and got on with her life, so none of this should matter anymore. Belle certainly hadn't been around lately, and Mae thought it likely she was getting along just fine. She probably didn't even know where Mae was living now. Damn, damn, damn! All she wanted was to get back to the way her life had once been, and instead she was plagued by the ideas and questions Leo had planted in her mind.

Maybe she just wouldn't go see him anymore.

But as soon as she settled on that idea, her thoughts overwhelmed her again, and a new feeling began to well up in her. Was it doubt? It felt like it. Now, what did she have to be doubtful about? Never had been that way in her life; always knew what she wanted and knew how to go after it. She looked around her at the house that had meant so much to her. Was she dissatisfied with it now because of her doubt? Or was she still thinking it was because she couldn't find Jim here? But she had found him in that dream, and maybe she would find him again. So, what was her problem? She was lost in trying to figure things out and was startled by the ringing of the telephone. Who could be calling at seven o'clock in the morning? Hardly anyone even had her number.

The caller quickly identified herself as a trauma nurse at Community Hospital. "Is this Mae Jameson?"

"Yes, yes it is. Why are you callin' me?"

"Your daughter, Mira Timkins, has been the victim of an assault. She is being treated here and has asked for you. Are you able to come and see her?"

Mae gasped in shock. Belle? Belle in the hospital? "How … what happened? How is she? Will she be all right?"

"I'd rather not go into details over the phone, but she's going to be all right. If you come in, she can explain some of it to you, and we can fill you in on her medical condition."

Mae's mind reeled, searching for an explanation. Had Timpkins assaulted Belle? How dare that worm take his anger out on Belle!

"Ma'am? Are you there? Are you all right?"

Mae realized she was still holding the receiver to her ear and breathing heavily into the phone. "Yes, I'm here. I'll get a cab and be there soon as I can."

On the way to the hospital she wondered how they had even known her phone number. Had Belle found it out and given it to them? But worry over Belle's condition pushed that question out of her mind.

Two uniformed officers were talking with Mira as Mae entered her room. A weak, exhausted Mira was describing the man who had attacked her. Coming into the middle of the conversation, Mae was confused about the details but gathered that Timkins had not been the assailant. Still, why hadn't he protected Belle?

"We'd like to send over a police artist to make a sketch of the man. You've given us a very good description, and if we can get a sketch and put it out we'll have a greater chance of catching him."

Weakly, Mira nodded. Then she noticed Mae and gave a little cry, holding out her right hand to her mother. Without thinking about it, Mae walked to the bed and grasped her daughter's outstretched hand. Mira tried to squeeze her mother's hand, but the attempt was feeble. Holding onto Mae's hand, Mira turned again to the officers. They thanked her for her cooperation and promised to do their best to find her attacker.

Left alone with her daughter, Mae wasn't sure what to say or how to say it. She wasn't even sure Belle had the strength to talk to her.

"Are you all right? How did this happen?" Mira lay tiredly against the pillows and described the attack. Mae was stunned to learn that Belle was working in a motel.

"Why are you even working there? Doesn't your husband provide for you?"

"Oh, Mama, there's so much you don't know. Arthur and I are divorced. He was angry with me because I went back to see you that one last time. He told me before I went that it would mean the end of our marriage, but I hoped he didn't mean it. He did. He gave me a day to pack my things and leave. Everything I thought was ours was in his name, so I had to find a job just to live, and that's the only one I could find without a reference."

"That don't make sense. You worked for years at that place before you married him. Why wouldn't you have a reference?"

"Mama, I'm just so tired I don't think I can go into all this right now. But I hurt so much, and I wanted you to come. I hope you're not mad at me for having them call you."

Mae realized that the emergency had blocked out her anger toward Belle. It would seem that she did have some feelings for her daughter after all. Bewildered, she looked at Belle, seeing that she was falling asleep. A nurse came in to check on her and told Mae quietly, "She'll sleep now, from the shock and the meds. You can call the nurses' desk at any time and get an update on her condition. She'll probably be here for a few days."

"And then what?"

"You'll have to talk with her doctors about that. They'll be making rounds tomorrow morning to check her. Maybe you could come back then?"

And Mae knew that she would definitely be there.

Chapter 29
Carla

It was mid-December, and things had been going a little better for Carla. Early this morning, though, Faith's insistent crying brought Carla out of a sound sleep. Groggily, she leaned over and picked her up from the basket. Faith felt unusually warm to Carla, and she wondered if the baby was ill. She'd definitely have to stay home if that was the case.

She changed Faith's diaper, noted that she had a slight rash, and thought she should get some kind of ointment for her. As she walked to the kitchen to warm a bottle, her mother appeared in her bedroom door. "Can't get no sleep at all with that caterwaulin' goin' on. Shut her up. I need my sleep." With that she slammed back into her room.

Faith grabbed onto the bottle, chewing on the nipple as if it was the nipple and not the milk that she wanted. Carla cautiously felt her mouth and found a hard little bump on her gum. She was sure it was some kind of growth. What should she do now?

Again, she made her way up to Lotte's to see if she could tell her what was wrong. Lotte was clearly unhappy at being awakened so early but listened to her concern. Finally, she put a finger in Faith's mouth and let out a loud snort. "Kiddo, you got so much to learn it's pathetic. Faith's teething, that's all. That's her first tooth you're feeling."

Relieved, Carla headed downstairs to finish feeding the baby and get ready for school. But Faith was fretful, and as soon as the bottle was empty, she started wailing again. Carla knew she would have to miss another day of school today. She took Faith back into her bedroom, closed the door and began to pace, holding the child against her shoulder and rubbing her little back. Nothing seemed to work. She took her into the living room to try to rock her back to sleep.

Ma came out of her bedroom again, dressed in a threadbare old shirt and grimy sweat pants, heading for the small kitchen. When she'd had her morning pick-me-up, she came back and stared at Carla for a few moments.

"I ain't puttin' up with being woke at this ungodly hour. You better figure out how to shut her up, or you're outta here."

Carla held Faith closer to her and tried to comfort her, but nothing seemed to make a difference. Finally, clearly exhausted, Faith fell asleep. Carla breathed a sigh of relief.

"Lotte says she's teething. I'll go get some stuff to put on her gums so she won't cry so much."

"It better work. I ain't puttin' up with that. My health ain't so good, and I need my sleep."

"Yeah, I know about your 'health' problems. I'll take care of it."

"You better."

While Faith slept, Carla went out to the drugstore to get something for Faith's gums along with ointment for the diaper rash. She paid for the two items and hurried home, not wanting Ma to be put out about Faith's crying and force them out of the apartment. When she got back, Faith was still asleep, so she figured she could get to her classes after all. She showed her purchases to Ma, who barely glanced at them as she headed back into the kitchen for another drink.

When Carla returned home from school there was no sound of crying. Relieved, she hoped that Faith had slept all the time she was gone so Ma wouldn't be so belligerent. She walked into her tiny bedroom, but the basket and Faith were gone. Alarmed, she ran back out and pounded on Ma's door. Opening the door, she saw the room was empty. Maybe they were up at Lotte's.

At the top of the stairs she ran into Ma coming out of Lotte's apartment.

"Where's Faith? Did you leave her with Lotte?" Ma tried to push past her and got one foot down a step, but Carla grabbed her sleeve and held her there. "Where's Faith?" she yelled.

"She started bawlin' right after you left and never quit. I told you that don't set well with me. I ain't puttin' up with that squallin' ever' time you're gone. You thought you were so smart about the booze, missy. Now you'll think twice before threatenin' me."

"What did you do? Where is she? Is she with Lotte?" Carla was shouting, clutching the sleeve as Ma tried to shrug her off. Ma twisted back toward Carla on the step, trying to pull her sleeve away from her daughter. Instead, she swayed dangerously above the open stairwell. She over-balanced on the narrow step, hanging there for a moment, groping for something to hold on to.

Carla watched in horror as the sleeve tore away and her mother seemed to fly through the air, hitting the landing with an ominous thud. Carla stood frozen in place, gripping the torn fabric. Below her she could see Ma on the landing, her body contorted onto the small space. She was not moving.

Lotte rushed out of her apartment and gasped at the sight. "Carla, what have you done?" she screamed at the frightened girl. Stunned, Carla just stood there, shaking. Lotte headed down the stairs, calling Gert's name. As she reached the landing, she could see that her friend would never answer.

"I'll call the police."

"But … but it was an accident."

"Maybe, but anything like this happens, they got to check it out. You were fightin' with her about Faith, weren't you?"

"Yes! She's not in my room. Where is she? Do you have her?"

"Honey, Faith is the least of your worries right now. You're probably gonna be in a lotta trouble over this, accident or not."

"I didn't do anything! She just fell, trying to get away from me. But Faith? Is she all right? Please, Lotte, you gotta tell me!"

"First, I gotta call the police. Then we'll talk about Faith."

And Carla knew in her gut that Faith was gone.

When Lotte came back out, she sat down on the top step and pulled Carla down beside her, putting her arm around the girl's shoulder.

"You know Faith was teething, and teething babies cry a lot. Your ma never woulda put up with that for long. She told me that right after you left for school, she took Faith to a hospital and left her there in the Ladies room. So I guess you at least gotta give her credit for making sure the baby was somewhere where she would be found."

Carla jumped up. "What hospital? Where is it? I've got to go get her."

"Oh, honey, I don't even know which hospital, and anyway you can't go anywhere until after you talk to the police."

"No, ain't nothin' more important than getting Faith back. This was an accident. I can't wait for the police — I got to go find Faith and bring her home!"

Carla looked down the stairwell; an officer was already in the lobby and headed up the stairs. She was more scared than she'd ever been in her life. Neighbors in the apartment building poked their heads out to see what was going on and gathered in small groups along the stairwell as the police interrogated Carla and Lotte.

After urging the onlookers to go back into their apartments, the police questioned Carla a second time at greater length about the quarrel she and her mother were having. It seemed they were more focused on that than on the "accident" itself. After the body had finally been removed, they told Carla she would have to go with them to the station and fill out a report. Although they read her rights to her, the words barely registered with Carla.

At the station she was put in a holding cell while the officers filed their report, then moved to an interrogation room where another officer told her she had the right to have an attorney present if she wanted one. Carla shrugged, saying she didn't know any attorney, and since anyway it was an accident, she didn't think she needed one. She just kept saying she needed to get out of there and go find her baby. The officer asked her again to tell him what had happened.

"I was arguing with Ma on the stairway about what she did with my baby, and she ignored me and started to go on downstairs. I grabbed her sleeve to keep her from leaving, and she tried to twist it away from me. She lost her balance and fell."

"Carla, your neighbor says your mother had just had a drink with her."

"Yeah, Ma likes … liked her booze and pretty much drank all day."

"Did you see her drink any other time this morning?"

"Yeah. She had herself a cup of coffee and then had a cup with booze in it. Said it helped her get going for the day."

"And you saw her do that this morning, as well? Be careful how you answer, Carla, because we'll know how much alcohol was in her system when we do the autopsy."

"Yeah, I know she had at least one drink before I left for school. More'n likely had one more before she went to Lotte's to talk to her. "

"So, you and your mother were having an argument. What were you arguing about?"

"My baby. Ma took care of her when I was at school or at work, and when I came home today Faith was gone. I was trying to get her to tell me where Faith was."

"And did she tell you?"

"No, that's why she was trying to get away from me. She wasn't going to tell me."

"Are you sure you didn't get mad at her and push her down the stairs?"

"No, I was mad, sure, but more scared than mad. I just wanted her to tell me where Faith was so I could go get her, and she just kept trying to pull away from me."

"So you still don't know where the baby is?"

"No … well sorta. Afterward, Lotte told me Ma took her to a hospital and dumped her there."

"Dumped her? You mean left her outside in this weather?"

"No, Lotte said she left Faith in the Ladies room."

"How old is the baby?"

"She's six months old. She's teething and she cried a lot, and that upset Ma, and that's why she dumped her at the hospital."

"Okay, Carla, we're going to keep you here while we check all this out. Is there anybody you'd like to call?"

Carla shook her head. "I ain't really got anybody." Desolately, she let herself be led back to the holding cell.

◈

The next morning Carla was again questioned about her mother's death. The questions were pretty much the same as they had been the day before, and her answers didn't change either. The autopsy had confirmed that her mother had a very high blood alcohol level, and there was no real evidence that her death had been anything but an accident. There was no reason to hold Carla, but they couldn't release her because she was underage. They asked about relatives.

"Don't know that I got any. But Lotte helped me when Faith was born and when Ma was drunk. Maybe Faith and I could stay with her for now."

"That may be possible, but you're underage, so you'll need a state-approved guardian until you're of age. We'll need to contact the Welfare office to handle this part of it."

The word "Welfare" jogged Carla's memory. "Ma got welfare for me. Why can't I get it for Faith? Then we could live with Lotte, and it'd be okay."

"We'll let them know that at the department. What is your case-worker's name?" Carla froze. She hadn't counted on having to talk with Miss Martin. She would probably be really mad at her for not telling her about Faith right at the start. And maybe Welfare would take Faith from her now.

"No matter. We can call the local office and give them your mother's name. They'll be able to take it from there."

Carla started to cry. She wasn't a crybaby; she mostly shoved her way through problems and setbacks. But this was too much. She was going to lose Faith and probably be put in some foster home herself. The officer waited quietly while Carla felt her world crash down. She handed Carla a box of tissues, and said softly, "Carla, level with us. You have some explaining to do, and maybe we can help you if you tell us the truth."

"Her name is Miss Martin. She's always been nice to me, but she didn't seem to like Ma at all. But Ma made me promise I wouldn't tell her anything. Said she'd just take Faith away and probably put me in a foster home. So, I did what Ma told me to do. I lied to Miss Martin or tried not to answer her questions. We never let on about Faith, and she never had a birth certificate. Ma said that was a sure-fire way for them to take her away from me."

"And then, in the end, your mother took her away from you, anyway. Did that make you angry?"

"Yeah, I was mad, but I was more scared than mad. And I didn't know she'd left Faith somewhere until after she fell down the stairs. Lotte told me."

"Carla, you can only be released into the custody of your caseworker. She'll likely find a temporary place for you to stay until all of this is straightened out, maybe at your friend Lotte's. I'm certain that there will be an effort to find your baby, so don't give up hope.'

Carla was crying again.

How could this woman say that? How could she not worry about Faith? She was so afraid that she would never see Faith again, and nothing else mattered to her.

Chapter 30
Mira

***

Mira awoke, a little disoriented by her surroundings and the ache in her left shoulder. Then she remembered. She tried to shift into a sitting position, but her arm was immobilized in a tight sling. She groaned with the pain. At that moment a nurse entered the room to check her vital signs and scolded her for moving her arm.

"Whatever you want, you ring for us. The cord is here, by your right hand."

Mira nodded sheepishly. Before the nurse finished her tasks, a doctor came into the room.

"How are you feeling this morning?"

"Pretty sore and achy, but I think okay. Well … a little woozy."

"That's all to be expected. So, there is some damage to your shoulder muscle, but the good news is that the knife missed major blood vessels. It was apparently a straight in-and-out stab. We cleaned it out and disinfected it thoroughly before stitching you up, but we need to monitor you for any sign of infection for a couple of days. Then, if it's healing well, we can release you from the hospital. However, the wound was fairly deep, and you'll need physical therapy and wound care after your release. Your best option would be a facility set up to do that. Do you have a preference as to where you'd like to go?"

"I know some of the people at Sunnyside Haven. That's the only place I know."

"Okay, we'll double check to be sure they can give you the kind of therapy you need and see about getting you moved in a couple of days."

At that moment, Mae entered the room. Mira told Mae the news the doctor had given her as he passed her on his way out of the room. Mae barked a brief laugh.

"What's so funny, Mama?"

"Well, don't you think it's a little interestin' that you're going to the same place you put me in last spring?"

"Oh, I guess it is. But I'm glad to be going to a place where they can help me get over this. At least it will be somewhat familiar to me."

"Well, I meant to be here when the doctor came around, but guess I was late. How soon will they move you?"

"A couple of days, he said. At least I know Leo, so I'll have someone to talk to when I'm there."

"How the Sam Hill do you know Leo?"

"Oh! Well, I went back to the home a while back to see you, and they said you'd moved. They couldn't give me your new address, but they were kind enough to let me know that Leo might have it, so I talked to him. Sure enough, he gave me your phone number, and then we talked a little. It was so nice to have someone to talk to that I asked him if I could visit again, and now we're friends."

"So you and Leo are buddies, huh? That explains some things I been wonderin' about. And gives me more to think about."

"What do you mean, Mama?"

"Got to think about it before I talk about it, Belle."

"Okay, Mama. And … could I ask you a favor? All my new friends call me Mira, and I really like that better than Belle. Would you mind calling me Mira?"

"Humph. Your Daddy was the one who nicknamed you Belle. Don't see what's so wrong with that name."

"Oh, Mama, if you don't want to change, that's all right. I just thought..."

"Don't make no never mind to me, I reckon. May take a while to get used to it, but I'll give it a go."

Mae could see that Belle … no … *Mira* was fighting sleep, so she grabbed her purse and stood. "I'll see about comin' in tomorrow. Have to watch my money some, and cab fare's expensive. But I'll see."

"Thanks for coming today, Mama." Mira fell asleep before Mae left the room.

As Mae rode back home in the taxi, her mind seemed to be scrambling. She felt like she was seeing a change in Belle, and she thought maybe it made her just a tad easier to be around. She *was* somewhat put-out by learning that Belle and Leo might have been talking about her, and she wondered how that fit with the advice Leo was giving her. So she had to think on that some. But there was something else pushing at her for attention, and she tried to let it in. She could sort out the Belle/Leo thing later.

It dawned on her that she was starting to think different about Belle. She guessed the word she wanted was "accept" Belle a little, and she guessed that was good. Maybe as good as it was ever going to get. But even that little bit gave her some satisfaction, as though she were somehow living up to a bargain she'd made, even though she couldn't think what that could be.

Now there was something different about Belle that she couldn't quite put her finger on, but whatever it was just seemed to make it easier to be around her. Not that she was over anxious to spend a lot of time with her. But at least maybe these visits wouldn't grate against her so much. *Mira*, huh? Well, guess that was as good a place to start as any.

Affording the cab fare was just a good excuse to keep Mira from expecting too much from her. Her daughter obviously didn't know anything about Mae's finances, so she would keep on with that while she decided how close she wanted to be with her daughter.

She also wanted to rethink the advice Leo had given her after hearing what Belle just said. If they'd become pals, then his advice to Mae might be fishy. She figured she could change some, but she wanted to be sure it would work out well for her before even trying. She sure didn't want her daughter to start getting clingy again.

Chapter 31
Leo

***

Leo shifted uneasily in his chair. The nurse's aide lowered his table and wheeled it up to him before going back into the hall to bring in his lunch tray.

"Haven't seen Carla for a few days. Is she taking some time off?"

The aide shrugged. "Don't know, but the word is that she just didn't bother to show up for work the last three days. No one seems to know why. The director is really ticked with her about now."

Leo frowned. That wasn't like the Carla he had come to know. Maybe her baby was sick. But she surely would have called in to let them know. He wished he had asked Carla for a phone number so he could check up on her. Of course, he hadn't been expecting anything like this, but he knew from what she told him that her situation at home was precarious. He was certain that she wouldn't just stop coming to work without letting the home know, and he felt she would also have touched base with him as well. At least, he hoped she would have. This turn of events alarmed him.

He mulled over the idea of calling Lynda and asking her to check on the girl. Carla might be mad at him for doing that, but he worried that she might be in danger and need some help. Without giving himself too much time to think about it, he called the attorney's office.

Lynda listened to Leo's concern but was uncertain if she could do anything to alleviate it. Leo had no idea where the girl lived or any idea of how to go about finding her. Leo told her that Carla went to school, and he was pretty sure her mother was on welfare. Surely the school system or the welfare office would have her address.

"Is this the girl you asked me about a while back?"

"Yes, she's the one. She was afraid to follow up on that call for fear that it would result in losing her baby. But I'm afraid now that something has happened in her life that she may not be able to handle by herself."

"Okay, at least I have the welfare angle to check on. I doubt they will be able to give me anything substantive, but they might take what I can give them and check it out. You know, however, that when I call them, keeping her circumstances private will pretty much be out of the question."

"Yeah. But I'm more concerned about her health or safety than her privacy, so I'm just not going to worry about that for now. Please let me know what you can, will you? And as soon as you know?" Leo found he had no appetite for lunch and left his tray untouched. The aide took it away without comment.

Lynda's call to the Welfare department went as she expected. The supervisor asked if she was Carla's attorney and refused to give her any information when she replied that she was not. She could only tell Lynda that they knew where Carla was and that she was not ill or hurt. She also promised that she would talk to Carla's caseworker to let her know about Leo's concern.

Lynda called Leo back to tell him what little she had found out. It only worried him more, wondering what could have happened to so abruptly interfere with Carla's life. Maybe Mae knew something.

Mae answered the phone on the second ring. "Oh, Leo! The phone ringin' shook me up a bit. Thought maybe Belle had took a turn for the worse or something."

"Your daughter? What's happened to her?"

"Probably more than you want to hear about right now, but she was attacked at work and is in the hospital. Stabbed in the left shoulder. She's gonna be all right, but it's still a worry."

"Oh, lord. Too much going on."

"What do you mean?"

"Well, Carla hasn't shown up for work for the past three days, and I can't find out why. I'm worried that something may have happened to her or her baby. And now you tell me Mira, uh, Belle has been injured."

"Yeah, and I found out that you and her have become pretty cozy lately. How come you never told me about that?

"Mostly because I figured Mira should be the one to tell you."

"Well, now she has, and I gotta think how that changes things for me."

"I see. But I actually called you to find out if you know anything about Carla."

"No, haven't heard from her since I left the home. Ain't she workin' there anymore?"

"No, she just stopped coming to work, and no one can tell me why. I'm worried that something has happened to her or her little girl."

"I don't know nothin' about that, but if I hear anything I'll give you a call. "

"Thanks, Mae. And tell Mira I'll be thinking about her."

Chapter 32
Carla

Lori Martin entered the station later that day to pick up Carla and find her a temporary place to stay. She was taken aback by the change in Carla's behavior. Where before there had been a taciturn, uncooperative teen-ager, there was now a defeated young person who had seemingly lost all hope. She quickly finished the paperwork to get Carla released and suggested they go to a nearby restaurant where they could have coffee and talk. Carla just shrugged.

"Carla, let me express my condolences on the loss of your mother."

"I don't much care, one way or the other."

"Well, I think I can understand; it seems your mother had a whole lot to answer for. And you and I are going to have to start putting back together the pieces of your life. I'll help you as much as I can; I only ask you to be more of a help to me than you have been. I can't do much if I'm always working in the dark!"

"Wasn't my fault. Ma told me that you would take Faith away from me if you knew about her. I did what she told me to do so I could keep Faith."

"I understand how difficult it must have been for you. But your mother gave you a great deal of misinformation, I'm afraid. I just wish you could have trusted me to help you work out those problems." Before Carla could respond, she hurried on. "I know you didn't think you had much choice, but clearly now things are different. I hope you'll let me help you put your life back together."

"Only thing in my life that matters is Faith — I want her back. Nothin' else really matters to me right now."

"Yes, but getting Faith back doesn't take care of everything else. You've got to figure out where you go from here. Everything in your life has changed, and you'll really need some guidance on a daily basis for taking care of her and yourself. How will you support the two of you?"

"Can't I get welfare like Ma did?

"That is a possibility, but you're young to go that direction; we'd need to do an assessment before we approve that. You really need a mature person to help you. Do you have any relatives or close friends who might help you?"

"Only friend I got is Lotte. She's sorta my friend. She might let me live with her."

"Who's Lotte?"

"She lives upstairs from us, used to be a nurse. She helped me get Faith born and sometimes after that when I didn't know what was wrong with Faith. She sorta taught me how to be a mother, how to feed Faith and stuff like that. She's the one who called the police when Ma fell."

Lynda jotted the name in her notebook, adding a question mark. "Anyone else?"

"Nope. Well, maybe Mae would consider it, since it's just for a couple of years. I think her last name's Jameson. But she's old, and I don't know."

"How do you know Ms. Jameson?"

"Ma made me take a job after Faith was born to pay her for my keep and for taking care of Faith. The only one I could find was in a nursing home, and Mae was in the Home. But she moved into her own place a couple months ago, so I ain't talked to her lately."

"Let me talk to Lotte. Maybe we can make some kind of arrangement for the time being, at least. I'm certain we'll have to have a more permanent situation before we can begin to plan for you to have Faith back. But try not to worry about her; we'll do everything we can to find her."

"Would you do somethin' else for me? I never got a chance to call the nursing home and let them know why I never showed up for my shift. Would you tell them?

"Of course! And, you know, that request tells me more about your maturity than you can imagine. I'll check with Lotte today and see if she's willing to have you. Otherwise, I'll take you to an intake home, just until we can find something more permanent."

"Now, Carla, tell me about Faith. About how much does she weigh, what color is her hair, and what color are her eyes? Does she have any moles or birthmarks or anything like that we can identify her by when we find her?

Carla hesitated. "Her hair was a different kind of color. Like mine, but lighter and more blond-red. Someone said it was the color of a ripe peach. Dark blue eyes. No moles or anything like that. I'm not sure how much she weighs now; never had a reason to weigh her. Lotte thought she was a bit over four pounds when she was born, and she's still kind of tiny for her age."

"Well, that gives us a place to start. And I'll check with Lotte. Maybe as a nurse she can give us better estimates of weight and length. But if you think of any other things that can help identify her, call me right away, okay?" Carla nodded. "Now, let's go and see what we can find for you."

Carla rose listlessly as the caseworker paid for the coffee neither had touched. Didn't much matter where she went. Nothing much mattered if she didn't get Faith back.

Chapter 33
Carla

Snow was falling as Carla stepped out of the apartment building on an early February morning and a brisk wind brought the temperature down into the teens. Before taking her to live with Lotte, the caseworker had stopped at a thrift shop and bought Carla some warm winter clothes and a down jacket. She couldn't remember ever being able to stay warm in the winter before, and she was grateful for the comfort. All the same, she was still focused on finding Faith and losing hope more with every day that passed. She and Lotte were managing together, although Lotte still seemed put out about Ma's death and Carla thought the woman blamed her, though she never said so. But then, they never talked about any of what happened and what troubled them the most, not about Ma and not about Faith and not about what was going to happen to Carla herself.

Carla attended classes regularly now that she was living with Lotte. She finally had more time to study, and her grades reflected the change. Classes and studying took her mind off her worry about Faith, at least for a while. Miss Martin had been quick to congratulate her on her improved grades. Carla just shrugged.

One day after school, Carla was surprised to find Miss Martin in Lotte's apartment. She was still wary around the caseworker but also hopeful that she had brought news about Faith. But the caseworker's solemn expression was guarded.

"We have located the hospital where your mother took Faith. Fortunately, there were surveillance cameras in the basin area of the restrooms because of prior vandalism, so we have a tape of a baby being left there in a basket. It's time-stamped the same day you lost Faith, so we're pretty certain it's her."

"Then where is she? Where's Faith? Why didn't you go get her and bring her here?"

"Wait, Carla, there's more. There is a later segment on the tape that shows another woman coming into the restroom, picking Faith up and carrying her out. Do you think your mother would have made arrangements with someone to find the baby there?"

Lotte and Carla both spoke up at once. "No way." "Definitely not." "She wouldn't have cared enough about Faith to do that," Carla added, and Lotte nodded in agreement.

"Then we have to assume this was someone who just happened to find her there. The police are enlarging the frames that show the woman, and they'll be asking hospital staff if anyone recognizes her. This is a *good lead.*"

Both women looked on helplessly as Carla began to cry. Lori moved over to the girl and put her arms around her, allowing her to sob hopelessly on her shoulder. Finally, Carla wiped her eyes and stared defiantly at the two women. "I gotta find Faith. That's all there is to it. Whatever it takes, I gotta find her."

"The police and the Child Protection agency are trying to do the same thing, so you're not alone in this, Carla. Don't give up hope."

Although Lotte had signaled her willingness to keep Carla there until Faith was found, Lori wanted to move her to a place less filled with the fear, stress, and memories that attended her young life in this building. So far nothing had panned out, most foster parents being unwilling to bring such a distraught young girl into their homes, especially one carrying the stigma of being involved in her own mother's death. As a last resort, she called Mae to sound her out about taking Carla in.

Lori brought Mae up to date on what had happened to Carla and then asked her if she would consider having the girl live with her until she was of age. Mae hesitated for some time but then said she'd think about it. Now Lori was about to find out what her decision was.

Ms. Jameson answered her knock quickly, as though she was watching for her. She was a dumpling of a woman, probably in her late sixties or early seventies, and Lori was immediately unsure of her quest. But she was here now so she might as well give it a try.

"Mrs. Jameson, I'm Lori Martin, Carla Wills' caseworker. I understand you know Carla from your time at Sunnyside Haven."

"Yep. We got along pretty good after a bad start. She sorta helped make bein' there easier to take, y'know?"

"I'm glad to hear that, because Carla needs some help now, and I'm hoping you might be willing to give it to her. I assume you know about her mother's death and losing her baby daughter." Mae nodded.

"I feel Carla needs a different place to live, away from the building where so much trauma has happened. As I told you on the phone, Carla thought you might be willing to take her in until she turns eighteen in a little over a year. You would receive a monthly allotment to pay her expenses, as well as the baby's when and if we locate her. Do you think you could do this?"

"Well, couldn't hardly think about anythin' else for thinkin' about it. I liked Carla and admired her spunk. Also felt bad for her 'cause of her situation. But I don't know about havin' her live with me. I'm just gettin' my own life back and don't reckon I can do that with somebody else in the house."

Lori sighed. "Well, you were my one hope of people she knew. I guess we'll just have to try to find something else for her."

"Can you find a place that will let her have her baby when she gets her back?"

"I'll admit, that will make it harder — but we might be able to do that. I just have to start looking for other possibilities."

"And if nothin' turns up?"

"Well, then, we'll have to rethink the situation. That would probably mean placing her baby, if and when we find her, in another foster situation until Carla reaches eighteen."

Mae thought about how much Carla loved that baby and how hard it would be for her if Faith was found but wasn't returned to her. "What if Carla came here to stay until you do find a more permanent fix for her? Her and the baby, I mean. I might could put them up until some-thin' better came around."

Lori hesitated. A more permanent arrangement now would be best for Carla, as battered as she was by all that had happened in her life this year. At the same time, being in the care of this older woman who could help her learn how to be a mother might be her best shot. "I think I could recommend that as a better solution than continuing to search for the ideal home under such pressure. Are you willing to do that, then?"

Again, Mae hesitated. Lori interrupted her thoughts. "Mrs. Jame-son, this is a young girl who has been battered around in her short life. It would be best for her to have a stable place to begin to heal and to learn how to lead a more normal life. I believe you might be the person to give her that boost up. But I'd certainly want to be sure that you would stay the course until we can find a better solution for her."

"What does that mean?"

"She needs stability. I'd like to be assured that she could stay here until we do find something as good or better for her. That you wouldn't be calling us in a week or two and saying she's got to go."

"Well, how do I know for sure? Can't guarantee anything. But me and Carla got along all right at the Home, and I reckon I should try to help her out some now. So, even though I'm a mite hesitant, I reckon I'll do the best I can for her for as long as it takes."

"I'm sure she's going to be relieved and very happy to hear that news. I'll help her get transferred to the school nearest here so you won't have to deal with that. And I'll try to help with anything else you may need, if you let me know." Lori knew she was promising herself more after-hours work and responsibility, but she'd worry about that later. "How soon would you be able to have her here?"

"Well, just about any time. There's a twin bed in the other bedroom but not much else. Reckon she may have to live out of boxes for her things for a while till I can get some more of my furniture moved in here for her."

"From what I've seen, she's no stranger to living out of boxes. To-morrow's Saturday. Would that be too soon for you?"

"No, it don't matter. We'll just have to figure it out as we go along."

"I think you'll find she's pretty adaptable. So, we'll see you tomor-row around 10:00."

Chapter 34
Mae

Leo was troubled about little Carla. Gossip around the home was that Carla's mother was dead and Carla was in foster care. No one seemed to know about her baby or what had happened to it. Leo was relieved that she was all right but worried about what might have happened. He worried it around in his mind for a while and decided to phone Mae to ask if she knew anything about it.

Mae answered on the third ring. "Mae, it's Leo. How are you?"

"Oh, my, things have been pretty bad lately, and it's sure a worry. I reckon you know about Mira being attacked at work."

"Yes. In fact, she's been to see me since she was moved here. She says you haven't been here to see her yet."

"Nope, and I don't reckon I will. It's kinda spooky to me now that the tables have been turned."

"Well, I hope that changes, for your sake and hers. But in the meantime, I see her nearly every day, so I'll let you know how she's doing."

"So you and her are getting' to be buddies, huh? She told me about comin' to see you all those times before. I been thinkin' that's what made you take up her side of things, so I ain't sure about what you been tellin' me about forgivin' her and all. Seems to me you been listenin' to her instead of me."

"Oh, Mae, please don't take it that way. Of course I listened to her, just as I've listened to you. Sometimes someone outside the picture can get a better handle on things. I only gave you advice that came from that understanding. From what you've told me of Jim, it seems to me that Mira has a lot of his traits. She's gentle like he was, caring and a caretaker, and maybe, like Jim, she's been misunderstood during her formative years."

"Humph. Sounds to me like another lecture comin' on, and I ain't got time for lectures right now. The welfare worker is bringin' Carla over to stay with me. I think they're here now."

"Carla? Carla's going to be staying with you? What a relief! She surely needs some TLC with all she's gone through, and I think you're just the woman who can give it to her."

Mae pondered Leo's parting words for a while, wondering what he meant by that. Didn't seem to her she was giving any TLC to anybody — just a place to live, until something better worked out. A knock at the door broke through her thoughts, and she dismissed them as she went to answer it.

Mae was a bit shaken up when she saw Carla. The teenager looked lost and sort of fragile. She barely acknowledged Mae's greeting and just stood there inside the door as though waiting for someone to tell her what to do.

"Well, come in, come in! Hello, Miz Martin. Hello, Carla. I'm sure sorry 'bout all your troubles."

Carla nodded but still didn't say anything. Lori Martin handed Carla the suitcase she had carried in and suggested she go look at her new room. Mae pointed her toward the small room, and Lori spoke softly to Mae. "She's becoming more depressed every day because we still haven't found her baby. I think maybe she's giving up on finding her, and I'm not sure what she'll do if we don't. I'm hoping that being here with you will help her work through some of her fear and worry. You might want to let her bring up her fear before you try to help her through it. Follow her lead, as it were."

The caseworker's words made Mae uneasy. "I wasn't figuring on dealin' with that. When's she goin' to snap out of it and get her starch back?"

"Right now, I can't answer that question. But I'm hoping that being here with you and starting in a new school will change her life enough to start the process. All you have to do is be there for her, if you can, and listen if she wants to talk. You don't really have to do anything more than that. I'll check back with you frequently to see if there's any progress. If not, we may have to consider some other kind of living arrangements. But for now, just give her as much TLC as you can."

"I ain't never been much good in that department. But I'll see what I can do. Maybe help her get some of her spunk back, anyways."

◈

Mira made her way down to Leo's room with the hope that talking to him would lift her spirits. Mama had not come to see her since she'd been moved here, and it disheartened her, believing as she had that the attack might bring them a little closer together. Now it seemed as if nothing had changed.

She found Leo sitting at his table, reading a book in Braille. "Oh my, Leo! That is so amazing, being able to read with your fingers."

Leo chuckled. "I suppose it seems so, but to me it's just everyday stuff. How are you, Mira? How's the shoulder today?"

"Still sore, but it's getting better. The therapist seems pleased with my progress. She's talking about getting me strong enough to go back to work."

"Wow, that seems fast. Good for you. I'd guess you are really working with her to move forward so quickly."

"Well, I want to get my life back as soon as I can."

"Sounds like someone else who used to be here. She couldn't wait to 'get her life back' as she put it. Guess you're cut from the same cloth."

Mira's face turned red.

"I surely did make a huge mistake on that, didn't I? I guess I let my need to keep her safe override her need to keep her independence. It's not a mistake I'll make any time again soon, I can tell you."

"Mira, don't give up on your mother. I think she's changing some. It's just that she's got a whole lot of catching up to do. I truly believe she's beginning to understand some things she didn't before."

"It's not as if I have a lot of choice. About being patient, I mean. And I'll keep trying to see her side of things. But at least we have a bit more of a relationship now than before my injury. Maybe it won't ever be all that I want — but it's likely it's all I'll get, and I'm willing to go with that. I think that's because I have some good friends now, people who accept me as I am. Before I felt I had no one but Mama, and that I didn't really have her."

"Oddly enough, I think you may be right, and that might be part of the solution. Anyway, keep the faith with her."

"Did you know that little nurse's aide is staying with her now? The one who was always so mouthy with Mama? That kinda hurts me … that she would want an outsider and not me."

"I'm not sure she exactly wants an outsider, as you put it. It's more like there's no good place for Carla to go right now, and your mother is just helping her until they find one."

"Did she tell you that?"

"Not in so many words, but I'm reading between the lines. She and Carla formed a fairly tight relationship while your mother was in here. Mae told me more than once that Carla was the only thing that kept her going. So, I'd guess she's trying to return the favor."

"Oh, my, I really did hurt Mama, didn't I? I guess I just didn't stop to think. I truly only wanted for her to be safe, but I never thought how it would affect her."

"No, I guess you didn't. But then, when we're worried or afraid, we don't always think things through too well. You made a mistake, but don't keep holding it against yourself. She's back in her own home now, so no real harm done. And maybe while she was here she learned some things about herself."

"What do you mean?"

"I don't want to talk about it right now, and I'm not sure I'm the person you should ask about it. Let's wait and see how all this turns out, and then I suspect you'll know exactly what I mean. So, how about you? Are you going to be all right?"

"How do you mean?"

"You've lost a lot of time from your job. Will it still be there for you when you're ready to go back to work? And how about your apartment?

And your bills? All this medical care is pretty costly, I'm thinking, and you've told me Arthur didn't give you anything in the divorce."

"No, no help from old Arthur. But, oddly enough, it feels pretty good to not be dependent on him. The motel's insurance is paying all the medical expenses and is even paying my salary until I can return. I'm hoping that will be as soon as I leave here. But my rent is paid up, and I don't really have any other expenses, since everything's furnished here."

"Well, good. Another worry off my mind."

"Why, Leo! You're just like a knight in shining armor, worried about me and Mama and Carla. You're just an old softie!"

"Have to have something to think about, sitting here all the time. This is the most I've had to sort out since I stopped hiking around the country."

Chapter 35
Mae

Mae was beginning to wonder if she had made the right decision in bringing Carla here. The girl was like a robot, doing all the things she was supposed to be doing, but with no apparent interest in any of them. There was nothing to fault; she kept her room neat and made the bed every morning. She ate when Mae called her to dinner, usually returning to her room "to study" immediately after dinner. She did her own laundry and carefully folded the clothing into the dresser Mae had provided. Her homework was completed every evening, and she was keeping her grades up. But the Carla Mae had known seemed to be lost somewhere.

Mae decided to be a little pushier in getting the girl to talk with her. At dinner, she questioned Carla about her day but got only very brief answers. Finally, in desperation, she said, "Seems to me you ain't livin' at all anymore. How long you gonna keep on this way?"

Carla shrugged. Mae persisted. "What happened to all that spunk you used on me back in the Home? Ain't you got any left to use on yourself?"

"What's the use? I'm never gonna get Faith back, and I just don't care about anything else."

"Well, I know the feeling. I thought I would never be able to leave that Home, but here I am! Maybe it would help if you talk some about Faith." Carla looked up and tilted her head. Mae didn't give her time to shut back down. "What was she like anyway? Was she a happy baby, or fretful, or what?" Carla thought for a moment and almost smiled.

"She was tiny, the littlest thing I ever saw. She had sort of red-blonde hair, not carrot-red like mine. And she had a lot of it for such a little thing! Somebody told me once that her hair was the color of a ripe peach." She paused to remember. "She was mostly good, didn't cry much unless she was hungry or wet or something. Could be she was more fussy than I knew … I'd never been around a baby before, so everything was new to me. She was – she was just getting her first tooth." With that last remark, Carla started to cry again.

Mae sat still, not knowing what to do. Finally, through her sobs, Carla talked about how much she missed Faith, what a good baby she had been, how she helped fill her own life with something that mattered. "She sorta gave me hope for myself and my life, y'know? Like, as long as she was depending on me, I had to make the most of myself to be what she needed. Now it just doesn't seem to matter."

Mae had no words of encouragement to offer, so she just stood and started to clear the table.

◆

The next morning, Mae's phone rang. "Dang, I never did have so many phone calls before in my life. Can't they leave a body in peace?"

She'd scarcely got the phone to her ear before the caseworker was talking.

"Mrs. Jameson, this is Lori Martin. I'm calling to let you know there's been a break in finding the woman who took Carla's daughter. A hospital employee identified her from the video — she was a clerk in the billing office at the hospital. She called in sick the day the baby was taken and has since resigned, also by phone. The officers are following up on this, starting with going to the address listed on her personnel records. I didn't want to tell Carla this yet, because there's a good chance the woman may have moved, and tracking her down may be difficult. But it's a break, and you can be sure they'll follow it through."

"Oh, my! But I shouldn't tell Carla yet, huh?"

"I'm thinking not, since it's so iffy. How is she doing?"

"She's pretty much down most of the time. Sort of like all the light has gone out — just doing what she has to do to get through the day and not much else."

"Well, use your best judgment, then. Maybe she needs some hopeful news to help her come out of that."

"I might could talk around it some, and see how that goes. Maybe then I'll know whether to tell her or not."

"Okay, that sounds like the best we can do. Good luck."

When Carla came home from school that afternoon, she seemed a little less bleak than usual. For a moment Mae wavered, hesitant to even bring up the subject that might push her down again. She decided not to say anything until she had more good news to add to it.

Instead she tried to get Carla to tell her about school, and her classes, and anything else she could think of. Carla's responses were brief, but she did respond. Later that night, however, Mae heard Carla's muffled sobs when she should have been asleep. Mae could almost feel her hurt and despair, and she was somewhat amazed at herself for that feeling.

The next morning, Lori called Mae again. "I've talked with my supervisor, and she thinks we should tell Carla what's happening. She believes it might help her. She also wants me to find out if Carla has remembered anything else that would help us. So I'll be dropping by this afternoon after school to talk with her."

Mae wasn't so sure this was a good idea, but the memory of Carla's sobs last night haunted her. She welcomed having the caseworker be the one to make the decision on how to proceed. Maybe Carla could take some comfort from knowing they were still working so hard to find Faith.

That afternoon, Lori was there when Carla came home from school. At Carla's startled look, Lori spoke warmly and firmly.

"Carla, we've had a break in finding Faith. We believe we've identified the woman who took your baby from the hospital restroom. She was a billing clerk in the hospital, but she hasn't been in to work since your baby disappeared. And three co-workers have positively identified her as the woman on the tape."

"So, if they know who has her, where is she? Where's my baby?"

"We don't know. The authorities have gone to her address, but she seems to have disappeared shortly after Faith was taken. No one in her building knew her well, so we couldn't get any information from them about where she might possibly have gone."

"So *what*, then? She took my baby and ran away with her?"

"That's about the size of it. We're pretty certain she couldn't have gone far, though. From what her co-workers told us, she likely didn't have the resources to leave town. So we're alerting every doctor in the area, especially pediatricians, to be on the lookout for her."

"How will they know it's her?"

"We're sending out the picture that was taken of her for her hospital badge. We'd like to have a better picture of Faith. We do have a picture of her from the security tape. It's not very good, but we'll use that and your description of Faith. A sharp-eyed nurse or receptionist might be able to recognize them from that."

Carla slumped against her chair in defeat. Lori reached out to her. "Don't give up hope, Carla. We're doing everything we can to find Faith."

"Faith was never sick. That woman will never bring her to a doctor."

"Let's hope you're wrong about that." But Lori knew the odds were not in their favor.

Chapter 36
Carla

Instead of being reassured by the development as they had hoped, Carla seemed to give up. Knowing that each passing day lessened the chance of finding Faith, Mae had no idea how to give Carla hope when she had so little herself.

Witnessing Carla's grief seemed to get through to Mae in a way nothing else had ever done. She would sometimes go back in her mind to the time when Mira was small and contrast Carla's feelings about her baby with her own feelings about Mira. She reluctantly admitted to herself that she had been a poor mother. *Piss poor*, she thought. She admitted to herself that her own actions had been responsible for much of the behavior she had faulted in Mira. She couldn't quite bring herself to believe that her poor mothering was the only reason Mira had been the way she was. Still, she knew in her heart that she hadn't been a very good mother to her daughter. She just didn't know what to do with this new information.

Lori came about once a week in the early evening to see Carla. Neither Carla nor Mae knew that she was using her own time to check up on the girl. Mae thought about talking privately with Lori about Carla but had no idea how to start such a conversation. So the weeks went by with a sameness that seemed to be endless. Mae floundered in the miasma of Carla's depression and her own helplessness.

Carla's routine seemed to be all that kept the girl going. She made it to school every day, did her homework every afternoon, and sat listlessly when she had nothing to do. She barely ate enough to keep up with her meager activities. Many nights Mae heard her crying quietly in her room.

The gloomy atmosphere worked on Mae's nerves, making her rethink her decision to keep Carla. Opposing that was her concern about what Carla would do if they moved her again. Unable to reconcile her dilemma, she finally decided to talk to Leo; he seemed to see things she couldn't see, so she hoped he could help her sort it out. She was still put out by his talking to Mira behind her back and how that might have colored his advice about their relationship, but asking him about Carla was a whole different thing. She hoped he would help her work out what she should do.

As Mae walked up to the door of the nursing home, she thought somewhat guiltily that she probably should go see Mira while she was here. She didn't want to do it, but her conscience was pushing her to at least make an effort in that direction. Well, she'd think about that after she had her talk with Leo.

Mae found Leo in his chair by the window, and they greeted each other warmly, Mae pushing aside her fretting about whose side Leo was on. She told him how it seemed as if Carla was going downhill, and that she didn't have any idea how to help her.

"So Carla has lost all hope, has she?"

"Looks that way to me. I don't know what to do. Seems like when I try to talk to her about it, she just cries more. Could I maybe bring her to see you and see if you can cheer her up any?"

"Mae, I wonder if anything can cheer Carla up right now. Somehow we need to get her thinking about something else instead of spending all her time grieving. You know, when she was working she didn't seem to let anything get her down. Maybe it was because she was so busy running from school to work to caring for Faith. Can you think of anything now that could keep her mind busy and not leave her with so much time to fret?"

"Nope, nothing. But I bet you're on the right track. As long as she's doing homework, she seems to hold herself together. Not havin' anything left to do brings on the waterworks.

"Does she help out around the house?"

"Nah, I don't need any help keepin' up with that little house. She washes her own clothes and makes her bed and stuff, but that's about it."

"What I'm thinking is that, for all this time, Carla has had to run as hard as she could just to keep up with all that was put on her. The baby, the job, school, and taking care of her mother sometimes, I suspect. Now she goes to school and does her homework, and then she has all that time left to think."

"And cry. She cries a lot of an evenin'."

"So, it sounds like she needs something more to do."

"Well, I reckon I could ask her for more help around the house. Not that I need it, but if you think it would do her some good?"

"I think it might. And I'm also thinking maybe you could talk to her social worker about getting her into some kind of volunteer program or something. Anything that wouldn't leave her with so much time to brood about her situation."

"Humph, don't know why I didn't think of that myself. That's a good idea, Leo. I'll give that Martin lady a call the minute I get home. She really seems to care about Carla."

"Good for you, Mae. I'm so glad Carla has you and maybe someone else to care about her. It seems she hasn't ever had that before in her life. Just be patient with her, try to keep her talking to you, and I'll bet she'll respond to you in time."

"Y'know, Leo, there's a lot of things I knew pretty good about my life and how I was livin' it before I met you, but now things are changin'. I'm not comfortable with what's happenin', but it don't seem as if I can stop it."

"Mae, if we're lucky we never stop learning. You have so much to offer that you never knew you had, and that's helping you see things in a way you never did before."

"Yeah, well, I'm not all that happy with how things are goin', but it is what it is, I reckon. I'm willin' to go along with it for now, but I'm thinkin' I'd like to get back to my own ways sometime."

"Speaking of going along with the changes, are you planning to visit Mira while you're here? I'm sure it would mean the world to her if you would."

"Don't push too hard, buster." Mae paused, and her voice softened. "But, yeah, I thought about stoppin' by her room for a few minutes to see how she's doing. Now that doesn't change things much yet," she warned. "She's still got a lot to answer for, so don't go imaginin' everything's fine."

"And I think she's beginning to realize that. Try to cut her some slack, Mae. She really does love you."

"Funny way to show love, shovin' me into a nursing home and all. Alright, alright, I'll stop by and talk to her. Just don't get too pushy." Leo chuckled as he listened to Mae leaving the room.

Mira was pathetically glad to see Mae. She sat aside the book she had been reading and jumped up from her chair. Then she hesitated, unsure of what to do next, waiting for Mae to speak.

"I see you're doin' right good now. When will you be leavin' here?"

"Maybe within the week. The therapist says I'm progressing very well and should be able to go back to work when I'm released." Mira rushed on. "Mama, thank you for coming by to see me. Being here has helped me reevaluate things, and I think I understand what I never did before. I'm sorry for making arrangements for you without talking to you about them. I know now that being helpless is an awful feeling, not thinking you have control over your own life. I was wrong to do what I did, and I'm sorry."

"Well, I'm guessin' you had ol' Arthur pushin' you to do that, so maybe I been a bit hard on you about it. Don't you never do that to me again, though."

"Oh, Mama, that's what I'm trying to say. I understand a little bit about how that made you feel, and I'll never, ever try to take over your life again."

"Well, now, that's all I wanted from you! All that you told me then was half-truths and outright lies, and you hid things from me so I couldn't do anything about any of it. Maybe if you mean what you say, we can get along alright — as long as you treat me like you oughta."

"How are you getting along in your new home? Do you like it? Does it feel like 'home'?"

"Don't reckon I'll ever feel as much at home there as I would if my old house was still mine, but I'm makin' do."

"And Leo tells me that Carla is living with you for the time being. How is that working?"

"Truth is, not very well. Can't seem to quit cryin' about her baby. I don't have any idea how to help her. That's why I came in today, to talk to Leo and see what he thinks. He gave me some things to think about, so I'll see how that works. Otherwise, I'm thinkin' she'll probably have to go to some other place to live where she can start to put all this behind her. But we'll see. Anyhow, guess I'd better get back home 'cause she'll soon be home from school. I want to talk to her about what Leo said."

When Mae arrived home, the house was quiet. Funny, Carla should have been home by now. Her bedroom door was closed, but she wasn't sure if it had been closed earlier in the day. Uncertainly, Mae stood listening for any sound from the room but heard nothing. She started to walk away and then turned back toward the door. Again, she turned away but immediately went back to the door. Something didn't seem right. Carla always studied with the door open. Had something happened today? Slowly, gradually, she turned the knob and pushed the door open a crack. Carla was lying on the bed, asleep. Mae started to turn away when Jim's old white robe caught her eye. It was flung across the desk chair. Mae's heart began to pound.

She rushed to the desk and picked up the sleeve of the robe. Turning it around in her hand, she couldn't feel anything in the cuff. Panicked, she shook Carla, calling her name, feeling the damp coolness of her skin. A black cloud seemed to envelop her as fear shot through her.

Unable to get a response from Carla, Mae hurried to the phone and dialed 911. It seemed to take hours before the ambulance arrived, and as soon as the paramedics entered the room, Mae was unceremoniously pushed back into the hall. They worked over the young girl for a short time and then brought in a gurney and strapped her in it.

"Do you have any idea what she might have taken?"

"Well, I sorta do, but I don't really know what it was. I think she found some pills I hid when I was in the nursing home. They're blue, but I don't really know what they're for."

"What nursing home? What's your name? We've got to call and find out what she took if we're going to help her."

Mae told them what they needed to know and watched helplessly as they wheeled the unconscious girl out, one of the paramedics already on the phone with the Home. Her heart pounded. Once settled into her home here, she completely forgot about the pills or that the robe where they were stashed hung in the closet in the spare room.

For a while, Mae paced the floor, wringing her hands and berating herself. What would Ms. Martin think? She would likely regret her decision to bring Carla here. It occurred to Mae that she should call Ms. Martin, but she could scarcely bring herself to do it. Finally, she acknowledged that putting it off was not going to make it easier, and she reluctantly placed the call.

Chapter 37
Mae

<hr>

Mae paced the floor wearily. She had paced through the long afternoon, waiting for a call from Ms. Martin about how Carla was doing. During all that waiting she had been beating up on herself for not remembering about the blue pills. She'd been a fool for not dumping those pills. She should have known better.

She thought about calling Leo, but why alarm him when she had almost nothing to tell him? She sat down briefly, tired to the bone, feeling totally helpless. She realized she cared about what happened to Carla, and she wondered at that: There were so few people in her life she truly cared about. She also wondered if, had it been Mira who took the pills, she would feel the same. She was surprised to realize that yes, she would be, remembering back to how upset she was after the attack on her daughter. She was turning this new development over in her mind when the phone finally rang.

"Mae, it's Lori Martin. I've just heard from the hospital. They believe Carla will be all right, although it was touch and go for a while. You were right about the medication. It was a mild sedative, but from what you told me and the hospital confirmed, she had a very large number of the pills, so the result could have been fatal. Thank goodness you checked up on her when you did. You saved her life."

"Well, I'm glad for that, but it seems to me that I nearly got her killed. I should have flushed those damn pills as soon as I moved here. I just forgot all about them. How long till we know she's for sure going to be okay?"

"The next twelve hours will tell us. They'll monitor her closely and intervene if it becomes necessary. But she's young and healthy, so that's in her favor. And she's getting the best of care. Try not to worry about her tonight."

"Can I go and visit her?"

"Let me check in the morning, and I'll let you know whether or not they'll allow that. Since you're not a relative, I do know you couldn't see her tonight, anyway."

Mae hung up the phone and was startled to realize there were tears on her cheeks. *When did Carla become so important to me?* Maybe it was just because she felt responsible for what happened, but it sure felt like more than that. She knew she would get little sleep that night from worrying about Carla and wrestling with her own feelings for the teenager.

Mae did sleep poorly that night, waking frequently, checking the clock, and wondering how Carla was doing. By morning she felt exhausted and barely had the energy to make herself a cup of tea. She tried to busy herself by straightening Carla's room and removing the sheets to launder so that Carla would have a fresh bed when she came home. *If* she came home. *Home!* When had she started thinking of this as Carla's home?

Mae did all the tidying she could think of, and still there was no phone call. Unable to carry this burden by herself any longer, she decided to call Leo, hoping he would reassure her as he had so often in the past.

"Leo, its Mae. I had to call you. Somethin' awful has happened. Carla tried to kill herself yesterday afternoon."

There was no response from the other end of the line. "Did you hear me? Carla took some pills and nearly died."

Still no answer. Oh, lordy, what if Leo had a heart attack because of what she had told him? She should have led up to it more gradually. "Leo, I think she's going to be all right. Are you there? Are you okay? Talk to me, Leo."

"I'm here Mae." *Finally!* "I just couldn't believe what you told me. Are you sure she's going to be okay?"

"No, not really. The caseworker promised to call this morning and let me know, but she said last night that they thought she would make it. I'm just waitin' for her to call."

"Where did she get the pills?"

"I don't hardly want to tell you, but she found them in the cuff of an old robe of my Jim's that was pushed way back in her closet."

There was another brief silence. "Ah. Would those pills have been your alternative if you hadn't been able to leave the home?"

"Yeah, how did you guess? I'm just sick about it, that I forgot they were there and that Carla found them, both."

"Mae, did you say the caseworker was going to call you this morning? Maybe we should hang up now. But would you call me after you hear from her? I do want to know how Carla is."

"Oh, shoot, you're right. I'm just so upset I can't think straight. I'll call you as soon as I hear from them." Moments after she hung up, the phone rang.

"Mae, this is Lori Martin. I called the hospital,and Carla's still asleep. But her breathing is normal, and I'm told she's out of the woods. *This* time!"

"I feel so bad about what happened. It's all my fault."

"No need for that, Mae. The doctors say that getting help as quickly as you did was exactly right. She's going to be all right. But if you can, why not go see her this afternoon? I think it might help."

Mae ended the call and then started pacing the floor. Lordy, she was too old for this. First Mira's attack, and now Carla's deliberately trying to kill herself. How was an old person supposed to hold up with all this happening? She needed someone to talk to. Oh, shoot, she had someone: She was supposed to call Leo back.

◈

Leo was relieved to hear Mae's report, but Mae was reluctant to hang up and just go back to pacing and thinking about all this again. So she asked Leo if they could talk for a while.

"I just feel so upset, like I'm to blame. And there's no one to tell me I'm not, and I should do something to make this right, but I don't know what to do."

"My goodness, Mae, that's a big load to carry! You had no idea Carla would find and take those pills. Yes, you were negligent not to have disposed of them, but Carla made the decision by herself. As to making it right, I'm guessing Carla will need even more TLC now to help get past her nightmare, and you *can* help her with that. Talk to her about her school work, or what she likes to do most, or anything that will help her get her center back. And remember to ask Miss Martin for suggestions! Maybe she'll have some more ideas about how to help her."

"Hadn't thought of that. Good idea — I'll check with Miz Martin."

Mira looked around the room. She was being discharged this morning, had called for a taxi to come about 10:30, and had packed up her few things. There was still almost an hour to wait for the taxi, so Mira headed down to Leo's room to tell him she was leaving.

"Hey, Leo, I'm going back to my apartment this morning. Thought I'd drop by and say 'good-bye' for now. Not sure how soon I'll be able to come back and visit you, but I'm sure I'll be back. I want to thank you for helping me see things better. I'm definitely going to think about all you said and try to make things right between me and Mama."

"Mira, there's something else you need to know. Carla tried to take her life yesterday afternoon, and your mother believes it's her fault. Maybe you could call her or go see her and help her deal with her feelings and her worry."

"Oh, my, that's terrible! But I don't think Mama would want my help."

"Maybe, maybe not. But this could be a chance to let her know that you are there for her. Let her tell you about it. It might be the opening you both need. Just think about it, Mira. Please, just think about it."

Mira did not have to go back to work until the following Monday, so she certainly had the time to think about Leo's words and to act on them. Try as she might, she couldn't imagine being of help to her very self-sufficient mother, but Leo seemed to think she should at least offer. As soon as she got settled back into her apartment, she called her mother.

"Mama, Leo told me what happened with Carla. I'm so sorry you have this to worry you now. Do you want to talk about it?"

There was a brief silence on the other end. "If you don't …"

"I'm not …"

"Well," Mira offered, "if you ever *do* want to talk about it, I'd be ready to listen."

"Don't know much yet what there is to talk about. Carla seems to be out of danger now, but no tellin' if she'll try again. That's a worry."

"Why did she try this time?"

"Well, it's about her baby, and she's givin' up hope of ever findin' her again." Mae realized that talking to Belle on the phone was enormously easier than talking to her in person. "I reckon she just decided there was nothin' worth livin' for."

"That's so sad. Is there any way I can help?"

"Well, I don't know yet. I'm not sure if she'll come back to live with me or if they'll put her someplace else. Don't know why they would bring her back here anyways. And if she ain't here, there's not much any of us could do to help."

"Why do you think she won't come back?"

"Well, she found some pills I'd saved up, so I suspect they're blamin' me for what she done."

"What pills? Why were you saving pills? Were they from the Home?"

"Yeah, well, I kept all these blue pills they tried to make me take there."

"But why did you keep them?" There was a brief pause, and suddenly Mira gasped. "You were planning to take them yourself, weren't you?"

"Yeah, that was my plan if I couldn't get outta there no other way. But I forgot I had 'em, and Carla found 'em."

"Oh, Mama, how could you even *think* about killing yourself?"

"I hated almost ever' minute I was in that place. Hated the food, hated most of the other people, and hated feelin' like I had no say in my own life. So I was goin' to get myself out of there, any way I could."

"I did that to you, didn't I? Why didn't you just tell me how much you hated being there?"

"Belle, I tried. Ever' time you came in, I tried. But you wouldn't even hear me. You just kept sayin' how wonderful it was for me to be there."

"I didn't understand. I thought your complaining was just … something to say, sort of. More of your usual. And I thought that once you got used to it, everything would be all right. But it wasn't ever going to be all right, was it?"

"Nope. I just wanted to go home, but you never heard me."

"Oh, Mama! I feel so bad. I didn't understand what you were saying. I always had a hard time understanding what you were thinking and feeling, so I figured this was just another time like all the others. Can you ever forgive me?"

"Well, now that my life is set back to rights, I'm workin' on that. Leo's been helpin' me see some things where maybe I kept you from understandin' me. So, I reckon maybe that makes it partly my own fault." As she said the words, they rang true to her for the first time.

"Mama, do you think we could sort of start over?"

"What does that mean, Be – uh, Mira?"

"I'm not sure. But now that *I'm* doing better in my life, I think I'm figuring out some things I never did before. Like, I never understood why you didn't seem to love me. And how maybe it was hard for you to have to take care of me when you were feeling like that. And how I made mistakes because I really didn't know how to be someone you might love, but I kept trying. I'm not saying this right, but can you understand a little?"

Mae felt as if all the breath had been knocked out of her. Every part of her body was rattled by Mira's words. She'd had no idea her daughter had been so affected by her lack of love, and yet how could she not have been? It's exactly what Mae had wanted her to feel.

"Belle, I can't talk any more right now. I'll call you some other time." And summarily she broke the connection.

Chapter 38
Carla

Carla awoke slowly, feeling an aching deep in her body and puzzled about where she was and why. She opened her eyes to a hospital room and was instantly angry. She hadn't done it. She was still alive. There was no one else in the room; she would get out of bed, find her clothes, and simply slip out. When she tried to stand up, however, the room whirled around and she nearly fell. She gripped the mattress with both hands and began to sidle around the bed toward the closet door.

At that moment a nurse entered the room, grabbed her arm, and led her firmly back to the side of the bed.

"Feeling frisky, huh? That's a good sign, but you're really not ready for a solo flight just yet. Let's just get you back in bed. The doctor will be in to see you shortly. He'll let you know whether it's all right for you to get out of bed."

Her aborted attempt to escape had taken away what little energy she had, so she settled back on the pillow and heaved a deep breath. As soon as she awoke, it had all came back to her: Faith being gone, her life in a mess, and her attempt at suicide. Didn't look like she could get anything right anymore. She felt the tears on her cheeks, but that seemed to be her new normal, so she ignored them. Now what? She was still alive, and Faith was still gone.

" — and she was trying to leave." The nurse was briefing the doctor as they walked into Carla's room.

"Well, Miss Wills, how do you feel?"

"Really awful, as if you didn't know."

"Aha. Got a little of your spunk back. That's good. Want to tell me why you tried to end your life?"

"Just seemed like the thing to do."

"Well, it wasn't. Now, you're going to be all right from this one. And I hope you'll think long and hard before you consider this again."

Carla knew the young doctor didn't have a clue. No doubt his life was just fine, while hers was already over. She'd just have to plan better next time.

"We'll be keeping you here for a couple more days to be sure all the toxins are out of your system and to help you get your strength back. Then you can go back home."

Home, Carla thought. *I've never had a home. How can I go back to a place where I've never been?* She lay listlessly in the bed, unable to sort out the thoughts that swirled about in her brain or even to make much sense of them. Next time, she promised herself, she'd plan ahead and get it right. With that thought, she drifted back to sleep.

A short time later, Mae peeked in and saw Carla asleep. She was about to turn away when a nurse came up behind her.

"I'm going to wake her up to take some meds, so you can come on in. I think some company would do her good. She's sort of down on herself right now." Mae followed her into the room and waited until the nurse left before talking to Carla.

"Why'd you go and do that, Carla? Do you have any idea of how I'd a felt if you had died while I was 'sposed to be takin' care of you?"

"Why would it matter to you?" Carl muttered. "I'm just in your way, and it looked like you'd be stuck with me till I'm eighteen. Can't imagine that makes you happy."

"Now, about that. I gotta tell you that I was getting' used to havin' you around ... and *sorta* beginnin' to like it."

"I don't believe you." Her voice was stronger and picking up steam. "Is that what the welfare worker told you to say? You wouldn't have come up with that on your own, I bet."

"I'm tellin' you, it would have made me feel really bad if you'd a died."

"Oh, c'mon, Mae. This is Carla you're talking to. I never heard you care much about anybody else in all the talking we did. You can't expect me to believe that suddenly you've found some reason to like me."

"What I'm thinkin' is that it wasn't so sudden. You and me did pretty good in that home, buckin' each other up over the lousy deal we both got. Reckon I got used to that."

"Yeah, so now that you have your life back the way you want it, you don't need me around reminding you of how bad it was before, I'm thinking."

"And that's just the problem. I don't have what I wanted. It ain't happenin' any more like I thought it was goin' to if I just got out of that danged home. And havin' you around was kinda helpin' me adjust to the way things are now."

"What you mean is, you gave up trying for what you wanted. And my being there was probably part of the problem with that. So my being there was keeping you from the kind of life you wanted."

"Okay, I'll admit that nothin' was workin' out the way I thought it would, and at first I wanted to blame you. But, to be honest, that isn't really the way it was. I see now it was just that I couldn't let go of my need to have my old life back. I didn't want to believe it was gone. And you were there, so I could tell myself it wasn't happenin' just because of you, and not because it wasn't ever *goin'* to happen."

"Right. Whatever. But it still comes down to my being in the way. And I didn't have anything to live for, either. So it seemed sort of useless to go on the way we were. I just wanted it all to be over and done."

"And I'm tellin' you I don't *want* it to be all over and done. I want you to come back and live with me and help me, like you used to do in the Home when I got so down. And I'll try to help you. Maybe neither of us has what we want, but maybe we can help each other through this like we did before. You gotta believe that they'll find Faith, and if you're gone, who's gonna love her anywhere near as much as you do? And while we're waitin' we could help each other figure out how to carry on without my Jim and your Faith."

"Okay, Mae, you win. I guess if you keep arguing with me about my life, maybe it will help me somehow endure it. I don't see how, but guess I can give it a chance."

"Good for you. So, when they let you go, you'll be comin' back to our house. We'll figure it out as we go along, okay?"

"Yeah. I don't see how this is going to work, but I guess I owe you that much … so you got a deal."

Mae left the hospital room feeling better than she had since Jim had passed away. Now she just had to convince the Welfare lady to let Carla come home to her.

◆

Mira was welcomed back to work with a small impromptu party. Everyone crowded into her small office, each with a gaily if awkwardly wrapped package. She felt her eyes tear up as she looked at the smiling faces of her co-workers. It felt very much as if she had friends who really cared about her! She hugged each one in turn and laughed at the jokes and quips that seemed to be coming at her endlessly. She had never felt so accepted in her life, and it felt good.

"Thought you'd like to know how your attacker got in that night," the night manager said. "Seems one of the guests dropped his key card just outside the back entrance, and instead of looking for it, they just used his wife's and left it out there. Apparently, that creep found it and managed to get all the way to your office without being discovered. The police still haven't found him, so we're being extra vigilant from now on."

Ernie jumped in. "Yes, Mira, I'm going to be checking up on you every so often, so just figure on it."

The night manager looked at Ernie curiously, but let it go.

"So, Mira, now that you've had your vacation, you'd better get straight to work. We had someone filling in while you were gone, and I think they've made a complete mess of everything. So, party's over. Everyone get back to work!"

With many "So glad you're back!" and "Good to see you at your desk!" and "See you at break!" comments, everyone left to start the night's schedule. Mira looked around and felt at home.

She quickly discovered that her replacement had not messed up, and everything was in order and up to date. True to his word, Ernie checked up on her every time he was in the area, and she blushed a little each time he did. She used the first hour to go over the figures and familiarize herself with the current numbers. Then the front desk clerk brought in the day's receipts and Mira got down to her job, humming a happy if tuneless ditty.

She had spent her last few days of recuperation in contemplation of her life and where she was in it now. She was content with how things had turned out and was hopeful that she and her mother were starting a closer relationship. She didn't dare hope for the love that she craved from Mama, but thought perhaps her new friends would help fill the gap. It surely seemed to her that life suddenly opened some new possibilities, and she was eager to make them work for her.

Except for Ernie's random popping in and checking to be sure she was all right, the evening went quietly, and she was feeling very good when it was time to go on break . There she retold much of what she had been through since last they were together and laughed at their silly jokes about how much extra work each had done to fill in for her.

She was at home.

As she rode the bus home the next morning, she thought about the night just past, and then the past few months, and then the huge changes in her outlook and image of herself. The old bewildered "Belle"was seemingly gone, and in her place was this apparently normal person who had friends, a good job, and a good life. Amazing! She got off at her stop and even hummed a little love song as she climbed the stairs to her apartment. She thought she might even try to tell Mama how good her life was these days.

Chapter 39
Mae

Mae hummed tunelessly as she prepared to spend her first day gardening since moving into her new home. The early March weather was mild, and there was some new green emerging. She wanted to put markers on the bright stems and tendrils while the old plants were still there to help her identify them.

She was more content than she had been for a long time, and it surprised her. She thought about why that might be. Jim had not come back to talk to her again, but she could bring his memory back in the evenings and talk to him in her mind. Somehow that seemed to be enough for now.

And Carla was doing better, too. Instead of going immediately to her room, she stayed and talked with Mae about her classes and her tentative plans for the future. Mae called Mira now and then to let her know things were going better; she found that focusing on Carla made it more comfortable to talk with her daughter now. And it seemed that all three of them were growing closer and feeling better about themselves and life in general.

True, Carla's eyes still welled up any time she mentioned Faith, but she was no longer crying herself to sleep. There were still gaps in her conversation with both Mae and Mira and some hesitation in expressing what she was feeling, but there was a new sense of relationship among them. They intuitively understood that their lives were tilting back to some kind of normalcy, different from before but so much more satisfying in most ways.

Mae and Carla regained much of their old camaraderie and even managed to zing each other once in a while. And Mira was dropping in on her mother more frequently and staying until Carla came home from school. Occasionally, Mae invited her to supper; Mira was more than willing to stay.

Over time it was as if the three of them formed a tentative family of sorts. There were still times when each slipped back into old patterns, but these were occurring less often and were less remarkable.

There was a definite bond being forged between them, with far fewer awkward moments. When she stopped to think about it, Mae was surprised by how much she now enjoyed the company of both Mira and Carla these days. She wondered sometimes when she was alone how this came about but, true to her nature, she didn't think about it too deeply. It was what it was, and it seemed to be good, so she just accepted it.

She stood now and massaged her back. That was about enough for one day's gardening. Mae looked out over her flower beds and was pleased with how much she had accomplished. She was also pleased with the direction her thoughts had taken as she weeded and trimmed. Life seemed to have a new normal for her, and she seemed to be accepting it. She wondered how all this had come about but decided not to dwell on it; it was nap time, so she let the thought drift away.

Mira opened the front door about two-thirty, just after Mae awakened from her nap. Mae was ready for the company and quickly made tea and put out cookies. Mira filled her in on what was happening in her life, all of it good: Her friends at works seemed to genuinely like her, she was happy with her new life and, she shyly reported, she was happy that she and Mae seemed to have met on common ground. Their talk seemed to come more easily these days, and Mae found herself enjoying the talk about Mira's work and her new friends but still inwardly resisted discussing their own relationship.

"Things are real good for me now. There's this fellow at work that kind of likes me. He hasn't asked me out or anything, but I think he might. And then my landlord just handed me a deal I couldn't turn down. He has a ground floor apartment that's vacant now, bigger than mine. Even has two bedrooms. He said I could have it, and it's only a little more than I'm paying for my small apartment on the third floor! I wouldn't have to climb the stairs anymore, and I'd have more room. I can't say I *need* more room, but I just couldn't turn it down."

"How you gonna get moved?"

"Oh, well, there's not much to move. Both apartments are furnished, so there's no furniture to move. It's only my clothes and dishes and things like that. And it's only down a couple of flights of stairs. Besides, I have all weekend to do that, so it shouldn't be a problem."

"Say, why don't you ask Carla to help you? It might do her good to get out of the house — give her somethin' else to think about for a change. She's younger than you, and she could climb up and down the stairs easier, I'm thinkin'."

"You know, I think that might be a good idea. It would also give us a chance to know each other better. I'll ask her this afternoon when she gets home from school."

"Yeah, but don't push her too much about what's goin' on in her life. I think she's still havin' trouble gettin' used to all that's happened. But she's managin' to work around it some."

"Oh, Mama, I'm more sensitive than that. I just thought we could talk about clothes and things. You know, girl stuff."

Mae regarded her daughter thoughtfully. She was learning that Mira wasn't the empty-headed girl she had always thought. In fact, she was turning out to be a much more interesting person than Mae had ever given her credit for. It seemed they could talk about almost anything and have a good conversation now. Sure looked like Mira had grown up at last.

Life was the best it had been since her Jim died. She wondered how this had happened, but decided Mira was just growing up at last.

◈

"Hey, Mae. Hey, Mira. Man, am I glad this day is over. Three tests today and I'm beat. Are there any cookies left, or did you two scarf them all down already?"

"Prob'ly just about enough for you. Looks like I'll have to make some more tomorrow, huh?" Mae heaved a theatrical sigh. "So, other than the tests, how was school?"

Carla waggled her hand while stuffing another whole cookie in her mouth. "So-so," she said around the mouthful. "Some of it boring, some of it interesting. None of it new."

"Carla," Mira began, "I'm moving to a different apartment this weekend and wondered if you would be willing to help me move my stuff into the new one. What do you think?"

"Sure, why not? Will there be anyone else helping?"

"Probably not. The new apartment is in the same building, and I only have clothes and dishes and stuff like that to move. No heavy stuff. And we'll be lugging things downstairs and not upstairs. I thought maybe we could go out to dinner to celebrate when we finish. How about coming over around two o'clock Saturday?"

Carla looked over at Mae. "That all right with you?"

"Oh, yeah! It would give me some time of peace and quiet."

"Ha! You mean you'd take a longer nap without me ragging you about it."

"Well, that, too."

Mae felt a sense of rightness about their bantering. It had been commonplace between them at the nursing home but missing far too long from their friendship since then.

◆

That Saturday the two women worked compatibly together, talking about inconsequential things for some time.

When there was a lull in their conversation, Carla hesitantly asked, "Mira, how did you work it so you and your ma are getting along better? I need to learn how to do that… Except for you and Mae, I don't seem to be able to make friends. Lotte was good to me, but only if it didn't make Ma mad. So we were never what you would call friends. The boy who knocked me up wouldn't even talk to me afterward. No one at school seems to want to have anything to do with me except to hassle me or laugh at me." The words fell heavily in the still room. "What's wrong with me that nobody wants to be my friend?"

Mira put down the dish she was holding and turned to Carla.

"Oh, Carla, I have to tell you that I absolutely know what you're feeling! Well, except for getting knocked up, anyway. I figured out that's why I married Arthur. He was the first one who seemed to think I was okay, but then I found out at the end that even *he* thought I was a loser. So I'm thinking my marriage was a lot like your one-night stand, only longer." They laughed. "And I'm guessing that all my life I felt a lot like you're feeling now. Then I reached rockbottom with no home, no job, no husband … Mama didn't seem to want me around … there was nobody and nothing there for me. I was down about as low as I could get. Nothing left to lose!

"So I decided to just stop trying to please everyone else so they would like me and find things I could do just for me, to make my life better. Somehow, that changed things for me. Now I think people tended to see me the way I saw myself and treated me accordingly. Even Mama did that. I wasn't sure just what would happen, but I tried to just not think about that and just do what felt good and right to me.

"I was scared at first, afraid I might be just setting myself up to get knocked down again, but somehow it seemed to work. Starting over in a new job and working with people who didn't know me from before probably made a big difference, too. I was still surprised when people started to treat me with respect and then friendship. And more so when even Mama seemed to change toward me. So things are the best they've ever been for me."

"I don't see how it can be that simple," Carla argued. "I never thought less of myself because of the way other kids treated me. I just never understood why it happened."

"Well, I'm no authority. It's all pretty new to me, too. But I think for me it's because I seem to be more sure of who I am and less in need of someone else's approval. I know that sounds strange, but it's what I'm feeling happened."

"Guess I got to think about that some. I'm not sure I understand it, but I'll think on it."

Chapter 40
Mae

It was a warm mid-May morning, and both Carla and Mae were sitting at the kitchen table. Mae was reading the Saturday *Indianapolis Star*, and Carla was boning up for the final exams which would be coming in about two weeks. But she was finding it difficult to concentrate, so she pushed her chair back and went to get a drink of water. Turning from the sink, she watched Mae for a moment.

"Y'know, I'm thinking that after all this time, it's not likely they'll ever find Faith for me. It's just too hard on me, this hoping and waiting to get her back." She swallowed hard. "So I think I have to figure out how to make my life work without her."

Mae looked up from her paper and watched Carla for a moment, trying to gauge her mood. "Why did this come up now all of a sudden? What's happened to make you give up hope?"

Instead of answering, Carla mused, "My friend named Faith was the first person ever to be my friend. She never put me down, she always hugged me when we said goodbye, and she taught me things that no one else cared enough to tell me. So when I think of 'friend' that's who I think of. That's what I wanted to have with my Faith, to make sure we both had that in our life. When I fed her, she would wrap her tiny hand around my little finger, and I couldn't help but think it was a little hug she was giving me. It just filled me up. But now she's been gone so long that the chance of them finding her is almost nothing. I only hope that whoever took her will give her what my friend gave me."

"But why are you thinkin' this way now?"

Carla returned to the table and sat down. "That Saturday when I helped Mira move into her new apartment, we spent some time talking. She's a pretty savvy lady when it comes to dealing with loss. She told me how much better her life has been since she stopped looking at what she doesn't have… and she said it made a world of difference. That made some kind of sense to me, and I've been thinking about it ever since." Carla swallowed hard.

"I want Faith back so bad it hurts. But I think I have to put that away and make my life work with what I have. Really, I have so much more now than I ever did before, and if I could get Faith back, I don't think I would ask for another thing in life. And I think I'll always hope to find her someday, and I truly believe I will. But whether I do or not, I need to make what I have now as good as it can be for me and not keep messing it up with feeling sorry for what I don't have. Does that make sense?"

"Well, I think you're right to get on with your life. Just don't know if you should give up on gettin' Faith back just yet."

"I'm not exactly giving up. It's more like I'm just not letting that be my only thing in life. It's too painful."

Mae didn't know how to respond to Carla's announcement. Secretly, she thought the girl was right; the chances of finding Faith were slim to none. And it looked as if the teen had found a way to accept that without letting it tear her apart. She needed to tell Leo about this development and hear what he had to say about it. It was about time to pay him another visit, anyway. The last time she was at the Home he didn't seem to be feeling too well, so she needed to check up on him anyway. She would go next Monday.

Meantime, she did something very uncharacteristic for her: She walked over to Carla and hugged her shoulder .

Carla jumped up and threw her arms around Mae and hugged her long and hard. Mae could feel Carla's tears against her cheek but could only pat Carla on the back, hoping that would be enough. Finally, Carla hiccoughed and drew back.

"Whew, don't know what brought that on, but thanks for the hug. Guess I needed it." Mae merely nodded and went back to her chair. But she felt something warm inside and savored the feeling.

◆

Mae's visit to the Home was disturbing. The administrator had seen her coming in and waylaid her for a moment's talk.

"Leo has had some health problems lately, so he isn't as alert and active as he has been. His diabetes has gotten worse, and he's feeling the side effects of that and some new meds they have him on. I just wanted you to know so you wouldn't be shocked."

When she stepped into Leo's room, Mae was still shocked. Leo was lying in bed although it was late morning; he appeared to be asleep. An untouched breakfast tray sat beside the bed. Mae touched his shoulder and called his name. Slowly, he woke up and considered her without recognition for a moment. Then he smiled.

"Mae ... I'm glad you've come."

"Gosh darn it, Leo. It's nearly eleven o'clock. What are you still doing in bed?"

"Little under the weather today, so I'm taking it easy."

"How long you been feeling bad?"

"Oh, not long," he said vaguely. "Couple of days, I guess. They're changing my meds, and maybe that's what's doing me in. Should be better soon."

"Anything I can do for you?"

"No, nothing. Sorry for being such poor company." And with that he seemed to slip back to sleep. Mae left the room, shaken by his condition and fearing what it might mean. She worried about it on the ride back home, wondering how much she should or would tell Carla. But she had to talk to someone about it. Maybe Mira would be over today, and she could ask her opinion.

Mira did come over just about two thirty, and Mae began to tell her about both Leo and Carla all at once, so that her words confused Mira.

"Wait a minute, Mama. I'm not understanding what you're telling me. Start with Carla. What's wrong?"

"Well, not wrong, but surely different. Carla told me on Saturday that she's pretty much come to terms with never finding her baby. I don't know if it's a brave front, but she seemed to be sure. She's given up, but she isn't broken up about it. I don't know if that's good, but I thought it might be. She said it was partly because of some of the things you and her talked about that Saturday she helped you move." Mira smiled warmly, but at Mae's expression she sobered. "So I went to talk to Leo about it and found out that he's in terrible condition. It's almost more than a body can take."

"Yes, I can see that. But back to Carla. How has she been since she told you that?"

"Well, not much different … but maybe not quite so mopey all the time? I don't know how to explain it, really. Maybe if you're here when she comes back from school you can see what you think."

"Of course I can stay. You know, we had a good talk when she helped me move. I tried to explain how I've found so much more than I ever lost by looking more closely at all that I have now. Maybe that helped her decide to move on in her life, too."

"Yeah, she mentioned that, so I'm guessin' you're right on that score. I just hope she doesn't go back into herself when Faith's birthday rolls around."

"So, let's you and I plan to be with her that day, to hold her hand, wipe her tears, and help her move past it."

"Yeah, it's about all we can do, and just hope it's enough. Now about Leo. He's really in a bad way, could hardly talk when I went in this mornin'. The head of the Home said his diabetes is worse, and they're havin' trouble adjustin' his medication."

"Oh, dear! Listen, I'll check in tomorrow afternoon and see what I can find out. Now, isn't it about time for Carla? Let's get the tea and cookies ready. I really want to hear from *her* the things she told *you*. I just hope for her sake that she's finally ready to move on."

After Carla reassured Mira that she truly was doing better, they all talked out their fears about Leo and admitted that he seemed like part of the family. At the word "family"' all three of them stopped and stared at each other. The word felt good, hanging around them like that, but it was new and somehow astonishing.

                    Ellie Pulikonda

Suddenly Mira laughed, Carla soon joined in, and Mae, staring at them as thought they were loony, finally began to chuckle as well. Mira reached out and took Carla's hand, squeezing it gently; Carla reached over and took Mae's hand, giving it a gentle squeeze. Mae just sat there, somewhat stunned by this turn of events.

Looking at Mira, Mae felt her hand moving toward the daughter she had ever wanted. Mira reached out as well, and their hands met halfway between them. After a few moments, they all began to laugh so hard that tears ran down their cheeks.

Just as suddenly, everyone drew back in embarrassment. All three started talking at once, trying to cover up the intimacy they just shared. But when Mira stood up to leave, she reached out to Carla and gave her a hug. The girl responded by hugging Mira so hard she squealed. Mae watched with a new feeling growing inside her. Longing? Something in her wanted to be part of this hugging, but she just couldn't bring herself to stand up and push her way in.

Chapter 41
Mae

The three women continued to keep some of the closeness that had started that day, but Mae was still holding back when it came to hugging. She had never been a hugger except with her Jim. Although Mae could feel herself wanting to be hugged again, she still felt especially uncomfortable being so openly affectionate with Mira and Carla. *Old habits die hard*, she thought. *Maybe I just ain't cut out for all this huggin'.*

◈

It was almost a year since the day Carla entered the nursing home as an aide and their unusual relationship had begun. The unseasonable late May heat seemed to take its toll. Tempers flared, and twice they had come dangerously close to losing their camaraderie. But they were able to repair the damage and move on. Mira initially came two or three times a week for cookies and tea, and although none of them admitted it openly, it was much more than that now. Leo's condition deteriorated, and he was moved to the hospital. The women missed him and his wise counsel and worried aloud about how he was doing. Their mutual concern forged another bond between them.

In early June they got word that Leo seemed to have turned a corner and was responding well to the new drugs he was receiving. They celebrated this news and spent most of their time talking about Leo, how he had helped each of them and how grateful they were that he was getting better.

And then the day came. June 10. Faith's birthday. She would be one year old today, and none of them would be there to see her blow out her one candle, sing silly songs with her, or help her open the birthday presents they so desperately wanted to give her. They met together anyway, just as they had been doing, but it was a somber time. All three wiped away tears from time to time, but each was determined to put the best face on it that they could. Still, for the first time in several weeks, Mae heard sobs coming from Carla's room that evening.

◈

The next morning Mae asked Carla to help in the garden, as much a diversion as a need for help.

"I'm gittin' a little behind on the weedin', and some of the earlier blooms need to be dead-headed. Sure could use some help."

Carla grimaced. Gardening wasn't her thing, and it was danged hot out there these days.

But she owed Mae something for all she'd done for her, so fair was fair.

"Sure. Just let me change into some old jeans, and we'll do it."

When Mira came that afternoon, she found Mae and Carla resting on two old lawn chairs, admiring their handiwork.

"Looks like my timing couldn't be better," she joshed. "But the garden surely does look well-tended! So how about we take the afternoon off and go to a movie? Tickets are on me, a reward for all your hard work."

Carla jumped at the chance, but Mae thought she'd rather have a short nap. "Come on back afterwards, and I'll have some dessert ready for us." It was quickly agreed upon, and Carla and Mira took their leave, bickering companionably about which movie they should see.

Their lives were forming a pattern, and the pattern was beginning to resemble a family.

◆

In late June two unexpected things happened. About ten in the morning, they had a call from Leo to let them know he was back in the Home and much improved. They all crowded around the phone, calling encouragement and love to him, promising to visit just as soon as possible. Then Mira and Carla went out shopping together. Carla needed some new sneakers, and Mira wanted to upgrade her wardrobe a bit more. Shortly after they left, Mae's phone rang.

"Mae, it's Lori Martin. Is Carla there?"

"No, her and my daughter went shopping. Should I have her call when they get back?"

"No, I wanted to talk to you first anyway. As hard as it is to believe, the authorities believe they have a strong lead on finding Faith."

"For sure? After such a long time?"

"The woman who kidnapped her had to take her to the doctor last week to treat a serious rash on her scalp. The nurse saw that her hair was an unnatural-looking black and guessed it had been dyed. She wondered why anyone would dye a baby's hair and figured it could only be to disguise her for some reason. Then, amazingly enough, she remembered the bulletin we took around last winter and found it in her files. The woman looked a lot like the picture on the bulletin, so they notified the police. But by the time the authorities got there, the woman had left."

"So, then, where's Faith now? Did they go to her place and find Faith? Will Carla get her back right away?"

"I wish it were that straightforward. First of all, the woman gave a false address to the doctor'soffice, so the police hit a dead end. But the doctor insisted that she bring the baby back next week so he could be sure the rash was healing all right. The staff thinks the woman is worried enough that she'll come. That would be next Friday. You can be sure that plainclothes officers will be there on Friday."

"Oh, my! Carla is just beginnin' to get on with her life, and she's doin' so much better. I'm wonderin' if we should even tell her all this. What if she gets her hopes up again, and that woman never comes back to the doctor?"

"That's pretty much why I called you first. I don't like keeping good news from her, but neither do I want to get her hopes up and have something happen."

"I don't like not tellin' Carla, either, but I'm thinkin' we should wait till next Friday. Would you be okay with that?"

"Like I said, I'm pretty much going to trust your judgment on this one."

◆

The next five days were the longest Mae had ever known. She kept second-guessing her advice to wait to tell Carla. Did Carla have the right to know how close they had come? Or would it simply push her back down into her sadness if they told her and she didn't get Faith back?

Carla and Mira guessed that something was chewing on Mae, and she worked hard to convince them that there was nothing bothering her.

Still, she intercepted some curious glances between them, so she knew that they didn't really believe her. Mae was jumpy and absent-minded. Mira decided to take the initiative once when Carla stepped outside to water the garden.

"Okay, Mama, I know something's up. Are you having health problems or something? You're so jumpy all of a sudden, and you don't seem to be listening when we talk to you. What's going on?"

"Listen, Carla might be comin' in at any minute. You'll just have to wait a few more days till I know for sure. Then I'll tell you both. Just don't push me."

Mira was certain Mae had discovered a lump or was having heart palpitations or something equally serious. She decided to ask Carla to keep a close watch on Mae in case things got worse.

Chapter 42
Faith

"Well, Ms. Cameron, the rash has not improved. In fact, it looks somewhat worse. Did you use the medications I prescribed last week?"

The dark-haired woman was jumpy and had to swallow twice before she could answer the doctor's question.

"Yes." She stopped to clear her throat. "Yes, of course. I want my baby to be well. How can you even ask that question? I take good care of her. She's everything to me."

"I must ask you again if you have used anything on her scalp that might have caused this rash. Any lotions or home remedies? Anything at all? And did you use it again this past week?"

"No, no, of course not. I resent your implying that I would, and I don't like your questions. I'm going to take her to another doctor, one who is more competent. It sounds like you're blaming me for her condition instead of trying to make her better."

The pediatrician nodded to his nurse, a pre-arranged signal for her to summon the officers in the waiting room. As they entered the room, the woman bolted forward, screaming and trying to snatch the baby from the doctor's arms. Two officers took hold of her arms, holding her in place, as she struggled against them.

"Ms. Cameron, I'm almost certain that the cause of the child's rash is hair dye. What reason would you have for dying her hair?"

She struggled unsuccessfully against their hold, screeching again and again, "My baby! You can't take my *baby!*" Getting an answer to the doctor's question seemed unlikely.

One of the officers slipped a pair of handcuffs over her wrists, and the two quickly escorted her out of the office. She cursed and screamed as they half-walked and half-carried her outside. In the quiet that followed, a third officer asked the doctor if the baby should be hospitalized.

"Definitely. Not only because of the rash, but because this child needs to be thoroughly evaluated. She told us the child was only six months old, but the number of teeth tells us she's closer to a year. Yet she has neither the skills nor the strength that a child her age should have. I'm guessing that the woman was deliberately trying everything she could to keep the baby's identity a secret – that's the only explanation I can provide for claiming she's younger than she is and for dyeing the child's hair. We need to be sure the woman has done nothing else detrimental to the child. If she has... well, we need to know. Perhaps it could harm her physically, as the hair dye did. At the very least, her development has apparently been set back a few months. This baby needs to be monitored and her health assessed."

About two hours later, Lori Martin received the call she was anxiously awaiting.

"Ms. Martin, we have the baby in our custody. She's been taken to St. Luke's hospital for tests and treatment. I don't have a complete update on her condition, although I've been told there doesn't seem to be anything life-threatening. But it will be a few days before she will be released from the hospital. While she's still there, they'll do a DNA test and will cross-match that with your client fairly soon. We'll stay in touch as things progress."

Lori was ecstatic. "I feel certain this is the missing Wills baby, but I do understand that it has to be legally established. Thanks for the update. Let me know when to have my client available for the tests. I'll be waiting for your call." Then she called Mae.

Mae answered on the first ring. Carla and Mira had just gone to the grocery store to re-stock the cookie-baking supplies, and Mae's hunch that this call was about the baby turned out to be right.

"Hello, Mae. Good news. The woman did bring Faith back to the pediatrician's office, and now the baby is in their custody and on her way to the hospital. It's just a precaution, because apparently the woman dyed her hair, and the rash on her scalp is worse."

"Oh, my! But she'll be all right, won't she? You said 'Faith' — ! Does that mean it really is her? Can I tell Carla that it is?"

"Well, I'm going to leave that up to you. I'm all but certain this is Carla's baby, but until the DNA tests confirm that, we can't be totally certain. On the other hand, Carla will have to know when we take her for a DNA test. So I'm thinking we should tell her now, but what do you think?"

"You're pretty sure this is Faith?"

"Yes, I am. The baby is small but about a year old according to the doctor. And her hair has been dyed, evidence that her natural color was a giveaway, and the woman didn't want her to be recognized. All these things point to it being Faith. Not proof positive, but it's hard to believe it's just coincidence."

"How soon will they be doing the tests?"

"I haven't heard yet, but probably within the next few days."

"Then I think we should tell Carla. I'll tell her the minute she gets in! … Unless you think you should be the one to tell her?"

"No, it seems to me that you and Carla have a very good relationship going. I think you should be the one to bring her the good news."

After hanging up Mae paced the floor, sat down, stood up, and paced again. It seemed to her as if the two had been gone for most of the day by the time they came back.

"Carla, I just had a call from Miz Martin. I think you'd better sit down for this." With a frightened expression on her face, Carla sat. "They believe they've found Faith."

For a moment, Carla just sat there in shock. "Really?" she whispered. All the color drained from her face, and Mae was glad she'd asked her to sit down. "Really?" she whispered again. "Where is she? Are they bringing her here? When?"

"Carla, the baby has a serious rash, and they took her to the hospital. They're just goin' to keep her for a few days until they can get the rash cleared up and check her over."

"What hospital? Can I go see her?"

"I'm sorry. I didn't think to ask. But you gotta know that you can't take Faith home until they check her over and do tests to prove she's your baby. Miz Martin said they'd probably do the tests in the next couple of days. She'll let us know when to get you to the hospital for your test."

Mira, who had been as stunned as Carla was, suddenly let out a big whoop. "Carla, you're going to have Faith back! That's the most wonderful news I've ever heard." She pulled her up into a big hug.

Carla was laughing and crying at the same time. She hugged Mira fiercely and wouldn't let her go. Mae watched the two for a moment and then went to them, putting her arms around both of them as far as they would go. She thought just maybe she was getting the hang of this hugging thing, and it felt pretty darned good. *Especially now.* They were all talking at once, none of them really hearing the others, but all three laughing and hugging.

Chapter 43
Carla

The next day in the early afternoon, the call came to let them know where and when to have the DNA test. Carla couldn't wait: She was ready two hours ahead of time and alternately paced the floor and stared at the clock, willing the time to pass. Mae was nervous, too. In fact, Mira was the calmest of all, so she took on the task of organizing the trip to the hospital. This was one time Mae was grateful that Mira took over for her.

Lori Martin met them at the entrance to the hospital.

"Well, Carla, I don't believe I've ever had a happier day than this. Let's get this test done, and then I'm going to take you up to see Faith."

Carla let herself be led to the lab where they took a swab inside her cheek. Told that the results should be back in two or three days, she was upset. She had hoped it would all be done today. She wasn't sure she could wait another three days to have Faith back for good. But she needed to see Faith,so she swallowed her disappointment and followed Ms. Martin out of the lab.

In the elevator, Lori cautioned Carla about Faith's appearance. "I'm pretty sure she will look very different from the last time you saw her. Not only is she six months older, but the woman tried to alter her appearance, we're guessing to disguise her. So, I don't want you to be alarmed by what you see. They had to shave her head to treat the rash adequately, and she's a little underweight for her age. So just look for the child you remember in the child you see today."

Carla's heart was pounding as they entered the pediatric wing. Lori stopped at the nurses' station to be sure Faith was still in the same room.

As they entered the room, Carla gave a little cry and ran to the crib. Faith was just lying there. Carla turned to Lori, a question in her eyes. "Yes, you can pick her up."

Carla reached down and touched Faith's face, gently caressing her cheek. Faith looked steadily at Carla but showed no recognition. Tears streaming down her cheeks, Carla picked up the baby, carefully supporting her head just as she had when she was a newborn. Faith responded with a small sigh.

Carla snuggled her up against her chest, and Faith was clearly content to be there. Carla began rocking back and forth with her, gently crooning to her. Faith reached up one hand, touched Carla's cheek for a moment, and then withdrew it.

A nurse, checking in to see how things were going, smiled warmly at Carla with the baby cradled in her arms. "We've been giving this little cutie extra love and attention. She seems to like it."

She held out her arms to take Faith from Carla. "Just for a few minutes, Mama. I need to take her temperature and check her scalp. Then you can have her back."

After transferring Faith to the nurse, Carla threw herself into Mae's arms. "It's Faith, it's really Faith. I can tell it's her." She began crying so hard she had to stop talking.

Mae held the girl close, awkwardly patting her back and making soothing noises. She looked helplessly at Mira, who came and pulled Carla into her arms for a hearty hug. She smiled at Mae as she did this, as if to reassure her it would all come together soon.

After the nurse finished checking Faith out, she handed her back to Carla as promised. Carla sat down in a rocker and began to rock the baby back and forth. She closed her eyes and relished the shape and weight of the small child she held. Faith's eyelids drooped, and she fell asleep. The others tip-toed out and left them alone.

It seemed to the three women that the wait for the DNA test results was an eternity. But true to their word, the staff had the results in three days and called Lori Martin in the late afternoon to confirm it.

There was no question: This was Faith.

Ms. Martin called with the good news and with the report that Faith would probably be released from the hospital very soon. The relief in the small home was tangible. They were laughing and crying and telling each other over and over again that they had known it was Faith right from the start. Not knowing what else to do, Mae put the kettle on and brought out the cookies for an impromptu celebration, but they were all too excited to think of anything as every-day as food. The tea grew cold as they talked over each other, swearing that they never doubted Faith would be found and what a miracle it was that she had been. Carla alternated between euphoria over having found Faith and fear that something would happen before she was able to bring the baby home.

Suddenly, Mira sat up straight and slapped her forehead. "We've been so focused on getting Faith back that we haven't planned for having her back! We need baby things, don't we?"

They all started chattering at once, excitedly calling out and writing down what they would need. Clearly, a crib was first on the list, and Mae and Mira argued a bit about which one of them was going to get to pay for it. They finally agreed to add up all the items needed and split the cost. Carla just stared at them, at a loss to understand their generosity.

"Wait, wait," she interrupted. "I think that Welfare might pay for some of the things we'll need. Shouldn't we ask Ms. Martin before we buy anything?" Mae and Mira looked at her for a long moment and then both broke out laughing.

"What, and miss out on all this fun?" Mira asked. "This may be as close as I'll ever come to having a baby to do for, and I want to enjoy every bit of it."

Mae agreed. She didn't say it aloud, but in her heart she was thinking that this might be a way to get back some of what she had missed through her carelessness in raising Mira.

They spent an hour listing everything they could think of that a baby could possibly use. The plan was for all three of them to go on a shopping spree and buy everything on their list.

They each sat back and sobered up a bit, thinking about all that had happened. After all the giddiness, the room was now curiously quiet. Carla was wondering at her good fortune to find these two women who had helped her put her life back together. Mira enjoyed a strong sense of satisfaction, not only about Faith, but also about how her mother had opened up to both of them. She never dreamed that a day like today would ever happen. Mae was contemplative, too, realizing how much she had relished the afternoon and the closeness to both Mira and Carla. She had a lot to thank Leo for.

At that thought, she bolted straight up. Mira and Carla jumped and then looked at her questioningly.

"We never called Leo to tell him how this was turnin' out!" Mae blurted. "We need to do that right now."

Mira agreed. "I feel kind of bad that we haven't checked in on him to see how he's doing."

Hesitantly, Carla asked, "Could I be the one to tell him?"

"Well, of course," Mira answered. "You absolutely should be the one to tell him." Mae felt a little deflated; *she* wanted to be the one to break the news to Leo, but in her heart she agreed with Mira. It should be Carla.

Seeing her mother's expression, Mira suggested that Mae dial Leo and find out how he was doing and then hand the phone to Carla. That didn't entirely satisfy Mae, but she knew it would be wrong to take the pleasure away from Carla, so she agreed.

"Leo, hello, it's Mae. How are you feelin'? Are you gettin' any better?"

Leo sounded weak, but he seemed to have regained his old interest in what was happening. "Mae, it's so good to hear from you again. How are you? And how are Mira and Carla? Seems like I haven't had any news for a very long time, and it's been troubling me. I think about you three all the time."

"Leo, there's someone here who has some news to tell you. Maybe you'll feel even better when you hear it." She handed off the phone to Carla.

"Hi, Leo, it's Carla. How ya' doing? I've missed being able to talk with you. It seems like forever since we talked."

"Carla! Oh, my, how I've worried about you. How are you doing? Where are you living?" Briefly, Carla filled Leo in on her life and then burst out, "Oh, Leo, you're not gonna believe this. They found Faith, and I'm gonna get her back!"

"Carla, that's incredible! After all this time … I want to hear all about it, but I don't want to hear about it over the phone. Will you bring Faith and visit me as soon as you can? And bring Mae and Mira, too, will you? I can't tell you how happy this makes me. And I can't wait to see you all!"

Chapter 44
Faith

"Careful, Mira. Don't be bangin' up my wall with that crib."

Mira looked at her mother in frustration. She was trying as best she could to wrestle the crib into Carla's small room, but the door simply wasn't wide enough. "I'm thinking we should have put this together inside the room. We'll never get it through the door this way."

Carla started laughing and couldn't stop. Both Mae and Mira looked at her as if she was crazy.

"It sure looks like we need a man here," said Carla and laughed heartily again. "And we don't have even *one* between the *three* of us!" Nobody laughed. Carla rolled her eyes, dusted off her hands, and got back to work. "Okay, Mira, let's look at that schematic again and see how far back we have to take it to get through the door."

Mira smoothed out the crumpled paper and handed it over to Carla. Surprisingly enough, between the three of them, Carla seemed to be the one who could understand the cryptic instructions.

"Look. I think if we just take this one side off and remove the bottom, we can collapse the two end walls in and get it through the door."

It was mid-afternoon, and the three women had been working at the task for over an hour. The nursery furniture was delivered that morning, but most of it was still in boxes, which took up much of the small living room, leaving very little room for assembling any-thing. Mae and Mira looked at the heap of boxes while they waited for Carla's next comment.

"Y'know, before we dismantle it and slide it in, maybe we should check the measurements. This may not fit in the room without taking the dresser out."

All three women slumped in defeat. "I'm guessing we should have done some measurin' before we ever went shoppin'. If only my Jim was here, he would know how to handle all this."

Suddenly, Mira snapped her fingers.

"Ernie!" she said. Mae and Carla looked at her expectantly. "The night janitor at the motel. He has to fix beds and chairs all the time. I bet he could figure this out easily and help us get it done."

"So what are you waitin' for? Get him over here." Mae's frustration was making her testy, and her tone of voice rubbed Mira the wrong way.

"Well, I could call him and ask him to come over. But I sure wouldn't want him to come here and be treated like hired help. He's a nice fel-low, and I would hope we'd be grateful for his help and not just order him around."

"Whoa," Mae said, bristling a bit. "Who said anything about orderin' him around? But we ain't got a lot of time to fuss with this. Faith comes home tomorrow, and we need help now." *Looks like Mira thinks she's in charge of ever'thing and ever'body once again.* It took Mae a moment to lay her resentment to rest.

Mira took an address book from her purse and went to the phone. "Ernie? I hope I didn't wake you. This is Mira, and I need to ask a huge favor of you."

Carla and Mae listened shamelessly, and it made Mira extremely self-conscious. "Um, yeah, we need help putting together a crib, and none of us can figure it out. Would you have time to lend us a hand?"

"… Oh, Ernie, you're a life saver. Let me give you the address. How soon could you be here?"

Carla looked at Mae. "You ever met this guy?" Mae motioned her to silence so she could hear Mira's side of the conversation.

" … Great! We'll be watching for you. Oh, and you better bring some tools with you."

◆

When Ernie walked into the house, he stopped and stared at all the boxes. "Does all of this have to be assembled? Where in hell are you going to put it all? Pardon my French, ladies."

"You're pardoned," Mae answered tersely. "Mira, where the hell are we putting this?"

Mira introduced Ernie to Mae and Carla, and then rushed to explain. "Yeah, I'm thinking we probably bought way more stuff than we have room for. But we *do* need the crib by tomorrow, so if you could help us assemble it, we'd really appreciate it."

Ernie eyed the crib. "Where are you planning to put it?"

Carla pointed to the bedroom door. "In there. But I'm wondering if just the crib alone is going to fit."

Ernie looked at the three women and shook his head. "Okay, I'll help, but you have to listen to me on this. I'm not a miracle worker who can create room where there isn't any. So let's do some measuring before we go any farther."

Mira led him into the small bedroom. Ernie looked stunned.

"No way are we going to get this in here unless we take out the bed that's here. How old is the baby, anyway? Maybe you could use a smaller crib for now."

"Well, she's a year old," Mira answered. "But she's small for her age, so maybe we should try to find a smaller crib." Ernie looked at Mira carefully, wondering if the baby was hers. And, if so, where the father was.

"Well," Ernie said, measuring by sight, "you might want to re-think your plan. Not only are you not going to get that crib in here, but this house is too small for all that other stuff you have out there." As he spoke he walked back into the living room. "If the baby's a year old, why do you need a changing table? Pretty soon you'll be potty-training her."

All three women looked at him in surprise. How did a middle-aged bachelor know so much about a baby's needs? But they realized he was right.

Carla started to laugh again. The others looked at her for a moment and then joined in. "Fact is, we got so excited about getting Faith back,

I guess we went a little crazy. Faith slept in a laundry basket by my bed for six months, and there's no telling how she's been sleeping since. She's not that much bigger now, so maybe we could just get a larger basket if we can't find a smaller crib."

That answered Ernie's question about who the baby's mother was. He watched the three questioningly. There was surely a story here, but he was hesitant to ask. "So, do you want to return this stuff to the store? I can load it into my pickup and take it back for you."

All three nodded their heads. "Maybe we could pick out one thing and keep it," Mae suggested hopefully. After all, this had started out as a lot of fun.They all agreed and decided to keep the little rocking chair for Faith.

Ernie began dismantling the large crib and returning it to the box. Mira and Carla started carrying out the smaller boxes and helped Ernie get the crib into his pickup bed. He asked Mira to go with him so she could handle the returns. Mae and Carla began to sweep up bits of cardboard and tape, tidying up the small living room.

"I think Ernie's kinda sweet on Mira," Carla said. Mae stared at her. "Why would you think that?"

"Well, because, for one thing, he jumped at the chance to help her when she called. Then, did you see how he looked at her all the time when he was here? And offered to take her and the stuff back to the store?"

Mae had been oblivious to all this but, thinking back, she could see how Carla had reached that conclusion. "Well, I just hope he treats her better than that husband of hers did. Or if he don't, then I hope Mira has the sense not to hook up with him."

"I do, too. But he seems like a really nice guy."

Mae studied on that for a moment. If nothing else, Mira did deserve a break in life. Maybe Ernie was the one to give it to her. In some ways, he reminded Mae of her Jim. That was a good sign.

When Ernie dropped Mira off, Mae and Carla saw that she was in sort of a daze. "Mira, what happened? Did you get the refund all right? I mean, was there any trouble or anything?"

Absently, Mira answered. "Oh, no, Mama, no trouble."

"So why are you acting so funny?"

"Am I acting funny? Well, I had sort of a shock. Ernie asked me out on a date."

"I knew it." Carla pumped her fist and giggled. "Mira's got a boyfriend."

Mira giggled, too. "It looks as if I just *might* have a boyfriend."

Mae went for the teapot and the cookies. It seemed like a celebration was in order. To her surprise Mae realized that she was pleased for Mira. Her life had definitely taken a turn for the better.

Chapter 45
Mae

For the rest of the summer things went smoothly enough. Faith seemed to have some difficulty adjusting to having three mamas most of the time, but she soon began to thrive on the attention. Someone was always available to pick her up, kiss her boo-boos, or cuddle her when she was cranky. There were now some temper tantrums that none of the three were prepared to deal with, but they were as short-lived as a brief summer storm.

Ms. Martin showed up every now and then, but her visits seemed to be more social than official. Even the Child Protection lady seemed pleased by the rapport they all had attained. Mae was enjoying her life and only occasionally wondering how much she had missed while raising Mira. On the whole, everyone seemed content with how things were turning out.

But in August, Carla entered school for her senior year, and Mae then found herself to be the primary care-giver during school hours. She had somewhat dreaded this, but for a while she seemed to cope well. Carla and Mira both wanted their "Faith time" so Mae had her afternoons for her tasks.

But Mae hadn't reckoned on having a teenager and a baby in the small house when she bought it, and the clutter, noise, and closeness took its toll when cooler weather kept them indoors most of the time.

A high chair and toy box showed up in the small living room, the toy box overflowing with the many baby toys no one could resist buying for Faith.

The resulting clutter took its toll on Mae's disposition. She tried to keep up, to maintain her little home's neatness, but there weren't enough places for everything, and anything that had a place didn't stay there long. In the afternoons while Carla and Mira played with the baby and chatted with each other, Mae busied herself with straightening and cleaning but was never able to keep her home as neat as she needed it to be.

Neither Carla nor Mira offered to help, knowing that Mae always wanted to do these things herself. Much as Mae had learned to love the baby, she resented the clutter, the scattered toys, and the over-flowing countertops she couldn't keep cleared. *And ain't it funny*, she thought often, *how Mira and Carla never notice the mess.*

Mae seemed to regress to her old nature, not asking for help but let-ting the resentment build up. In fact, she carried her resentment close and added to it every day. *It's just too danged much to ask of a body. I was gettin' so I could live with all the noise and fuss of havin' Mira and Carla underfoot so much, but I wasn't never cut out for all this mess and clutter I got now. And I ain't got any idea how to make it right again.*

Mae found herself revisiting all the old animosities she had felt when Mira was small. Most mornings Carla had to leave for school be-fore Faith woke up, so it fell to Mae to feed her, bathe her, dress her, and amuse her until Carla returned. Mae's mornings were all about child care, and that didn't set well with her.

She nursed her ill will and blamed Carla and Mira for all of it. "My garden is choked with weeds and stuff needs to be pruned back some," she muttered aloud when she was alone, "but I ain't never got the time. Can't even keep the floor picked up. And I can't turn my back on the baby for a minute she isn't into somethin' she shouldn't be. How can a body keep up with everything?"

It was into one of these mornings when Mae was seething with re-sentment that Lori Martin dropped by.

"Had a home visit near here and thought I'd see how you all are doing." Cheerful as Lori was, that was all the opening Mae needed to unload on the unsuspecting caseworker.

"I'm way too old to be doin' all this. Never was much cut out to be a mother, and I surely didn't bargain on this when Carla first came to stay here. It's all just too much."

"Mae, I'm sorry you've been loaded down with so much. Ordinarily, I'd have been by before now to see how things were going," Lori confessed, "but there's never enough time. So, now that I am here, tell me what would make this work for you."

Mae felt a small pang of guilt for dumping on the caseworker, but waking-up sounds from the bedroom told her that her brief respite was over. Her frustration outweighed any guilt.

"I don't know how to make it work. I need some time for my own self, but there's almost never any. I don't blame Carla, she can't help it, but it's always somethin' needs done, and no time to do it. Always Faith of a morning and then Carla comes home. And I think maybe I can get a break, but generally Mira stops by shortly after that, and lately she's been bringin' Ernie so there is all this stuff goin' on and no time for me to hardly catch up." She paused now to take a deep breath. "It's just too much. I hardly ever get a moment to myself and when I do, it's used up with all the chores I can't get done when I'm tendin' Faith."

Lori regarded her thoughtfully. Mae got up to see to Faith, and Lori thought about the problem. Mae was clearly overwhelmed; her lifelong patterns and her age made it almost impossible for her to adjust to this situation. Lori realized she should have checked in on the situation earlier; her heavy caseload hadn't allowed for that. But she knew that she couldn't walk away from it now, whatever it took her to sort out the situation.

Mae brought Faith back into the living room and offered her a bottle of juice before sitting her down on the floor. Mae and Lori watched the child as she sat the bottle down and crawled to her toy box. Faith's hair had grown back again, and the unusual color made it a pleasure just watching her crawl around so happily. Her emerging personality added to the joy. Soon, all the toys Mae had just picked up were scattered across the floor, and Faith was chortling with glee. Clearly, Faith was thriving in her new environment, but the more she thrived, the more work that fell to Mae. Clearly, the family could never work through this near crisis if Mae continued to act out her frustrations instead of seeking solutions.

Lori realized this was the type of personal support she had hoped to provide as part of her job but never had the time for. Without thinking about it further, she made the decision to give herself this gift of feeling professionally competent even if it meant using some of her own time to do it.

"Mae, I'm thinking we need to have a family council. Since all of this has just fallen into your lap, I doubt that Carla and Mira have even thought about what you're dealing with. How about if I come back ..." Lori flipped open her appointment book and continued, " ... say, Friday afternoon? I'm confident we'll be able to work this out."

The look of gratitude Mae flashed her more than compensated Lori for giving up on the first day she had taken off in some time. Lori added, "You let Carla know not to plan anything else so she can be here, okay?"

"I'd like Mira to be here, too. Both of them are still so dang pleased spendin' time with each other and the baby, they never think about how I'm doing."

"Sure, we'll get Mira here, too — a real family council."

◆

Both Carla and Mira wondered what the "council" was for, but neither was greatly concerned. They were still riding on the high of having Faith with them and the joy of how everything worked out for the best. As far as they knew, everything was running perfectly. They took over Faith's care in the afternoons so Mae could tend to her beloved housework. It seemed to them to be just right for everyone concerned. They entered the house together smiling and chatting comfortably.

Once they were seated, Lori directed the conversation.

"Okay, Carla, you're up first. How are things here going as far as you're concerned?"

"Perfect! This is the best I've ever known! I have my Faith back, and I have a family like I always wanted. Ms. Martin, honest, I've never been happier. I feel like I really have a family, and so does Faith." Carla's eyes were sparkling.

"And that makes me very happy for you. Now, hold that thought for a moment. Mira, how do *you* feel about how things have turned out?"

"It just couldn't be better. It's everything I ever wanted it to be! Mama and I are closer now, and Carla and Faith seem like part of the family. I always wanted to be part of a larger family, and now I am."

"And we're all happy for all you've gained. Now, Mae. What about the way things are going here for you? How do *you* feel?"

"Frustrated, tired, and sometimes just plain angry!"

Mira and Carla stared at Mae. They'd had no idea she was so upset. Both started to talk at once, directing astonished questions at Mae, but Lori stopped them.

"Carla and Mira, one of the reason things are so great for you is that Mae is picking up most of the work, and you are benefiting from that."

"Yes, but Mama — !"

"Oh, Mae —!"

Lori cut off their comments with a politely raised hand.

"Mae is not a young woman, and taking care of a small child has never really been her thing. Nonetheless, she's been trying to handle it. Add to that the frustration of seeing her tidy house strewn with baby paraphernalia which she feels she has to keep picked up. She has always delighted in her garden and specifically chose this house because of the garden. But now she frets because it's so neglected, and she has no time to work out there now. All this is making her irritable and testy." Lori enumerated these points by raising one finger for each one. "So, Mira and Carla, you've been happy, enjoying it all, and have not noticed how it's affecting Mae. This is all definitely taking a toll on her."

Lori paused a moment to let the two women consider her words. "Now, this isn't just a meeting to air complaints; it's a family council to work out a better plan. Since you can see how difficult this is for Mae, what solutions do you have to offer her?"

Carla was clearly frightened, afraid she might be homeless again. "Mae, why didn't you tell me? I thought you liked us being here, and everything was good."

Mae sighed. "I do — or at least I did, but now it's just got to be too much. I didn't never figure when Miz Martin asked me to take you in back then that it would end up with all of this."

"But, Mama, you should have told us! I thought you were as happy as we are with how it all worked out."

"Yeah, at first I was tickled pink. But now …" Mae gestured toward the toys strewn across the floor and the breakfast dishes she still hadn't had time to wash.

Lori cut in. "Let's do some creative thinking and see if we can come up with a better plan. In the meantime, would you both agree to start picking up more of the load here?" Mira looked confused.

"But Mama never wanted my help. She always said I did it wrong."

"Things have changed, Mira. I think your mother would welcome your help now. But talk to her first about what would help. For example, maybe Carla and Faith could spend weekends with you once in a while! Or maybe the three of you could go to the mall or the movies some afternoons."

Carla and Mira were silent.

Lori sighed and tried again. "If you don't like those ideas, try to come up with some of your own. But include Mae so she can tell you what would be most helpful to her. Will you do that?"

After Lori left, the three women sat silently for some time, each lost in her own thoughts.

Finally, Mira spoke. "Mama, would it help if maybe I take Carla and Faith to my apartment some weekends and give you two days to yourself?"

"It would sure be a start."

Carla looked at Mae with guilt written large all over her face. "Wow, I guess I took you for granted, Mae. It was so amazing to have a family, and this really great place to live, and someone there to help me and understand me that I just didn't ever think about how you felt." She chewed at a nail for a moment, and then her face brightened. "I could tend to Faith and pick up after her every day after school so you could do what needs doing. Or I could help with the housework if you teach me how you want things done." Mae was feeling justifiably self-righteous. "Seems to me you'd of both figured this out sooner." She didn't think it necessary to admit that she could have simply asked for more help. "We can try these things and see if it's gonna be enough. What Miz Martin didn't think of was that I need some kind of peace and quiet in the day! It's just too much goin' on for someone old as me. So we gotta figure that out, too, one way or another."

Carla and Mira promised to start looking for ways that would give Mae her quiet time, and Mae felt triumphant. Maybe this was going to work out at last.

And so it did for the rest of that school year. Mira and Carla were careful to help with the daily tasks as much as possible. They took Faith off to a movie or a walk in the park on a regular basis to give Mae some quiet time in the afternoon. Faith flowered in the attention, and Mira and Carla bonded in their friendship and mutual concern for Mae's wellbeing. Carla managed to do her homework after Faith was down for the night and still keep her grades up. She couldn't squeeze in the extra class to insure graduation in the spring, but that seemed not to trouble any of them. She could still take the class in summer school and get her diploma at the end of summer.

◈

Lori checked on Mae by phone from time to time and assured herself that things were going more smoothly. In early spring, Lori scheduled another family council to see how everyone was faring.

As the four of them were talking things over, Mira made a suggestion. Her voice was warm, but tentative, and she glanced at Mae to gauge her reception to the idea. "Lori, if you could arrange for Carla to attend her summer school class in a school close to my apartment, maybe Carla and Faith could just move in with me for the summer." Everyone agreed this was a good idea, and Lori promised to look into it.

Mae was particularly pleased. She was all but certain that once she was alone in her home again, Jim would come to her. And Mira and Carla were happy to have more time together to foster the friendship that was becoming so important to them both.

Chapter 46
Mira and Carla

Mira and Carla worked out an amicable schedule early in the summer. Carla's class met only in the afternoon each day, and Mira enjoyed that time with Faith. The little girl was endlessly curious, and Mira loved the feeling of bonding with her. Little Faith seemed to take for granted that she had two mommies and gave out hugs and kisses indiscriminately. The friendship between the two women deepened with each day as they talked easily about the pain of their respective childhoods and the joy of having so much to be thankful for now.

"Are your co-workers still teasing you and Ernie?"

"Not much. I think they've moved on finally." Mira smiled. "Once in a while someone says something, but mostly we seem to be old hat now. And that's just fine with me."

"You're so lucky to have each other. He's such a nice guy and obviously thinks the world of you. When are you going to kick it up a notch?"

"I think we're being cautious about that. He says he loves me, and I feel that I love him. But we both had disastrous first marriages, and it makes it harder to be sure of each other and even sure of our own feelings." Mira's face grew somber as she reflected.

Arthur managed to erase what little self-esteem I had, and I still wonder sometimes why any man would want to be with me. I think that if and when we kick it up a notch, to borrow your words, we'll both want to be very certain of each other and of our love. But we talk about it, and I think we both hope it will happen. Things are good for us just as they are now, so we're willing to let it develop as it may."

"That is *so* cool. I hope someday I have a chance to be so wise."

"Oh, I'm sure you will. And I'm going to watch very closely to be sure you are. I feel like your big sister, and I'm going to look out for you, so just expect that."

"And I can't tell you how much that means to me." Carla jumped up and put her arms around Mira, giving her a bone-breaking hug. "You've been better than a big sister to me, and I'll always think of you like that."

They were both quiet for a while. Finally, Carla broke the silence. "You know what? I've been really missing Mae this summer. Don't you miss her, too?"

"I do miss her, but not the way I used to. I think part of missing her before was because I needed affirmation that I mattered, and I believed she was the one person who could give that to me. But she never did, at least not in so many words. So I was still straining to have her approval, and that tied me to her. With Mama, I felt crucial parts of me were missing. Now *I* know I'm whole, that nothing is missing. I don't need anyone else to affirm that."

She paused for a moment to think. "You know, I even think I married Arthur because I thought he would give me that affirmation. I realize now that he was only using my uncertainty to feed his ego."

"Wow, how did you learn all that?"

"Well, having wonderful friends helped me to learn that. Even you! In spite of all life threw at you, you never seemed to think you were at fault. Even when you tried to take your life, I somehow knew that it was despair over losing Faith and not because you didn't think you mattered. But other things have conspired to help me see what is real … being able to fend for myself when Arthur kicked me out, finding great friends at work, listening to Leo's wise counsel, learning that I mattered to Ernie. When you get all these affirmations, you become a believer."

Carla became thoughtful and let her original suggestion about Mae slip away.

◆

A few days later, Carla stood filling the sink with dishwater and soap as she balanced Faith on one hip. "Mira!" she called, and Mira stopped sweeping to listen. Carla tossed two plates, two forks, two glasses, and a plastic cup into the water and turned off the spigot. "Say, we haven't even checked up on Mae for some time. What if she's been sick or had an accident or something?" Mira said nothing. "Don't you think we should go see her?" Mira thought about that.

"I'm sure if she needed us, we'd have heard about it by now. But if you want to call her, feel free." Mira gazed about at the trail of toys and baskets of folded clothes. She pointed at the petite hand and nose prints on the slider glass about two feet off the floor and laughed. "I don't think our comfort level for clutter and Mama's come close to meeting. But, hey, if you want to call her up and ask if we can drop by, that's fine." Mira shrugged. "Maybe it is time to touch base."

Carla understood Mira's lack of enthusiasm, and she hated to push. Still, she couldn't completely let it go. She jostled the flailing child to the other hip. Faith was already crawling when they moved in with Mira, and now she was a speedster on the floor and eager every waking moment to explore.

"You know, as cranky as Mae could be sometimes, I always thought she really cared about me but just couldn't admit it. And when I was living with her and you came over all the time, I think in her heart she really loved that." Mira looked doubtful. "But see, something in her doesn't let her admit it, even to herself."

Mira smiled, shrugged her shoulders, and returned to her sweeping. Carla waited a moment for Mira to push dust bunnies and floor debris into a pan, dump them into the trash, and move on before she set Faith on the floor; she wanted to wash enough dishes to get them through dinner. The baby rolled rapidly onto all fours, sped across the tiny room like a wind-up toy, and tipped the bin before either woman could catch her. Carla apologized as she picked up Faith, pushed the spilled dirt and debris back into a kind of pile with her free hand, and tried to quell the noise from the frustrated baby.

"I miss the tea parties," Carla hollered cheerily above Faith's indignant screams, "and the joking," as she struggled to detach the baby's dirty hands from her mama's hair, "and zinging each other." Carla pursed her mouth and blew a dust bunny from her own cheek as she turned on the tap. Mira watched, fascinated. "I even miss working in her garden with her. Mira, don't you think by now Mae's missing us a little, too?" Carla stuck Faith's filthy hands under the flow of water and over the sudsy dishwater.

"Whew, I'm ready for a break! Um, I'll do the dishes in a few minutes while you feed Faith." They settled on the apartment sofa, each relieved for different reasons, and Carla set Faith between them. The baby immediately rolled over the edge and bee-lined toward the toy box. "Carla, I've been thinking about that, too. It seemed as if for a while there we were really a family. It felt so good to me, being with each other each day and just hanging out."

They talked comfortably, each with one eye on the baby. "I wonder sometimes if Mama misses us, too, or if she's just content to have her own company without us interfering. She loved Daddy so much, you know, and I don't think she has ever loved anyone else like that." Mira had spent a great deal of time trying to analyze her mother since their new relationship began to blossom. "So I think she pushed us away so she could try to remember her life with him. She wants to relive it, somehow. And Carla, I'm not sure if she's missing us at all." Carla nodded and stepped over the toys to catch Faith before she made it to the kitchen. She picked up the baby and set her on the sofa again. That might give them another few minutes.

"Maybe you're right — you know her better — but somehow, I just can't get it out of my head that we should try to go see Mae." Carla sighed. "But I'll let it go for now."

Chapter 47
Mae

Mae sat despondently at her kitchen table, sipping tea. The house was quiet around her, just the way she had wanted it for so long. After school was out in June, Carla and Faith had moved into the spare bedroom at Mira's apartment for the summer so that Mae could have her quiet, orderly home to herself again. It had been pure joy to get her life back to the way she had wanted it for so long: She was sure to have the time she needed to find Jim's presence again. He had come to her once here in a dream, and although that seemed distant, she was sure that it would happen again. And the tidiness of the little house pleased her. Now, after a couple months, she wasn't nearly so pleased. It hadn't worked out at all like she planned. *I hadn't reckoned on how empty and silent the small house would seem after the happy racket of the past months.*

Where once she had cherished the silence, she now felt it as a heavy blanket wrapped around her.

Dusting and sweeping and scrubbing had once given her immense satisfaction and comfort, and now that seemed to her to be pointless busy-work. Acerbically, typically, she blamed it all on Carla, Faith, and Mira. "Seems like all this they put me through last year has plumb ruined everything for me," she grumbled.

She reminded herself of the activity and bustle of how things had been and how she had resented it, but instead of reassuring her, those thoughts only made her sad. Reluctantly, she finally admitted to herself that she missed the conversation and tea parties and noise and confusion and laughter and tears that had become the norm while Faith, Carla, and Mira were the constants in her world. But she had pushed them out of her life so she could bring back her former patterns and her memories of Jim.

Now those memories had faded to the point that she believed she would never feel him here again. Her little house was silent and lonely. It was just a house now, giving her no joy, no frustration, no comfort, no anger, no small victories. It felt huge with emptiness.

Dang it all, they spoiled it all for me!

But blaming them didn't even help. Something nagged her until, in frustration, she brought it out and considered it. And she felt the breath rush out of her when she did. All the things she had resented and pushed away from her after Jim died were the very things she was missing now. Maybe that was what life was all about, what it was for. *Peace and quiet is for dead people.* She had been living as if she died when Jim did, not wanting life to intrude on her memories and becoming belligerent and angry when it did. Maybe that's what Jim was trying to tell her the last time he came to her. But she had been too sure of herself to even consider it.

◈

For a few moments her epiphany filled her with joy. It amazed her that she had never, ever thought of it this way when now it was so clear. The joy was short-lived. She had obviously slammed shut every door to the life she now wanted and her characteristic pride and stubbornness allowed her no way to even try to find an opening. She allowed the bitterness to reclaim her.

"Apparently," she thought sourly, "the four of them are having a high old time in their new set-up, so much that they don't even think of me." Telling them that she needed them went against her pride, and it purely did not look as if they would ever try to reach out to her again. The frustration of her dilemma kept her awake at night and deprived her of any satisfaction in her orderly days. She needed help to find a way out.

◆

She took her dilemma to Leo. "It just don't seem to work right either way. When they was livin' with me, I resented the time and energy I used up to just have them there. Now that they're over to Mira's, it just makes me fume that they don't even think about coming over to see me once in a while."

"So, you're feeling they were just using you and now that they don't need you, they don't want to spend any time with you?"

"Maybe somethin' like that. I don't feel like they just used me, exactly, but like when it all got too much for me and they moved over there, they just stopped thinking of me at all. You'd think they would at least call me sometimes to be sure I'm okay."

"That hurts, doesn't it, Mae? Do you think that may give you some idea of how Mira felt all those years?" The words were gentle but the impact was fierce.

Mae automatically started to argue with Leo, but then stopped. "Well, yeah, I been thinkin' on that some. But what good does it do to drag up all that old stuff now? I can't go back and undo what was! So feelin' sorry about it ain't gonna help me or her none. And I don't reckon she even thinks on that anymore."

"How do you know unless you talk to Mira and let her know how you feel now?

"She don't come around anymore so I don't get the chance. Anyway, I never put much stock in bringin' up old stuff. Seems like it nearly always makes things worse."

"Mae, don't take this the wrong way, but I'm thinking that much of what has gone wrong in your life is because you made up your mind that a situation couldn't be changed, so you just charged ahead and pushed through it or around it instead of studying it. Don't you think that so much of what happened over the past year has actually turned out to be a good thing for you? Even now, when you're angry with Carla and Mira for leaving you alone, it's unlikely you would have thought through things the way you have unless you were alone. The good is almost always there, you just don't seem to want to see it."

"Don't know why I ever try to tell you about things. You keep comin' up with stuff that doesn't even have nothin' to do with what I'm talkin' about."

"Oh, Mae, darlin', think about what you're saying. When you came into the home, you were dead certain that you couldn't change what had happened to you. But, look at how much you've been able to do just that! And yet, before you consider changing anything now, you seem to have to throw up every reason you can think of why it won't work, and then you throw up an obstacle to make sure you were right. Do you want to know what I think?"

"I suspect you're going to tell me whether I want it or not." Leo took that as a *yes.*

"I think all the things you've complained about have actually worked for your benefit. If you hadn't been in the Home, you wouldn't have met Carla. And you wouldn't have found a new relationship with Mira. And you wouldn't have Faith, who I'm thinking is very important to you, whether you'll admit it or not. And now, because you're unhappy with the way things are right this minute, you won't even consider all you've gained over this past year. Mae, you have been blessed."

"Well, I ain't blessed now, am I? I don't have my Jim, I don't have Carla and Faith anymore, I don't even have Mira. I don't have nobody."

"You have me, Mae."

"Oh, Leo, I didn't mean it like that. Sometimes, I don't know what I mean."

"Mae, if you want Carla and Faith and Mira — and now Ernie! — in your life, go after them."

"Leo, sometimes you can't make it up when it's gone wrong. You just got to make do with what you got left."

"How did you leave it with Mira and Carla?"

"What?"

"Did you leave a door open, a welcoming word for them to return? What was the last thing you said to them?" Mae gave it some thought.

"Don't skin my door with that danged toy box?"

Leo closed his eyes.

And with that, Mae quietly left the room, without seeing Leo shake his head sadly. "And that conviction," he said, knowing perfectly well he was alone, "is what's keeping you from having it all."

◆

Leo's advice kept echoing in her mind, and Mae couldn't seem to argue her way out of it as she was used to doing. It nagged at her to do *something*. She just couldn't think what *something* was, and that exasperated her even more.

As she went about the chores that had brought her so much contentment before, she found that her comfort in a tidy house was replaced by the nagging problem looping over and over in her mind. Leo was so danged sure there was a solution but, shoot, she just couldn't see what it was. Still, the thought wouldn't let her be. She worked hard each day scrubbing already clean floors, dusting surfaces that weren't dusty, pulling nonexistent wrinkles out of the bedspread on Carla's bed. She thought she could sidestep the nagging thoughts by keeping busy. By bedtime, night after night, she was too tired to think and too wired to stop thinking.

One evening, in exhaustion, she dropped into Jim's old recliner, pulled an afghan around her and made up her mind to forget about it, once and for all. Almost immediately, she fell into a sound sleep. Her last conscious thought was that it would take a miracle to straighten this out.

She woke up sometime around midnight; her heart was pounding and she was gasping for breath. Her first thought was that she was having a heart attack and she was curiously unafraid. Slowly, the sensations receded and Mae moved on to wondering what had brought them on.

Gradually, the dream came back to her. She had felt Jim's presence with her once more. She was excited and happy to be close to him again. For a second she thought that maybe it wasn't a dream, that being close to death had summoned Jim to her. *Maybe this means I'll be with him soon.*

Then she gradually remembered what Jim had said to her in the dream, almost word for word.

"Mae, darlin', you are surely not thinkin' straight. You know deep in your heart you want Belle and Carla and Faith back in your life. What you don't know is that they want you back in their lives,too. But because you pushed your family away, they don't know if they'd be welcome. You've made those gals feel you don't really need 'em or even want 'em. Now you got to make the first move, sweetheart. You pushed 'em away, so you got to invite 'em back. You're smart, Mae. Figure out a way to do that."

Humph! When did Jim start soundin' like Leo? But she allowed the dream to replay in her mind, remembering his words so clearly. Surely he had come to her, had been here in this room with her. If her Jim said it, she ought to listen to him. But how did she go about putting things back to rights with Mira and Carla?

Almost as if Jim was hearing her thoughts and answering them, she had her answer: *Make the first move.* Her ingrained resistance stopped her there, so she went back to the dream. What did Jim mean? Maybe she could call over to the apartment and ask how everyone was. Then they would know she was still thinking about them.

Sorta a half-assed move.

Now, where did that thought come from? Was Jim still here, listening to her thoughts? Putting his own in her head? Those were just the words he would have used! Just seemed like he was nudging her to do something much more definite than just call over there. She recalled Leo's words.

"If you want them in your life, go after them."

Jim and Leo seemed to be on the same track. Their prompting made her come up with what was, for her, a startling idea. She would invite them all over for a tea party like they used to have when things were good among them. It could all work out, without the need for apologies and explanations. She wasn't quite ready for explanations yet.

An afternoon tea party would fit into Mira's and Ernie's work schedule just fine. And she had some new recipes she'd been wanting to try out but just couldn't work up the effort when it was only her. And it would be good to hold that sweet little baby girl one more time. *Who woulda figured babies could get under your skin like that? And, of course, it wouldn't have to last too long this first time. Sort of like a trial run to see how it turns out.*

This first time! She realized she was already thinking ahead of being together other times — and it felt good.

She was so worked up that she went into the kitchen, switched on the light, and took down her big old cookbook, flipping through it looking for recipes. She paused briefly to let that good feeling rekindle itself. Maybe, if this worked out, she could have another party on a weekend and ask Carla and Faith to stay the night afterwards. That way, Mira and that nice Ernie could have time some time alone together.

Well, she'd think on that some more before she said anything. *Just to be sure.* But she was pleased with herself for thinking of all of this and so excited about her idea that she danced a little way around the kitchen. Why had she never thought of this before? Her breath caught. She hadn't "thought of it before" because it was precisely what she had been pushing away for so long. *Why was I so slow to figure it out?* True to her own nature, though, she didn't dwell on the questions or what she had lost out on by her stubbornness. She figured it was enough that she had figured out a way to fix things up now. She cautioned herself to go slowly; she surely didn't want them to take advantage of her again; she figured she still needed to be careful of that.

She'd want to be careful, too, not to let things get to be too much for her. *Don't want'em all to start takin' me for granted again.* But for now, at least, she could — she would — move just that little bit closer and see how it worked out.

She couldn't wait to call Leo and tell him all about her amazing idea. The old boy was in for a huge surprise.

Finally her brain slowed, and a pleasant fatigue caught up with her. Mae returned to the recliner, pulled the afghan up around her shoulders again, and muttered sleepily to Jim, "I'm proud of me, Jim Jameson. And you'd be proud of me, too." As sleep claimed her, she felt just as if Jim was cradling her in his strong arms.

ABOUT THE AUTHOR

Ellie Pulikonda is a retired librarian who lives in southwest Oregon. She stays active by writing and volunteering, as well as reading and socializing. Her constant companion, a Shih Tzu named Cookie, sees to it that she exercises daily, weather notwithstanding. She is the author of two novels, *Split Second* and *Finding Faith*, both of which explore the value and effect of our relationships.

She is hard at work on her third novel.

www.amazon.com/Ellie-Pulikonda/e/B00LY3LLXM/
elliepulikonda.wordpress.com
plus.google.com/+ElliePulikondaAuthor
www.goodreads.com/author/show/8226102.Ellie_Pulikonda